CAP

by

SARAH FISHER

The characters and situations in this book are entirely imaginary and bear no relation to any real person or actual happening.

This book is sold subject to the condition that it shall not, by way of trade or otherwise, be lent, re-sold, hired out or otherwise circulated without the publisher's prior consent in any form of binding or cover other than that in which it is published and without a similar condition including this condition being imposed on the subsequent purchaser.

First published in 2000 by Chimera Publishing Ltd

CHIMERA

Captivation published by
Chimera Publishing Ltd
22b Picton House
Hussar Court
Waterlooville
Hants
PO7 7SQ

Printed and bound in Great Britain by
Cox & Wyman Ltd, Reading.

CAPTIVATION

Sarah Fisher

This novel is fiction – in real life practice safe sex

'Woman's destiny is to be wanton, like the bitch, the she-wolf; she must belong to all who claim her.'

The Marquis de Sade (1740-1814), from In Philosophy in the Bedroom, Dialogue the Third (1795).

Chapter One

Peter Tourne ran his hand over the shaft of the whip his handsome face was closed and expressionless. Against the wall the blonde girl began to writhe, pulling frantically against the manacles that secured her. Her struggles raised a fine slick of sweat over her slim body. He let the end of the whip drape across her narrow shoulders – just the lightest of caresses. He watched with pleasure as her breasts spread and pressed against the cold wall in an effort to avoid his attentions. The girl whimpered, closing her eyes to block out the images. They both knew what was to follow.

'Please, Peter,' she hissed, her words barely more than a sigh. It was difficult to decide whether she was begging him to stop or imploring him to begin.

He swung the whip, watching the tip flick back in a wide arc. As he brought it down the fine leather caught the girl squarely across the shoulders. Her cry came an instant later as the pain coursed through her. Her body bucked away from him, her instinctive movements exposing the soft pink crevices between her heavy buttocks. A thin red weal lifted on her flesh. Peter Tourne smiled, relishing the delicate flush that crept across her body.

She broke into a sob. 'No, Peter,' she shuddered, tears coursing down her face. 'Please! Don't hurt me. Please…!'

He swung the whip back again, concentrating on the satisfying hiss it made as it cut through the still afternoon air.

'It'll be all right,' he said softly, almost to himself, feeling the excitement building low in his belly. 'It'll be all right. Just trust me.'

The girl screamed again as the whip found its mark for the second time.

In her studio, Alex Sanderson heard the phone ring and then the tone of the answering machine as it cut in.

'I know you're there, Alex. Pick the bloody phone up,' snapped a familiar voice.

Alex grinned and climbed off the stool near her drawing board.

'Morning, Laurence,' she said, cradling the receiver on her shoulder as she wiped her hands on a rag. 'You sound as if you're in a good mood today. What can I do for you?

At the end of the line her agent snorted angrily. *'I had arranged for you to come in to see me first thing this morning. Remember?'*

Alex groaned and felt a sickening lurch in her stomach. She'd been on Laurence Russell's books for less than a year. He was an established agent with connections in all the right circles – as a virtual unknown she'd been lucky he'd taken her on. She grimaced – besides being a damned good agent he was also extremely good looking in an intimidating sort of way, and it didn't do to upset him.

'God, I'm so sorry Laurence, I'd completely forgotten about it.'

Laurence Russell sighed. *'You really must learn to take business commitments more seriously, Alex. You're not in college now, you know.'*

'I know, I really am sorry,' she said apologetically.

'Okay, enough said. Now, I've got a commission for you.'

'I'll get my notebook.' Alex stretched across the workbench on which the phone, the answering machine, and a thousand other things were piled with careless abandon.

'It's for a mural.'

Alex frowned. 'Oh God, not more *trompe l'oeil* for the rich and famous.'

'*No. One of my existing clients saw the piece you painted at Vernis Restaurant and asked me if you could do something similar for him.*'

Alex paused. Vernis had given her a free rein. She'd created a tableau of medieval images in rich golds and reds on a huge wall in their function room. It had been one of her most successful pieces of work so far.

'I'd be delighted,' she said enthusiastically. 'I've still got all the preliminary sketches. Who's the client? Have you got the address?' She teased a pen out of a pot on the bench and scribbled it into life.

Laurence laughed. '*Not so fast, not so fast, there is a slight problem with this one.*'

Alex groaned. 'I knew it. Go on, tell me.'

'*That's why I wanted you to come in this morning, so we could discuss it. The site is in a place called KaRoche, D'arnos.*'

Alex pouted. 'Run that by me again.'

'*It's on a Greek island. My client lives there in his villa.*'

'So, are you saying I've got to do it all on panels, and then we'll ship them out?'

'*No, not exactly. The client, Mr Peter Tourne, has suggested you fly out there and work on site.*'

Alex let out a low whistle. 'In Greece?'

'*That's right, all expenses paid. Would that be a problem?*'

Alex glanced around her tiny studio apartment. Rain lashed at the skylight above her drawing board. She grinned. 'No, I think I could manage that,' she said. 'Would you like me to come over right now?'

Less than a week later Alex found herself leaning against

the handrail of a little Greek ferry, surrounded by local people making their way back from the mainland. Despite it being the beginning of the tourist season, hers was the only foreign face amongst the passengers on deck. She stretched, letting the warm fresh breeze tug and tumble through her long coppery coloured hair. Above her the sky was clear and cloudless. She closed her eyes, enjoying the sensation of the sun on her body.

This has to be the life, she thought, drinking in the heat. The sea was as blue as any of the brochure photos she'd ever seen. Ahead, a cluster of islands rose from the water like glistening white pebbles.

When the ferry chugged slowly into port, it looked as if the harbour was sleeping in the midday heat. At the far end of the jetty Alex could make out a motley collection of dusty cabs waiting for the passengers to disembark.

She glanced at the piece of paper in her hand and murmured under her breath, 'The Villa KaRoche, D'arnos.' She wondered if she would be able to make the local taxi-drivers understand her phrase book Greek.

White painted houses gleamed around the quay. Above the harbour the landscape was verdant green with dramatic outcrops of rock pressing up between the trees and foliage. Dotted here and there were villas, clinging precariously to the rocky hillsides. It was stunningly beautiful.

Must remember to send Laurence a postcard, Alex thought wryly, shouldering her bag and picking up her suitcases.

At the far end of the pier a man in peculiar mongrel uniform, made up of a smart military jacket worn with tattered cream cotton chinos and sandals, was holding a cardboard sign that read 'Alex Sanderson'. She pushed her way towards him, relieved that she wouldn't have to tussle with the language, and extended her hand.

'Alex Sanderson,' she said cheerfully.

The man's eyes roamed over her body, drinking in the

details, lingering on the curve of her breasts where a thin cotton shirt clung to her warm skin. Alex shivered as he licked his lips and spoke.

'Not taxi,' he said in an accent so thick that she could barely make out what he was saying.

She pointed to his sign. 'Alex Sanderson,' she repeated more slowly, enunciating each syllable.

The man raised his eyebrows and muttered something she didn't understand, while his eyes continued to work across her travel-weary body. Feeling uneasy under his undisguised interest, she pointed to herself, repeating her name for a third time.

The man's reaction was to pull a face and then say very slowly, 'Alex Sanderson. I pick him up from ferry, today.'

Comprehension dawned: someone had assumed Alex was a man! She pulled her passport from her bag and showed the driver her photograph and name. 'It's me!' she said slowly and loudly as though speaking to an idiot. 'I'm Alex Sanderson, Alexandra! I've come to paint a mural for Mr Peter Tourne, at...' she showed him the piece of paper upon which was written her destination, '... KaRoche!'

The man barely glanced at her passport, but at the mention of his employer's name, rolled his eyes heavenward and snatched her suitcases. Reluctantly Alex fell into step behind him.

Parked a little way from the jetty, surrounded by village children, was a sleek black Mercedes. The driver opened the boot and slung her suitcases inside. Alex winced, obviously she was a great disappointment to him, and as if reading her mind, he glowered at her.

'You should be man,' he snorted disjointedly.

Alex shrugged philosophically and climbed into the car, which the man immediately gunned into life.

The main road meandered up around the island, taking in spectacular views of the coast and the sea below. Alex peered out from the cool confines of the car's luxurious interior, while in the front her driver turned up the radio and watched her face in the rear-view mirror.

Finally, as they rounded a steep bend, Alex saw a huge pair of wrought iron gates with the name 'KaRoche' set into them.

'Is this it?' she asked, hoping to finally break through the uneasy silence between them.

He nodded. 'You should be man,' he repeated.

Alex sighed with exasperation. 'Well, I'm not – I'm really very sorry.'

The drive through the island had not prepared her for KaRoche. The villa, built on a series of broad terraces, seemed to grow straight out of the hillside. Set amongst a tumble of vines, trees and fragrant shrubs, it was breathtaking. Alex gasped. The driver lifted an eyebrow at her reaction, but said nothing.

The car purred to a halt outside the front door. The driver unceremoniously dumped Alex's bags on the doorstep before disappearing inside. Alex, perturbed by the man's rudeness, picked up her luggage and followed him nervously into the villa.

The interior was cool and dark. It took Alex a few seconds before her eyes adjusted to the gloom. She glanced around the hallway. It had a red tiled floor and pale cream walls, set with a wealth of ferns and plants in huge urns. In the centre of the room a fountain and pool added a crystal babble of water to the cool and elegant interior.

Alex hesitated on the steps, uncertain what she should do next. Her thoughts were interrupted by a low melodious voice.

'Alex Sanderson?'

She turned towards the sound. Across the room, a tall slim man in his early forties stepped forward. He was dressed casually in a soft white shirt and cream slacks. His features were refined and aristocratic, the impression heightened by his dark hair, shot through with grey, which he wore in a ponytail.

Alex smiled and extended her hand politely. 'Mr Tourne?'

The man nodded, lightly pressing her fingers between his. His touch was cool and disturbing. Alex fought the urge to shiver as he lifted her hand to his lips.

'There seems to have been a misunderstanding,' he said, with the slightest trace of an accent. His dark eyes moved slowly and confidently across her face and body. 'You are Alex Sanderson, the artist?'

'Yes, and from the reaction of your driver, I assume you were expecting a man?'

Peter Tourne nodded, his eyes lingering on the curve of her breasts.

'Does this cause a problem?' she continued unsteadily. 'My agent said you'd seen my work at Vernis.'

He nodded. 'Indeed I have, and I was very impressed. But you're right – please forgive me, I had no idea you were a woman. Your agent – Mr Russell – is perhaps having a joke with me?' His eyes held hers. 'But I am forgetting my manners. I trust your journey was a good one? My housekeeper has already prepared the guest cabin for you.' He paused, and she detected the slightest flicker in his dark eyes. 'Or perhaps you might prefer to stay here, in the main villa?'

Alex shook her head, a peculiar feeling of unease growing in the pit of her belly. 'No, the guest cabin will be fine, thank you.'

The man pressed a bell set into the wall. Alex wasn't sure what kind of reception she had expected, but this certainly wasn't like anything she could have imagined.

'Please don't think me rude, but I am working at the moment. My housekeeper will ensure you have everything you need. We will discuss my plans for the mural when you have had a chance to recover from your journey. You will join me for dinner?'

11

Alex nodded. 'Of course, that would be very nice. Thank you.'

A small woman, dressed in a faded cotton smock, appeared from the far side of the fountain. She eyed Alex suspiciously and then murmured something to Peter Tourne in Greek. He glared at her, his icy look stifling the words in the old woman's mouth.

'This,' he said, with a hint of annoyance aimed at the elderly woman, 'is Alex Sanderson. Would you please show Miss Sanderson to the guest cabin.'

The woman snatched up Alex's cases and bustled across the tiled hall.

'I'll see you at dinner tonight,' said Peter Tourne.

Alex turned to thank him, but he'd already vanished into the shadows. With her sense of unease growing alarmingly, she followed the old woman out into the sun-drenched garden.

The cabin, almost completely obscured by creepers, stood away from the main house, up a steep flight of steps. The housekeeper hesitated at the open door of the little building, her face closed and stormy.

'You shouldn't have come here,' she said flatly. 'It's very bad place.'

Alex glanced back at her, uncertain that she'd heard the words correctly. 'I'm sorry?'

The woman lifted her hands in resignation. 'Mr Tourne, he very bad man,' she snapped. 'Better if you were man.'

Alex sighed and glanced around the sparse but comfortable interior of the little cabin. 'Well, I'm not, and I've come to paint – not to discuss the morals of my client. What time is dinner?'

The woman pulled a face. 'Eight. You find everything you want here; kettle, tea, bottled water.' She paused. 'He make you do terrible things, you know.'

Alex swung round, her degree of unease increasing her annoyance. 'I'm painting a mural, that's what he's paying

12

me for!'

The woman stepped back out onto the sunlit steps. 'Mr Tourne, he a wizard, he make a magic on women. Much better you had been a man.' She closed the door behind her.

Alex wondered what on earth she had got herself into. She glanced anxiously back through the windows, watching the elderly woman bustle down the steps, and wondered why her agent, Laurence, hadn't let Peter Tourne know that she was a female. As for the housekeeper – what could she make of someone like that?

Grateful to be alone, Alex slipped off her sandals and turned her attention to the chore of unpacking.

Outside, the afternoon sunlight touched everything with a brilliant exotic hue. Creepers and flowering plants that had been trained around the windows and doors filled the air with an heady exotic scent. Alex yawned, suddenly feeling tired and dirty from the journey. Her arrival at KaRoche had not been exactly auspicious, but surely things could only get better from here on in? Once she had unpacked her things, Alex slipped off her clothes and headed for the shower.

Under the refreshing torrent of water Alex soaped her aching body and thoughtfully considered her host. Peter Tourne was an odd man, but it was difficult to define exactly why. She thought about the housekeeper, and smiled at the woman's melodramatic pronouncements.

Clean and rejuvenated Alex turned off the taps, wrapped herself in a towel, and lay down on the comfortable bed. She closed her eyes, and within seconds travel weariness led her gently into sleep.

In the villa Peter Tourne poured himself a drink and looked out into the garden below his office. Amongst the intricate tumble of foliage and heavily scented flowers he could make out the tiled roof of the guest cabin.

13

He was both surprised and delighted that his resident artist had turned out to be female – and Alex Sanderson was quite beautiful. He let his mind conjure up a picture of her slim muscular frame, her deliciously firm breasts, and the way her hair curled into the curve of her long white neck.

He had planned on a mural, something cool and green in the long gallery overlooking the swimming pool, but now – he smiled and sipped his aperitif – now perhaps the mural could wait awhile. He sat down by the desk and opened the top drawer. Inside, in a small box, were a set of ornate body rings. He stroked the cool silvery metal and let his mind picture a dozen erotic possibilities. He imagined Alex tied and subdued, completely at his mercy, bucking against her restraints as he taught her the lessons he loved so well. She would learn to be compliant and obedient, and she would learn to understand that his word was law, and that her body was his alone to command or give away as the fancy took him.

He imagined her nipples, puckered and dark, pierced by the silver rings. He could see them glittering in the gloom, and below them the subdued flash of the one that would nestle in the lips of her sex. The rings, and other sets like them, were reserved as a gift, as markers for members of his discreet and beautifully trained stable of girls. He lit a cigar and then picked up the phone. He knew someone else who might enjoy the education of Miss Alex Sanderson.

Alex woke just after seven. Outside the light had subtly changed to a softer evening glow. Although the sun was lower it was still pleasantly warm. Alex pulled a thin cotton dress off its hanger and slipped it on. Glancing at her reflection in the bedroom mirror, she twisted her thick copper hair into a bun and secured it with a clip. The effect was soft and feminine. She stretched and smiled at herself. Recovered from the journey she felt relaxed and ready to face whatever Peter Tourne might have in mind. At least this time she would be ready for him. As she leant forward to add the lightest touch of lipstick there was a knock on the door. It was barely ten to eight, fleetingly she wondered if it was the housekeeper returning with another dire warning.

'Come in,' Alex called.

The door opened slowly to reveal a beautiful blonde girl, dressed in a cream evening dress. The girl hesitated in the doorway.

'Hi, can I help you?' said Alex, spraying on some cologne.

'I come to invite you to join Peter for drink before dinner,' she said slowly, struggling with the English words.

Alex turned and extended her hand. 'I'd love to, my name's Alex – Alex Sanderson.'

The girl smiled and blushed. 'I know. I'm Gena.'

'Right, and are you Mr Tourne's girlfriend?'

The girl's colour deepened and she shook her head. 'No.' She paused for a moment, considering her reply. 'I am his slave. He understand me.'

Alex turned to pick up her handbag. Gena's words must have lost something in translation; surely she really meant servant, or secretary.

In the hall of the villa Peter Tourne was sitting by the little fountain waiting for the two girls to arrive. Beside him stood another man, dressed in expensively casual clothes. As Alex and Gena came in through the French windows the other man stepped proprietarily towards Gena. Peter Tourne smiled a welcome towards Alex.

'Good evening,' he purred as he got to his feet. 'You look lovely.'

Alex smiled politely. 'Thank you,' and then glanced back at Gena and her companion.

'Forgive me. Let me introduce my friends,' he said, taking her arm. 'May I present Starn Fettico and Gena?'

Starn Fettico's smile was fixed as he stepped forward to shake her hand. His eyes moved slowly over her face, as if he could look inside her mind, whilst his other hand rested casually on Gena's hip. Alex sensed there was something wrong, something unsettling, but didn't resist as Peter Tourne led her up a sweeping flight of stairs into a sitting room.

'Would you like an aperitif?' he asked, indicating a tray on the side table. Alex nodded and accepted the glass he offered before turning back towards Gena and Starn, who had followed them up.

What she saw made her gasp. Starn was standing close behind Gena, his hands reaching around and cradling her large breasts, his tongue lapping at her throat. Alex looked away quickly, feeling her colour rise. Peter Tourne lifted an eyebrow as Alex fought to compose herself. Behind her she heard Starn moan.

Alex coughed. 'Look, Mr Tourne,' she began uncomfortably, 'if I'm interrupting something…' her voice faded away.

He casually sipped his drink. 'They disturb you?'

Alex shook her head. 'No, but I'm employed to—'

Lifting his hand he silenced her. His eyes were dark and hypnotic and did not leave hers as he spoke. 'Gena, take off your dress.'

Alex blushed furiously. 'Please, this is hardly what I'm here for!' she blustered indignantly and turned to leave.

Behind her, framed in the doorway, Gena had already slipped off her evening dress. Alex swallowed hard, feeling the heat flooding through her body. The blonde girl was naked beneath the creamy silk sheath, her body as pale as snow, but what was more startling was that she was shaved, her sex as pale and vulnerable as the rest of her body. Alex froze, feeling a thread of panic bubbling up inside her. The girl's heavy breasts were pierced with silver rings and below her outer labia were similarly adorned.

'What is this all about?' Alex hissed, suddenly remembering the housekeeper's words to her earlier.

Peter Tourne laughed softly. 'Perhaps you would like to paint Gena for me?'

'Perhaps not! Usually I'm told before I get a life model!' She struggled to regain her poise. 'And they don't usually strip off just before dinner!' As she spoke she noticed the way Starn's eyes slithered over the ripe and vulnerable curves of Gena's body. She shivered and then swung back to face Peter Tourne. 'Is this some kind of test?'

He lifted his hands. 'No, not at all. Gena, come here.' The blonde moved closer, so close that Alex could smell her expensive perfume and feel her body heat.

'Closer,' he coaxed.

Alex stepped aside as Gena glided towards him, and then watched mesmerised as he stroked the girl's heavy breasts without her offering any form of resistance. His fingertips lingered over the puckered outline of her nipples and the glittering silver rings that hung from them. Gena, eyes downcast in submission, moaned softly as he caressed her.

Alex shivered, wondering why the exhibition excited her almost as much as it repulsed her. 'Please,' she murmured, uncomfortably aware of the fluttering sensation deep in her sex. 'I think I've seen quite enough of this.'

As she spoke, his fingers moved down over the soft swell of Gena's belly. He looked across at Alex, his eyes reduced to dark pinpricks.

'Don't tell me this doesn't move you, Miss Sanderson,' he said softly, his fingers tracing the plump outer lips of the other girl's quim.

Gena shuddered under his touch and to her horror Alex

felt the flurry of excitement flare white hot deep in her belly.

She swallowed hard and took a deep breath, controlling her voice as she spoke. 'I'd have to be dead not to be moved by something so erotic, Mr Tourne, but I think you're making a grave mistake.'

Peter Tourne chuckled, his slim fingers parting the moist lips of Gena's sex, sliding unhindered past the heavy ring. Alex gasped, unable to look away as he caressed the girl's compliant body. It felt as if his fingers were on her own flesh.

He looked at her levelly. 'A mistake? I don't think so,' he said softly. 'Do you?'

Alex felt her colour draining. From the corner of her eye she could see Starn moving around to get a better view. He moved silently, like a predatory wolf.

Alex stared at Gena. 'Is this what you meant when you said Mr Tourne understood you? That you were his slave?' she asked. The blonde girl nodded, her excitement was obvious.

As Alex spoke, Tourne tipped his glass, trickling the wine over Gena's gorgeous body. She shivered as the sticky liquid trickled down over her breasts, leaving a slick glistening trail in its wake.

'Wouldn't you like to lick it off?' he said quietly, staring at Alex. 'Wouldn't you like to taste her sweat and her juices mingling with the bittersweet taste of the wine?'

Alex didn't move.

Tourne shrugged and then glanced at Starn who was now standing beside him. Starn grinned and stepped towards Gena, his tongue already protruding between thick red lips. Alex closed her eyes and looked away as Starn's lips closed around one of Gena's engorged nipples.

Tourne laughed. 'Open your eyes, Miss Sanderson, we'll leave them to play while we have our dinner.'

Alex flinched as his fingers closed around hers, but she

did not protest as he led her away. As they moved across the room, she heard the soft little noises of pleasure as Starn sucked greedily at Gena's willing body.

Alex let her host guide her up another set of steps to a large airy dining room. From the windows she could see the garden below, and beyond that the rich blue waters of the sea. Her discomfort was rapidly turning to anger.

She swung round to face him. 'I think,' she said with great deliberation, 'that you would be better getting someone else to paint your mural, Mr Tourne. I am not particularly impressed with your behaviour so far, and I am not sure that I can give you whatever it is you want.'

Peter Tourne smiled. 'So spirited – I like that. Just tell me truthfully that Gena's activities didn't excite you?'

Alex swallowed. 'I'm really not into women or voyeurism,' she said flatly.

He laughed. 'Perhaps not. But her obedience, her compliance, tell me that didn't fascinate you.'

Alex slammed her glass down onto a side table. 'I'm really very sorry, I'm not sure what it is that you want from me, Mr Tourne. What do you want me to say? That you shocked me? Well, you did. That what I saw excited me? Well, as I said just now, you'd have to be made of clay not to find…' she hesitated, wondering why it was she didn't just walk out.

Why on earth was she arguing with him? All she had to do was collect her things and leave. What held her back? She realised with horror it was because there was something about this bizarre and stunning scenario that had electrified her. She could still feel the little frisson of excitement that Gena's performance had ignited in her belly. She couldn't define what it was, or perhaps she was afraid to admit that the blonde's unquestioning obedience to Peter Tourne had mesmerised her. Sex without responsibility, an unquestioning obedience to another's desires, wasn't that a dark dream she had always

19

denied existed in her heart? Alex felt herself flush scarlet.

Tourne smiled warmly and guided her to the exquisitely arranged table.

'Don't worry about that now – let's eat,' he purred softly. His powerful self-confidence frustrated Alex. 'Let me tell you about my plans for the mural. Perhaps you and I can take a walk down to the gallery after dinner?' His tone was now matter of fact. Alex nodded dumbly and didn't resist as he poured her another glass of wine.

Dinner was exquisite, served by Peter Tourne's houseboy who moved like a ballet dancer between them. Despite the convivial surroundings Alex found it impossible to concentrate on the meal, her mind drawn again and again to thoughts of Gena and Starn in the room below. Peter Tourne reverted to the role of perfect host, spoiling her and asking questions about her trip, her life her art.

She willed herself to relax. The combination of wine, food, and conversation slowly eased away the tension. If it hadn't been for the recurring images of Gena's smooth excited body and Starn's glittering predatory eyes constantly bubbling up in Alex's mind, the meal would have been perfect.

The young servant served their coffee on the balcony outside the dining room. As Alex and Tourne stood side by side, looking out over the evening, watching the light changing on the sea and sky, he turned to her.

'You will stay.' It was a statement, not a question.

Alex bit her lip, not letting her eyes meet his.

'Yes,' she said, in a voice barely above a whisper. As she said it she knew that she'd agreed to more than just painting the mural – and the forbidden, unspoken possibilities excited her.

He nodded. 'Good, in that case I think we should go and look at the gallery,' he said, indicating she should follow him. When she finally caught his eye she could see the gleam of desire there. Alex swallowed hard as she allowed him to take her arm, her heart beating like a drum in her chest.

Below the terrace a winding stairway threaded a path around the outside of the villa. Alex tried to keep her eyes on the sea, resisting the temptation to look in through the windows in case she caught sight of Gena and Starn. Finally Tourne led her under an archway and into a wide gallery overlooking a swimming pool below. She could immediately see why he'd commissioned the mural; the gallery was a superb site. She turned round, about to congratulate him, but something about the way he looked made her swallow the words. His eyes glistened, while the rest of his face seemed devoid of expression. She stared at him, all her previous fears returning.

'What do you want from me?' she stammered, backing away from him.

He smiled thinly, though she noticed the smile did not quite reach his eyes.

'Oh Alex, you disappoint me. Can't you guess? I want to instruct you, to teach you to obey, to let go—'

'Like Gena?' she whispered.

He watched her slow retreat along the gallery, the heady mix of emotions propelling her back towards the steps.

'You'll be better than Gena – far, far better,' he said. 'Come with me.' He turned his back on her and walked towards a door set in the far end of the gallery wall.

Alex felt the flutter of fear growing with every passing second into something more electric and enticing. She stood frozen by the archway, afraid and yet some how compelled to follow. He opened the door, his face now obscured by the evening shadows. They stood there, unmoving, for what seemed like an eternity. She could feel the pulse rising in her throat.

'Come.' His voice was stronger now; firm and authoritative. He held out his hand and Alex knew then that she was lost. Slowly she walked towards him through

the fading evening light, knowing that some part of her
longed to experience whatever Peter Tourne had to offer
her.

Above her, unseen amongst the verdant green climbers,
the housekeeper watched from her apartment window.
The old woman let out a thin, bitter sigh.

'You should be a man, Alex Sanderson,' she whispered,
and closed the window quietly.

Chapter Two

The room beyond the gallery was gloomy, lit only by skylights that caught the last rays of the evening sun. Alex stood in a pool of light, losing Peter Tourne in the shadows.

'Where are you?' she said unsteadily, unable to disguise the tremor in her voice.

'Here,' said he from behind her.

Alex trembled. 'Please... what do you want me to do?'

He stepped closer. 'Everything,' he purred. He stroked her neck. He touched her gently, his tenderness surprising her. She let out a thin hiss, jumping at his caress. His fingers were cold, almost unnaturally so.

'You will learn to obey me,' he murmured. 'You won't need to ask me what I want, you will know instinctively. You will be available for everything I desire.' He paused. 'All the time, night and day.' As he spoke his fingers caught in her hair, jerking her head back. The pain made her gasp. 'Do you understand?'

Alex shrieked as his fingers tightened in her curls, his lips pressed into the soft curve of her neck. 'Tell me you understand,' he said.

She grimaced and twisted as his fingers tightened again, pulling her closer. She whimpered and then whispered, 'Yes – yes I understand! Please, you're hurting me!'

Peter Tourne stepped away from her. His expression was one of triumph.

'Good,' he said. 'Now take off your clothes.'

Alex flushed. 'No,' she said immediately.

He pouted in displeasure. 'You tell me you understand,' he said flatly, prowling around her. 'But you obviously don't understand, or you would obey me at once – like Gena does.'

Alex started to justify herself, but to her horror he sprang forward fluently and grabbed hold of the neck of her dress, his fingers closing tight round the fabric. Alex shrieked, feeling the cloth bite into her flesh. Before she had a chance to resist he pushed her violently against the wall. Hitting the cold bricks knocked the breath out of her. She struggled to regain some shred of control, fighting her fear and surprise.

Peter Tourne's fingers tightened on her dress, wrenching at the thin material. She twisted and turned under his grip.

'Let go of me!' she hissed in terror. Looking up into his face all she could see were his eyes, bright and catlike in the gloom. She knew he was relishing her struggles – the realisation unnerved her and she froze. He gave the material another sharp tug and the summer dress ripped to the waist, revealing her delicate lacy bra beneath.

He grinned as she instinctively tried to cover herself. He pushed her hands away and traced the soft curve of her breasts. She whimpered as his fingers tracked across her nipples, roughly brushing and nipping at their sensitive peaks. She let out a sob and then pushed against his chest, trying to break away.

He let go of her, the smile fading. 'Why are you fighting me, Alex? We both know this is what you want. Take off the rest of your clothes.' His voice was low and hypnotic. 'Do it now before I lose my patience with you.'

Alex watched him like a hunted animal, glancing instinctively towards the door. He followed her eyes.

'You may leave if you wish,' he said evenly. 'But we both know you want to stay, don't we?'

He was right – and she knew now why Gena had said Peter Tourne understood her. She shivered and caught hold of the ragged remains of her dress, pushing it down over her hips. In the gloom he watched her coldly.

She stood on the stone floor in her underwear, the dress around her ankles.

He waved his hand towards her. 'And the rest, take everything off,' he whispered. His eyes travelled down over her body. 'Come along don't disappoint me now, Alex. I have so much to teach you. Tonight is merely your first step of a wondrous journey.'

It suddenly seemed to Alex as if her body had a will of its own. She undid her bra, letting it drop to the floor, then slid down her knickers; both excited and at the same time frightened and acutely conscious of her vulnerability. From the shadows she could see his eyes and knew he approved of what he saw.

'Turn round slowly,' he murmured.

She did, teasingly, deftly. When she had her back to him Alex felt his hands on her shoulders. She yelped as his fingers pressed into her flesh. His voice was a threatening murmur in her ear.

'Don't flirt with me, Alex. There is no need, you are mine already.'

As he spoke he pushed her to the floor. She stumbled forward onto the cold flagstones, landing heavily on her hands and knees. Before she had time to recover he grabbed hold of her arms and jerked her towards him. His face was impassive as he produced leather cuffs from the pocket of his dinner jacket. She watched in stunned surprise as he slipped them round her wrists and then tied them down into rings set in the floor. It wasn't until she had let him put them on that she realised he had rendered her completely helpless.

'Mr Tourne,' she gasped in horror, suddenly afraid. His response was to turn his attentions to her ankles. When she started to strain against the straps he tightened those around her wrists, jerking her face closer to the floor, so that she was crouched on all fours. She let out a thin desperate sob as his hands moved slowly across her body, 'oh Alex, you will be perfect – just perfect,' he said on an outward breath. 'I knew it as soon as I saw you. It will give me the greatest of pleasure to be your first teacher.' He paused as his fingers circled her hardening nipples. 'A good teacher can always bring out the best in his pupil, I will bring out only the very best in you.'

Alex shuddered as his hands moved slowly round to the curve of her buttocks. As he got to his feet, the feelings of vulnerability and exposure overwhelmed her. She trembled, listening to his footfalls in the gloom. She wasn't sure what was more frightening – the sound of his moving away from her, or the sound of him returning.

The shadows subtly changed and she guessed he had altered the lighting in the room so that he could admire his new prize. As he stepped closer she held her breath. He let something cold trail along her spine. She could hear his breathing in the empty silence and closed her eyes, fighting the growing sense of terror.

Peter Tourne let the leather belt rest for a moment on Alex's beautiful bound body. He smiled to himself, relishing the fear and the anticipation he could feel rising from her. She looked divine. Her buttocks were thrust up towards him, accentuating the erotic 'hour glass' shape of her body. Between the cheeks of her bottom he could see the lips of her sex, just parted to reveal the delicate inner pleats, and above them the tight dark bud of her anus. Her sex was framed with a delicate flush of coppery curls. The kiss of the belt made her shiver and wriggle, revealing a little more, opening her a little wider. Already he could make out the glistening moisture of her juices, gathering in the sensitive folds, betraying her excitement.

He let the belt move on, relishing his sense of power, drinking in the heady cocktail of emotions her body created in him. As the seconds passed, he could see her desperately fighting to retain some vestige of dignity, or control. Her breath came in shallow gasps as if she were straining to hear his every move. He saw her relax momentarily, and in that instant he drew the belt back and hit her squarely across the plump orb of her buttocks.

Alex screamed, twisting away from him, her belly dropping to protect the soft exposed areas of her body, while her face pressed down onto the cold floor. Before she could brace herself for the next stroke he brought the belt down again, harder this time.

Peter Tourne grinned, relishing the desperate noises of her humiliation and pain, delighting in the angry red glow that flushed across her skin. She struggled and writhed, trying to avoid the next blow, but he had bound her too well, and the stroke exploded across her buttocks, which clenched as she fought to evade his attentions. Between the heavy curves he could still see the lips of her sex gaping, glistening in the soft light. As if she could read his mind she clenched her muscles tighter still, trying to hide the secret parts of her body from him as the belt swept viciously back again.

Alex gasped as the next blow struck. The soft leather bonds creaked quietly as she jerked and vainly tried to twist away from her assailant. Tears of pain and shock bubbled up in her eyes. Whatever she had anticipated from Peter Tourne's instruction, it had not been this. The overwhelming red hot bite of the leather belt made her gasp and buck with surprise. She could feel the glowing pain in her buttocks spreading up through her whole body. She tried hard to control herself, not wanting to cry out to let him know how much it hurt – or more telling still – how much the hot stinging sensations and the sense of exposure and helplessness were awakening something deep and hungry in the darkest recesses of her mind.

She arched against his next blow, letting out a strangled sob as her face and breasts pressed down onto the cold floor. Behind her, she heard Peter Tourne moving. For a few seconds, she thought the beating was over and let out a thin whine, letting the tension ease in her back.

Before she had time to catch her breath the belt caught her again, hard and hot. The sensations spread out from her bottom in incandescent ripples. She knew she was losing control and let out a dark wailing moan as he hit her again, her rational thoughts were being overcome by the scorching arc of sensations. She bucked and strained against her restraints, letting instinct take over. She felt as if everything she had ever known was slipping way, as Peter Tourne ministered his own particular brand of instruction.

Suddenly there was stillness. The only sounds in the room were those of her desperate and ragged breaths. This time Alex didn't relax, fearing that it would herald another volley of blows from the belt. Instead she held herself taut, waiting for whatever torment might follow.

After a few seconds Alex felt fingers splaying the glowing, stinging contours of her buttocks. She shuddered as long fingers dipped inside her – she knew she was wet – and whimpered as they commenced their exploration.

From behind her, she heard the raw metallic sound of Peter Tourne's zip, and then the brush of his engorged cock against her inner thighs. The contrast to the hot angry glow of her bottom was electrifying. Brutally his fingers opened her sex and he slid into her without prelude. She bayed as his cock filled her and stifled a sob as he grabbed her hips and dragged her exhausted body back against his.

The friction of his clothes against the tender, glowing swell of her bottom made Alex shriek, but Peter Tourne was oblivious to her discomfort. He hauled her into his groin again and again, plunging deeper and deeper into the wet confines of her body, his fingers crushing down on the delicate folds of her inner lips.

Despite the sense of pain and humiliation, or perhaps

she realised with a sense of horror – because of it – she could feel the pleasure growing deep inside. Dark crystals of excitement glistened and grew as he locked his fingers into her hair, arching her back against his thrusts. She screamed again as he jerked her hair harder, his fingers now moving to nip and drag at her breasts. As his fingers tightened around her engorged nipples she felt the glowing crystal sensation in her belly explode into glistening shards that ripped through her. Her bruised, aching body closed frantically around the shaft, sucking at him, milking him, and a second later she heard him groan and then join her in a wild and desperate race towards oblivion.

Finally Alex collapsed onto the cold hard floor, huddled to save her screaming shoulder muscles and glowing buttocks. Peter Tourne remained buried deep inside her, his breath ragged and uneven on her bare skin.

Eventually he slowly peeled himself away from her, leaving her feeling open and exposed.

Alex eased herself into a more comfortable position, afraid to speak. He turned his attention to the leather ties around her ankles and relief swept through her. It was short lived though; once he had untied the straps around her ankles, he moved away. She stretched out on the flagstones, waiting for him to come to free her hands. Instead he lifted her head and slipped a thin pillow beneath it. She started to protest but he seemed unreachable. She wanted to see his face, his eyes, but could only focus on his expensive shoes as he walked slowly past her. She felt him fold a blanket over her bruised and sated body, and then she let out a thin unhappy cry as she realised he intended to leave her there, tied to the floor.

'Mr Tourne,' she sobbed, all her senses alight and afraid. 'Please, Mr Tourne. No, don't leave me here! I'll do whatever you want. Please, untie me…' but her cries fell on deaf ears. She heard the sound of his footfalls recede as he left the room, and seconds later she was plunged into total darkness. She screamed out at the indignity, the unfairness, and the memory of the dark insistent call of her own desire.

Finally she realised it was pointless. Peter Tourne had gone. She began to cry aware that in her struggles to call him back she had dragged the blanket down off her shoulders.

Between her legs the sting of the belt still throbbed, while her sex, wet and bruised, still glowed with the aftermath of her excitement. She lay still for a few seconds, hot tears rolling down her cheeks, wondering whether she could untie herself. Her fingers fumbled with the thongs, but in the dark she couldn't see how or where the ties where held.

She listened to the unfamiliar sounds of room and the night outside. It seemed as if she were totally and utterly alone. The tears came back with a vengeance – tears of fear and tears of shame, for she knew that some part of her relished what the virtual stranger had done to her, however much her rational mind denied it.

In the darkness Alex rolled over onto her side, making the joints in her shoulders scream. She tried to slide down under the blanket to keep warm. Her body protested as she felt the cold floor beneath her biting into her hips and knees. She shivered. It was going to be a long, long night.

Easing herself onto her back she concentrated on the stars, which were clearly visible through the skylight above, trying to take her mind off the pain and the strange dark thoughts that emerged again and again in her mind. Slowly, despite everything, she felt exhaustion creep over her aching body, and did not resist as she slipped into a light and fitful doze.

It was still dark when something woke Alex. Instantly she knew exactly where she was. Her body was cold, her muscles and bones aching with strain and cramps.

She peered into the gloom, wondering if Peter Tourne had taken pity on her and returned to untie the straps. His name conjured up the images of her excitement and of his body pressed intimately against hers, but more compelling still, the memories of the belt biting into her delicate flesh.

Alex swallowed hard and listened. Close by she could hear someone moving about in the room. She licked her dry lips, struggling to find her voice.

'Mr Tourne?' she asked uncertainly into the darkness. The movement in the shadows stopped. Alex held her breath. 'Who's there?' she eventually called uneasily, unable to keep the tremor out of the words.

She heard the soft footsteps moving closer, and then in the starlight caught the glint of dark eyes. Instinctively she drew herself up into a small tight ball. Her unknown visitor moved closer – so close that she could hear his breathing. He was excited, struggling for control.

There was the sudden flare of a match, and in the flickering light she saw the heavy features of the driver who had picked her up earlier in the day. His lips were slack and wet, his eyes bright with excitement. He lit a candle and stood it on the flagstones beside her. His face contorted into a lustful grimace as he took in the details of her vulnerability.

Alex shuddered, fearing the sickening desire in the swarthy man's eyes. He knelt at her feet, which she protectively curled up against her body, and grabbing hold of the corner of the blanket, whipped it away. Alex let out a thin, strangled squeal.

'No – no please,' she whimpered, as his lecherous eyes roamed eagerly over her naked and bound body.

He grabbed hold of her ankles and jerked her legs apart so that she was totally exposed. He leered at the junction of her legs where her sex, the curls damp and matted from Peter Tourne's use of her tied body, gaped to reveal the damp folds within.

He grinned triumphantly, but didn't look at her face. Instead his stubby fingers moved to her sex, splaying the lips wider so that he could explore her. His thumb brushed her clitoris and she gasped as a lightening bolt of sensation roared through her slim body. The driver grinned again and plunged his fingers inside, playing in the mingled juices of her orgasm and that of his employer's. He spread the moisture out over her thighs, letting it dribble onto her cold skin then bent closer, sniffing at her sex like a dog. Alex flushed scarlet as he lapped tentatively at the pooled moisture.

'Please,' she whispered as he pressed her legs further apart, drinking in the flavours from her helpless body. 'Please leave me alone. Mr Tourne said he would come back. Mr Tourne...'

The man snorted in derision as Alex's voice faded – they both knew she was lying.

Her body felt leaden, touched by cold and cramp and the hideous hypnotic caress of the peasant driver. He sat up, his lips obscenely slick, and grinned as he moved his fingers to open the cheeks of her bottom. For an instant his finger caressed the dark forbidden closure behind her sex. Alex, suddenly terrified, squealed and tried to wriggle away from him, realising the direction in which his desire was developing.

The horrible man sniggered, pressing his finger speculatively against the tight, puckered closure.

'You should be a man,' he murmured dryly.

Alex snorted. Fear fuelling her anger, she tried to disentangle herself from his disgusting fingers.

Grunting, he knelt on his haunches, the same wet fingers working now on his ragged trousers. His cock – dark and meaty – sprung forwards like a wild animal. She let out a terrified sob as his hands moved back to her bruised sex. Dipping into her with his dirty fingers he spread the fragrant juices of his employer and Alex around her quim, lubricating, spreading. The thick liquid cooled as it touched her body, leaving shiny slick trails. He grinned and leant forward, outlining her nipples with the juices. She could smell the warm ocean musk of her sex.

The driver crouched over her, the pungent smell of his sweat overwhelming and repulsive as he lapped at her breasts, dragging them into his mouth, milking her, sucking her breasts as if he were feeding.

Alex tried to unseat him, but it was impossible, he was far too large and heavy to fight off. Roughly he spread her thighs, twisting her body painfully and stroking her juices over his dark and threatening cock. She shivered and then gasped as he drove his phallus home into her open quim. His yellowed teeth closed around her nipples, biting hard. She yelled out in desperation, and her body bucked instinctively, impaling her further onto his vile cock.

The man sat back a little, his eyes fixed on the junction were his body entered hers, and then he began to pump deep into her, his fingers returning again and again to the tight dark closure behind her quim. She bucked as his finger tried to work its way inside her. He leered down at her and then spat onto his other hand. She flinched – she knew now that he was intent on buggery and there was nothing she could do to stop him. As she felt him working the saliva into her anus she struggled to blank out the terrifying sensations. His fingers eased their way into the forbidden place, making her flinch as he finally breached the tight band of muscle. With each passing second her rogue body gave him greater access, until through the walls of her sex she could feel him stroking his own cock.

She shuddered, bright tears of pain rising behind her eyes, fearful that if she fought too hard he would hurt her.

Unbuttoning his shirt he pulled her up towards him so

33

that he could brush his torso against her pale breasts. His chest and shoulders were thickly carpeted with wiry, grey hair that scraped her sensitive nipples. He sniggered again as their skin touched, then he leant forward to kiss her. His thick wet lips tasted of beer and cheap cigars – and the heady aroma of her own body.

As his lips brushed hers again she bit him. His reaction was to growl angrily and sink his teeth into her bottom lip. She felt the bright metallic taste of blood, then surrendered, knowing it was pointless to resist; tied to the floor, what Alex didn't give him, he could easily take. Fighting her revulsion she opened her mouth to his filthy, invasive kisses.

Above them, unseen by Alex or the driver, Peter Tourne watched the desperate attempts of his gorgeous new guest to unseat her unwanted lover. He lifted a wine glass to his lips and smiled. He'd let his driver know the girl was available, and the man had needed no further encouragement to go and explore his employer's new house guest. He moved closer to the glass at the edge of his hidden gallery. He knew his driver's special predilection and wondered if he would indulge himself.

Below, the man pulled his thick cock out of Alex's slim pale body and lit another candle. It seemed he wanted to see his victim better; wanted to revel in her bondage. Peter Tourne sat back and watched as the man moved closer to Alex and slid his hands under her buttocks. He lifted her pelvis up to his lips, plunging his tongue deep into her sex, lapping and lubricating, whilst, even in the gloom, Peter Tourne could see his driver's fingers moving back between his victim's buttocks, fingering the dark tight closure that he preferred.

Alex's face was contorted, fighting the sensations that threatened to overwhelm her. Her body moved instinctively against the man's broad tongue, unable – despite her fears

– to resist the temptation to accept his caresses. Beneath her the driver's slick cock glistened in the candlelight, waiting for Alex to submit, waiting for the moisture to smooth the way into her most secret place.

Peter Tourne held his breath. The driver lifted the girl higher, holding her open so that his mouth could lap greedily at her tight little arsehole. Peter Tourne could sense Alex's horror and the driver's growing desire. The man moved back to Alex's clitoris; she moaned, afraid even now to relinquish her control. Her beautifully pert breasts were flushed, her nipples puckered and dark from the excitement and the cold.

Peter Tourne could sense Alex's climax approaching as her body began to tremble. Just at the instant when it seemed she would tumble headlong into ecstasy, the driver pulled his mouth away from her and spat into his hand again, rubbing his saliva between her buttocks. The girl's expression changed and froze as she anticipated what was to follow. The driver eased forward, his raging phallus all but invisible between the cheeks of her bottom.

Alex mouthed the word *NO!* but the man was relentless, and then Peter Tourne heard her throaty groan as the driver slid his cock into the darkest recesses of her body. She seemed afraid to move, her face pale and desperate, unsure of whether she hated this new sensation... or whether she adored it. The driver looked down at her, his eyes glittering with triumph. He crept closer, sliding deeper and deeper, then his thumb moved to Alex's clitoris, and roughly, persuasively he began to circle it. Peter Tourne could see the pulse twitching in her throat, while her face was still frozen with confusion.

Fear flickered in her eyes as the driver began to move – gently at first, slowly, feeling his way into her. Suddenly she twisted instinctively against his circling thumb and then screamed out as she dropped down, unable to hold herself up any longer, completely impaling herself onto his cock. Her body twitched and turned with the first desperate flurries of the orgasm the driver had lit in her belly, while he began to work more insistently, set now on his own frantic release. His fat lips contorted into a maniacal grin as he reached his climax, fiercely driving his phallus as deep into her as he could.

Finally there was calm; an eerie brittle stillness that hung like smoke between the two figures on the floor. The driver slid out of Alex's body without a second thought. She shuddered, her breath coming in ragged sobs.

The driver grinned at her, his fingers moving back and forth across her body, slipping inside her sex. He leant forward to drag her nipples deep into his mouth, sucking and biting. Alex lay motionless, staring up into the dark night. The man shrugged, pressing his lips against her sex for one last caress, and then slung the blanket over her. She didn't respond, her eyes were focused on the middle distance as the driver leant over her to blow out the candles, his cock dragging, wet and flaccid across her exhausted body.

Chapter Three

'Wake up.'

Alex blinked, hearing a female voice close by. She tried to turn over, feeling unbelievably uncomfortable. Her waking mind was flooded with images from the night before. She gasped and struggled to sit up. Her arms were so numb she could barely feel them. The tight leather straps still held her firm. She groaned and then licked her lips, aware of the stale taste of sleep in her mouth. Above her the face of the elderly housekeeper came into view. Alex blushed furiously. The older woman shook her head.

'I tell you Mr Tourne is wicked man,' she said flatly. 'You should not come here.'

'Have you come to let me out?' Alex asked, wincing at the ache in her bladder.

The woman sighed theatrically. 'Yes, I let you out, but first Mr Tourne he want you shaved. Turn onto your back.'

Alex began to protest, thinking about Gena's slick and exposed sex.

The woman above her just shrugged. 'If I don't shave you, you stay tied on floor. Mr Tourne, he say so.'

'I want to use the bathroom,' snapped Alex, turning so that she could catch the woman's eyes. The housekeeper shrugged as if she didn't understand.

'The toilet,' Alex repeated desperately. 'Please!'

Comprehension dawned at last, and the older woman smiled. 'I shave you first, then you go to toilet.' As she spoke she jerked the blanket back off Alex's body. She looked over the girl's slim well – proportioned frame with something akin to professional coolness.

'You have nice body,' she said as she fingered Alex's

37

tender breasts. Alex flinched at her touch, the single pain awaking a thousand others. 'Mario, he come to you also?'

Alex pulled a face. 'Mario?'

'Mr Tourne, his driver, he like to bite, you have bruise here.' She poked the sore area again and Alex winced.

'Mario, he like boys best.' She lifted a questioning eyebrow at Alex, who felt hot threads of humiliation course through her. The old woman's words conjured up the driver's leering, ugly face and his thick meaty phallus pressing home into her. Alex reddened; there had been no way to stop him. She could still feel the pain.

The old woman pouted. 'But he don't mind girls too, and you can't stop him like this,' she indicated Alex's bonds. 'Now, I shave you.'

Alex looked way, feeling her colour deepen under the woman's scrutiny. What could she say? She was as powerless to resist the old woman as she'd been to stop Mario or Peter Tourne from doing exactly as they wished with her.

The woman made a clucking, motherly noise. 'You stay very, very still. I don't want cut you.'

Alex shivered at the possibility, listening now to the slosh of water. The woman returned.

'Open your legs, little one,' she said, prising Alex's aching thighs apart. 'Open them real wide.'

Alex closed her eyes as the housekeeper began to lather the coppery curls around her sex. Her hands were practised and confident. Alex shuddered as she felt the first cold rasping stroke of the razor and then froze, remembering what the housekeeper had said about staying still. She tensed, listening to each compelling stroke, resisting the desire to shudder at her exposure. She held her breath, willing herself not to move, trying not to even think, until the old woman finally struggled back to her feet.

'There, you are done now,' the housekeeper said with a smile. 'You need to rinse soap off.'

Alex wriggled. 'Let me get up now, please.'

The woman mumbled something and then reached above Alex's head. Alex felt the leather thongs give and them lifted her hands slowly until she could see them. Every muscle in her back ached.

'Thank you,' she whispered as she struggled to sit up. Her head span.

The woman crouched over her with a look of concern on her face. 'Slowly,' she said, 'don't rush.'

Alex nodded and finally, if unsteadily, sat upright. The icy touch of the floor was like a balm against her glowing buttocks.

The woman glanced across the room. Alex followed her eyes – the interior was bare except for a series of rings in the floors and walls and ceiling and an expanse of cupboards. At one end of the long room were two doors set into the wall.

The old woman handed Alex a thin cotton robe. 'There is bathroom there,' she said, pointing towards one of the doors, and then glanced down at the remains of Alex's dress on the flagstones. 'I bring something clean to wear.' She bundled up Alex's clothes and then, carrying them and the bowl of water, hurried away.

Once she'd left, Alex grabbed the robe and dragged it around her shoulders. Her body protested, every muscle and sinew felt knotted and sore. She clambered unsteadily to her feet, and hobbled towards the bathroom door. As she walked the slick fragrant remains of her night spent with Peter Tourne and Mario trickled out onto her thighs. She shuddered and pushed the door open.

In the bathroom the walls were lined with more built-in cupboards. She opened the first one – it contained perfume and toiletries, the next one a pile of thick luxurious towels. Alex turned on the taps, ran a deep bath and then gratefully slipped into the warm water. She sighed as the water eased away the pain. Stretching, she took in the startling, naked contours of her sex. The clean lines were shocking, and at the same time deeply erotic. She looked way, feeling the mixture of intense emotions bubbling up through her. Soaping herself, her fingertips sought out the aftermath of the damage from the previous night.

On her breast were the deep navy teeth marks of one of Mario's bites, other lesser bruises pinched and ached as she touched them. Finally she let the soap slide down between her legs. The naked mound of her pubis felt strange under her fingers. She opened her legs wider, wincing as she felt the bruising inside, and behind it the sensation of raw violation that she didn't feel ready to contemplate.

A picture of Mario's eager, lascivious face filled her mind. She shook her head and tried to drive his image away when she succeeded his features were replaced by the cool and aristocratic face of Peter Tourne. She swallowed hard and slid further down into the warm water, willing it to heal her body and soak away the desperate aches and stiffness.

Finally dried and feeling somewhat restored, Alex glanced into the mirror above the basin. Her blue eyes were bright, despite her lack of sleep. Her lips and breasts were bruised from Mario's attentions – but what surprised her most was that other than the obvious bruising she looked no different; she was unchanged by the events of the night before. Thoughtfully she ran a finger over the livid purple mark inside her bottom lip, wincing as she found the tender spot where Mario had bitten her. Her mouth still felt dirty. She shuddered as she remembered the driver's filthy kisses and the odour of tobacco and beer. She opened another cabinet and found a toothbrush and paste. Gratefully she spat into the sink and attempted to scrub away the last physical remains of the peasant's invasion of her body. She pulled the robe tight. Glancing back at the mirror she smiled; at least her body now felt clean – although her mind was a very different matter.

Outside the bathroom, on the floor, lay one of her favourite floral dresses that the housekeeper had obviously collected from the guest cottage. Alex picked it up and pulled a face – the woman had forgotten to bring her any underwear, and had already taken away the things she had been wearing the night before. She sighed and pulled the dress over her head, ignoring the complaints from her body as she moved.

By the rings in the floor where she had spent the previous night were her sandals, discarded at some point, but not forgotten. Alex slipped them on and then made her way out into the bright sunlight.

It took her a few seconds to work out exactly where she was – she had no desire to go back into the house – instead she went back to the steep path around the outside of the villa and climbed up until she found a way into the garden that would lead to the guest cabin.

Inside, on the table in the sitting room, someone had set out a breakfast tray with orange juice, coffee and hot light rolls. Alex ate ravenously, cramming the delicious bread into her mouth as if she hadn't eaten for a week.

She had barely had a chance to collect her thoughts and finish her breakfast before Gena appeared at the open door. Her sudden appearance made Alex jump. Gena's expression was dark and unreadable, but there was a split moment when their eyes locked, each female understanding fully what the other had recently experienced.

Gena was the first to break the silence. 'Peter wants to see you in sitting room.'

Alex hesitated. 'I'm not really dressed,' she began, glancing down at her thin dress. Through the lightweight fabric she could make out the shadowy outline of her nipples, and the curve of her breasts.

Gena's eyes flashed. 'He said you are to come.'

41

Alex nodded, remembering Peter Tourne's reaction to her disobedience. 'All right,' she said quickly, standing the cup down.

Gena turned so that the sunlight shone through her elegantly tailored dress. Picked out by the sun her silhouetted figure was stunning. Alex swallowed hard, knowing from the events of the night before that Gena too, was naked beneath her dress.

She followed the blonde down into the main house, struck once again by the peaceful qualities and the elegance of the hallway and the rippling sounds of the fountain. Ahead of her Gena mounted the staircase that led up to the sitting room.

The blonde opened the door and let Alex go in first. Peter Tourne was sitting across the room in an armchair, looking out into the garden below. Starn was standing behind him. His eyes roamed slowly over Alex and then to Gena as the two women stepped into the room.

'You wanted to see me?' Alex said softly.

Peter Tourne said nothing – he didn't even move. It was Starn who stepped closer, his eyes resting on the curve of Alex's body where it touched the thin fabric of her summer dress. Under Starn's unsettling gaze Alex was astounded to feel her nipples hardening, pressing forward to reveal themselves through the material.

'Did you have her shaved?' asked Starn over his shoulder to Tourne. His eyes gleamed as he noticed the outline of her nipples.

Peter Tourne was still looking into the garden outside. 'Show him,' he said flatly.

Alex felt herself flush scarlet, and she hesitated.

His voice lowered to a menacing purr. 'Don't make me ask you again, Alex. You know how I reward disobedience.'

Knowing she had no other choice but to obey, Alex gathered up the hem of her skirt, lifting it slowly to reveal the soft vulnerable curves of her naked sex. Starn licked his lips greedily. He stepped forward as if he intended to touch her. Alex flinched and instinctively stepped back towards the door.

Peter Tourne turned to look at her, his eyes resting first on her sex, and then her face. He smiled. 'Very good.' He glanced across at Gena. 'Take off your dress, Gena, then come here and stand by me.'

Without any hesitation Gena began to undo the buttons of her shirt-dress, revealing the heavy swell of her breasts. Alex stood motionless, her fingers knotted in the thin material of her frock, while Gena let her dress fall into a silky puddle around her feet.

Peter Tourne glanced back at Alex. 'I want you to kiss Gena,' he said softly. Alex shivered but didn't move. His penetrating eyes never left her face. 'Am I not making myself clear?' His tone hardened. 'Let me explain. I want you to kneel in front of her, part her thighs, and then kiss her, caress her. Use that tongue and those pretty lips of yours to bring her to the very brink of ecstasy.'

Alex gasped; she had thought he meant a real kiss on the lips – and that prospect had abhorred her – but what he actually meant completely astounded her. She dropped the hem of her skirt.

'No,' she stammered, 'I won't, I can't!'

Peter Tourne lifted his hands in resignation. 'Why do you insist on fighting me, Alex? What I ask is so easy. All you have to do is give yourself to me. Let me guide you show you, teach you. Ah well.' he looked at Gena and then at Starn. 'Lift your skirt up again, Alex.'

She did so very slowly, with great reluctance.

'Now Gena will show you how it's done.' He fixed her eyes with steely determination. 'And you will let her. Do you understand me?'

Alex couldn't bring herself to answer him.

'Do you understand me?' he snapped again.

This time she nodded and Starn stepped behind her. One of his hands slipped round her wrists, holding her fingers tight in the skirt. He jerked them higher until her whole belly was exposed. His other hand snaked around her shoulders until one of her breasts rested in his palm. He squeezed firmly, his thumb and fingers seeking out her nipple, which to Alex's horror, hardened again under his touch.

Gena walked slowly across the room. It was impossible for Alex to ignore her pale and delicate eroticism. Peter Tourne nodded towards a stool and the gorgeous blonde pulled it up in front of Alex, before arranging herself onto it on all fours.

She glanced up at Alex, her eyes glittering as she ran her tongue around her red painted lips. Alex let out a desperate whine and then closed her eyes as she felt Gena's warm breath on her belly. An instant later she gasped as Gena planted the lightest of kisses on the junction where her heavy outer lips met. Behind her she heard Starn sigh and felt him tighten his grip on her. He slid his knee between her thighs and forced her legs wider apart.

In contrast to Starn's touch, Gena's tongue was soft and enquiring, her mouth planting delicate kisses on the lips of her quim. Her tongue eased Alex's sex open, probing and seeking out the hard ridge of her clitoris. Alex gasped softly as the blonde found her goal and then started to nibble and suck at the little throbbing bud. Behind her Starn changed position, his fingers now dropping from the hem of her skirt to the naked contours of her sex. She tried to push him away but he was strong and persistent. His fingers slid down to hold her body open for Gena's probing tongue.

The blonde girl's attentions were frightening in their intensity. Within seconds Alex could feel the spiral of her excitement growing. Gena's fingers joined her tongue, stroking and caressing and teasing. Alex gasped, feeling

44

as if she was losing the control of every part of her body. She found herself leaning back against Starn, and could make out the pressing of his penis through her dress. She moaned as Gena plunged her fingers up into her willing body, exploring her sensitive and moist interior. Her fingers stroked along the inner lips, dipping in and out of the wet slit between. Alex let out a long wild sob as Gena returned her attentions to her clitoris and dragged a perfectly painted fingernail across the throbbing hood that protected the little bud.

The sheer intensity of the sensations threatened to drown her. Alex writhed helplessly, opening her legs wider, her body's desire suppressing her mind's revulsion. She thrust herself onto Gena's waiting tongue, straining to catch every last electric caress.

Moaning and twisting, with Starn supporting her, Alex surrendered herself totally to the feelings Gena lit in her. All restraint and all embarrassment was pushed back by her body's single-minded struggle for satisfaction.

Suddenly Alex knew she couldn't resist the spirals of excitement any longer. She screamed, letting the heat of the climax engulf her. As though in a dream she heard Starn laughing softly, still holding her tight. Even before the last waves of pleasure had crashed through her she heard Tourne say:

'Very good, Gena. Now come to me.'

Alex opened her eyes in time to see the luscious blonde crawling towards her master. As she reached him she lay her head in his lap.

He looked up at Alex whilst he ruffled Gena's hair playfully – it looked as if he were stroking a kitten.

Alex watched, mesmerised, as Gena began to undo the zip of his trousers. Before she could free his cock, he tipped her head back and kissed her full on the lips. Alex shuddered, imagining the salty taste of her own juices on Gena's mouth.

Behind her Starn relinquished his grip. His voice was thick with excitement.

'Take off your dress, bitch,' he said huskily. Alex looked over at Peter Tourne in desperation.

He merely smiled arrogantly as Gena ran her expert tongue along his engorged shaft. 'Do exactly as Starn tells you,' he said quietly.

Alex thought about the night before. Hadn't he said that she would learn to obey him? She could hear his voice in her spinning head: 'you won't need to ask me what I want, you will know instinctively. You will be available for everything I desire. All the time, night and day'. Was this what he meant?

Alex pulled her dress up over her head and dropped it to the floor. Naked, she turned to face Starn.

'That's better,' he said, and sneered victoriously. 'Now come closer.' She did as he ordered, trembling as he lifted her right breast to his lips and lapped at the bruise Mario's bite had left. Cradling her breast in his fingers he closed his lips around her nipple, sucking it hard into his mouth. Below, he delved into the fragrant moist confines of her body. Her sex, so close to orgasm, tightened around him. Starn grunted appreciatively.

Eyes alight with sexual hunger, he guided her back towards a sideboard. Resting her weight against the edge, he slipped his hands under her thighs, lifting them to encircle his waist. With one hand he unzipped his trousers, letting them slide towards the floor.

His cock was slim and arched towards Alex with a single glistening drop of moisture clinging to its tip. He let the swollen helmet nuzzle between her throbbing lips. The sensation made her shiver. He sneered again as he saw her reaction, and then pulled her forward roughly so that he could slip into her.

As her body closed around him, his face contorted into an expression of pure victorious pleasure. She glanced down and was shocked by the image of his slim phallus sliding into her, her naked sex gathered and puckered around the junction were their bodies met. Above his cock, the little bud of her clitoris throbbed, revealed and then hidden by each of Starn's eager thrusts.

Alex could sense it wouldn't be long before Starn lost control. Across the room Peter Tourne watched their coupling dispassionately, despite the ministrations of Gena. In his lap her red lips closed again and again on his erect penis. Only a slight tightening around his mouth and jaw gave lie to the sensations the blonde was lighting in him.

Alex held his stare, watching every nuance of his expression, whilst Starn forced himself deeper and deeper into her. His thrusts were wild and ragged now, making her already aching body feel sore and beaten.

From across the room, perched as she was on the ornate piece of furniture with Starn thrusting maniacally at her, Alex watched Peter Tourne swallow hard. He seemed to momentarily lose his concentration, and she knew he too was losing control. In his lap Gena moaned as she swallowed, lapping against the pulsating ejaculation of his phallus.

The sound of Gena's muffled little cry was enough for Starn. He lurched forward. Deep inside Alex felt the energetic throb of his orgasm breathlessly he leant against her, his heat seeping through into her naked skin. She gasped and trembled again as she felt his seed fill her to the brim.

Peter Tourne pushed Gena away, letting her collect her clothes, whilst Starn stepped away from Alex, his spent cock trailing its juices onto her thighs. He grinned lazily at her, his eyes glistening.

Peter Tourne stood up, still holding Alex's gaze.

'I want you to begin the preliminary sketches for the mural today,' he said, as if they were both stepping away from a consultation meeting. 'Perhaps you would start after lunch. I'm sure you could now do with a little rest – after all your exertions.'

Alex nodded, 'I'll begin this afternoon,' she said with equal coolness, and stooped to pick up her dress, slipping it easily over her shoulders. She followed him to the door, her expression as impassive as that of the man she knew she would learn to relish; the man she knew could guide her to the dark heights of ecstasy.

Back in her cabin Alex showered quickly, her mind desperately trying to blot out the exotic images of Gena crouched between her legs. She turned the water to a roaring bore to drive away the smell of Starn's body and the warm glow that still pulsed from deep within. Naked and still damp, she threw herself onto the bed and dragged the quilt up and over her body. Seconds later she fell asleep, her dreams alight with the new sensations Peter Tourne's tuition had awakened in her.

When Alex awoke the afternoon sun was streaming into the comfortable bedroom. Outside in the cabin's sitting room someone had opened the French windows and left a tray of food on the table outside on the terrace. The tray was complete with a bowl of tiny roses. Alex stretched, feeling the aches and pulls of the exertions of the last twenty-four hours.

As she dressed she caught sight of herself in the bedroom mirror – her shaved pussy gave her whole body a strange alien quality. She stopped for a few seconds to examine her reflection. Her eyes glittered, fresh from sleep. Below on one breast were Mario's teeth marks, like a livid blue badge. Lower, below her waist, her body ached, but even so it was still only the exotic naked lips of her sex that really marked the changes that had taken place.

She slipped on a light Indian cotton smock with sandals, deciding – in view of Peter Tourne's apparent tastes – that it might be better to leave her underwear off. After she'd eaten she collected her shoulder bag, picked up a sketchpad, pencils, and her tape measure, and then set off into the garden to begin work on the site of the mural.

The long gallery was deliciously cool. It was thrown into deep shadows, and it didn't take Alex long to find a comfortable spot to contemplate her new commission. She chose not to consider what lay beyond the door at the end of the gallery.

In Vernis restaurant she had painted a banqueting scene, showing wild revellers in beautiful medieval costume. The overall effect had been rich and colourful, not unlike a tapestry. But what would she create for Peter Tourne?

She smiled to herself – a Bacchanalian orgy would be most appropriate, she thought darkly, as she began to make a few preliminary sketches.

On the ceiling of the long gallery the reflections of the swimming pool below shimmered and glinted. She stretched, enjoying the luxurious setting and the quietly calming sounds of the water. She didn't hear Peter Tourne's soft footsteps as he came in through the archway, and she jumped when he appeared in her field of vision.

He smiled at her discomfort. 'I'm sorry, I didn't mean to startle you.'

Alex shook her head, glancing up at the enigmatic man who had discovered the way to set her body alight. 'I was miles away, thinking about what I could do with this.' She lifted her hand to indicate the blank walls.

He moved a little closer his eyes were dark and mischievous. 'How quickly your mind moves onto other things – I'm impressed. May I ask what you have decided to paint for me?'

Alex sighed. 'That isn't exactly how this works. You're the client, you tell me what you want, and then I do it.'

He stared at her. 'An arrangement I approve of.'

Alex blushed and lay down her pencil. She could feel his eyes on her body. She stood up to face him, feeling the little flurry of excitement and fear returning in her belly. He lifted a hand and ran it gently over her breasts. Her nipples hardened at his touch. Lower still he stroked at the contours of her sex. She moaned as his knowing fingers traced her heavy outer lips. He smiled at her, like a dark and dangerous wolf, and then stepped back as if satisfied.

Alex was astounded by the intensity of feelings he lit within her, realising too that he had been exploring her to see if she was wearing anything beneath the smock.

'I like my pupils to be ready for my lessons, whenever I want to instruct them.' His voice dropped to a low purr.

Alex shivered.

Tourne glanced towards the door at the end of the gallery.

Alex laughed nervously and tried to tear her mind back to the mural. She focused unsteadily at the blank gallery wall. 'What do you imagine when you look at this wall?' she said as lightly as she could.

The question seemed to break the spell. He stepped forward to touch the smooth white plaster. 'A forest,' he said. 'A magical, wild, green place, full of angels and devils and exotic mythical beasts.'

Alex nodded it was an idea that smacked of sheer genius. The gallery, with the water below and its backdrop of tangled rich green creepers, would be an ideal setting for his fantasy forest.

'That's a wonderful idea!' she said enthusiastically. 'Do you want people in your magical forest?'

Peter Tourne looked back at her, his eyes alight and glistening. 'Oh yes,' he murmured. 'What would fantasy be without people to enjoy it?' He touched the wall again. 'Lost souls playing games in amongst the trees.'

Alex looked at him levelly. 'Lost souls?' she murmured.

He shrugged. 'Players then, lost souls is not quite what I mean.' He paused and stared at her. 'What I am striving to create here at KaRoche is a game,' he said softly. 'A dark magical compelling game.'

Alex swallowed hard and forced her eyes to hold his, knowing that somehow they had strayed away from the mural and back into the electric desires of Peter Tourne's mind.

'And what do you want me to do with your mural, Mr Tourne?'

'I would like you to reflect my intentions,' he whispered. 'Hint at the magic that can be had if you just submit to it; lay yourself bare to its enchantment.'

Alex felt her colour rise. 'And if your players submit themselves to your magic?'

He moved closer, his fingers returning to the hard puckered buds of her nipples. 'Then they can choose how long their enchantment lasts. Some will choose to stay in my wood forever. Others will leave and plant a fantasy of their own.'

Alex shivered, but did not resist as his lips pressed to hers. His fingers on her breasts became rougher, twisting and nipping at the sensitive buds. Alex moaned, feeling the heat rekindling between her legs. She pressed herself to him. Instantly he froze and pulled way, his eyes darkening into unfathomable pools.

'Let us not forget, Alex Sanderson, who the master is here, and who the pupil is.'

Alex blushed. 'But I thought…'

He ran his hand down over her belly. His touch was totally possessive.

'There is no need for you to think, Alex, I will think for you. You have chosen to stay, now you must realise that you have joined my game and you will play by my rules.' He let his hand drop away and walked back towards the archway. 'I will see you at dinner.'

Alex nodded instinctively and picked up her drawing pad, clutching it like a touchstone against Peter Tourne's dark enchantment. After he left she stood staring at the blank wall of the gallery, her mind reeling with erotic images that he conjured in her mind, and a peculiar sense of frustration.

It took time for Alex to regain her composure. Despite Peter Tourne's unexpected intrusion she knew she had to get on with the sketches and lay her tape out to measure the walls. A residue of excitement glowed in her belly with an intensity that both surprised and unnerved her. Her hands shook as she scribbled down the measurements and then some ideas for the mural. The words *'dark enchantment'* appearing again and again on her list. Finally she sat down by the poolside and began to sketch.

Drawing was like an addiction to Alex. Its magic pulled her in so that it was easy to forget everything else – or at least, almost everything else. She worked single-mindedly until the fading light made it impossible to continue. Glancing at her watch she realised with surprise that most of the day had gone. She lay the sketchpad down and collected her pencils together. As she took one final look at the pictures she had drawn she realised that every man's face bore an uncanny resemblance to that of Peter Tourne.

She stared at the drawings as if she was seeing them for the first time: Between two trees a nymph was tied and blindfolded, awaiting the attention of her master, her pert breasts pressing through the gossamer of her robe, her sex open and exposed. On the adjoining page a second girl lay spread-eagled. She struggled and fought, her hips lifting instinctively, while the satyr who crouched above her looked on with a riding crop in his hand. On the next sheet, in a shady woodland glade, two women embraced, one kneeling before the other, her tongue deep in the other woman's quim, while their master looked on with pleasure. Alex reddened furiously and snapped the sketchbook shut. Stuffing it into her shoulder bag she hurried back to the cabin in time to change for dinner.

Back at the cabin Alex quickly got ready for dinner. Sitting by the dressing table, adding the final touches to her make-up, Alex wondered if Gena would come to call for her again. She leant closer to the mirror, adding a final touch of lipstick. The soft coral pink complemented her light tan. As she drew the stick across her lips she thought about Gena's mouth pressed close to her sex, its contours working on the delicate folds of her body, bringing her closer and closer to the moment of release. The intense images brought a flush to her cheeks. How was she going to face Gena or Starn after the earlier events in the sitting room?

Meeting Peter Tourne had changed her life forever. Trying to dismiss the erotic thoughts she picked up her bag and turned off the lights. Standing in the darkness she wondered for a moment what other lessons he had in mind for her. Outside, the night closed around her like black silk, adding to the sense of expectation. She nibbled her lower lip; was it possible to live so close to the edge? With every minute that passed something seemed to make her think about passion or pain. As Alex reached the doors to the villa she hesitated, hearing the sounds of voices from within. She wondered what she might discover inside.

The doors opened before she touched the handle. Peter Tourne's housekeeper stood in the hallway, her dark eyes expressionless. Alex nodded her thanks, wondering whether the old woman's tense demeanour was one of excitement or anger.

'They waiting for you upstairs,' she snapped and hurried away into the shadows.

Alex climbed the stairs and found Gena and Starn sitting on one of the long leather sofas in the sitting room. They were each cradling a glass of rich red wine. Alex felt herself blush even before anyone had a chance to speak.

Starn nodded towards the next flight of stairs that led

up to the dining room. 'Peter is waiting for you, he would like you to go up to him.'

Alex went without hesitation, relieved not to have to make polite conversation with her two morning lovers.

Peter Tourne was standing by the window speaking into a mobile phone.

'Yes, it's working out fine, we're just about to have dinner,' he said, watching Alex's progress as she crossed the room. 'In fact she's here now, would you like a word with her?' He handed her the phone. 'It's your agent.'

Alex felt a sense of relief; Laurence Russell represented normality and real life. While in London he'd always seemed a little disturbing, on D'arnos even the sound of his name lifted her spirits. She glanced at her host, and immediately realised he had no intention of leaving. 'Hello?' she said.

'Hello, Alex. I thought I'd give you a day or two to settle in. How's it going?'

The tension in Alex's stomach eased with the sound of Laurence's familiar voice.

'I hope Mr Tourne's treating you well. He's a very important client of mine.'

Alex swallowed hard, staring at Peter, who was standing beside her.

'I'm fine,' she murmured. 'I've started the first sketches today.' She imagined Laurence in his London office. He often worked late, and as he made enquiries about the job she visualised him seated behind his impressive oak desk, his grey eyes flashing. Odd, she thought, until she'd met Peter Tourne she'd always found Laurence Russell intimidating. He had an upright, military bearing that made her feel uneasy, and sometimes she sensed, when she looked up at him, that he'd been watching her. She had wondered several times whether his interest in her was purely professional. Now she was just relieved to hear him – a voice of normality and reason amongst confusion.

Laurence Russell's artistic empire couldn't be further away from the events at KaRoche.

As Alex spoke Peter Tourne lifted the hem of her dress. She shivered.

'The only thing is that they were expecting me to be a man,' she said.

Laurence laughed dryly. *'Really?'* he said. *'Perhaps I ought to have warned Mr Tourne that you're all woman. It hasn't caused you any problems, has it?'*

Alex felt strong fingers seeking out the folds of her sex. How on earth could she answer Laurence's question? 'No,' she said softly. 'I think he's quite pleased with me.'

'You sound somewhat subdued. Are you okay?'

Before she had a chance to reply Peter Tourne took the phone from her, and in doing so he let a long finger snake around to find a way inside her. She let out a strangled gasp as he found his mark.

'I am very pleased – I just wish you'd told me. Alex is proving to be extremely talented,' he said with a smile, tucking the phone under his chin. 'I am delighted with her efforts so far.' His fingers moved to and fro in an intimate, invasive arc. 'I think she'll do very well here.'

Alex didn't quite hear Laurence's reply at the other end of the line, but Peter Tourne laughed. 'Oh yes, I'm sure she'll prove to be more than satisfactory. I'm afraid we have to go now, we're just about to eat.' While he made his goodbyes his finger remained in place. Alex stood frozen to the spot, afraid to move.

He looked at her as he placed the phone on the side table.

'Well done,' he said softly, while pulling his finger from her body. She flinched, but didn't resist as he lifted his hands to her face and pressed the finger into her mouth. The heady musk of her own body flooded her taste buds.

He smiled. 'We will eat, and then later we'll continue with your education.' Alex's eyes didn't leave his. He took her hand and led her to the table, seating her beside him. A second or two later Gena and Starn appeared, and dinner was served.

As each course was completed Alex couldn't help but wonder what would happen once they had finished their meal. A little spark of tension hung in the air, and by the time coffee was served the atmosphere was so expectant that Alex could hardly bear the wait. Finally Peter Tourne looked at her.

'Go down to the room near gallery and wait for me there,' he said softly. She felt a little tremor of excitement and hesitated for an instant – did she really want her education to continue? He looked at her again, but by this time she was on her feet and moving.

Afraid to look back in case her courage failed her, she hurried down through the house and out into the garden, imagining his footfalls on the stairs behind her. Scurrying through the velvet shadows of the gallery above the pool she opened the door of the room where she had spent the night, and gasped – waiting inside was Mario, his dark feral eyes glistening in the gloom.

Alex glanced back over her shoulder, wondering where Peter Tourne was. Across the room Mario leered and licked his lips.

'No – you shouldn't be here,' she stammered, as the rough looking man crept towards her. 'Mr Tourne said,' she began, and then remembered that he'd told her to wait for him. She had to obey his instructions – she couldn't leave. She had to stay if she wanted what Peter Tourne had to offer.

Alex moved towards the door until her back was against the wall. She trembled slightly. Mario's eyes wandered over her body, as cruel and obscene, as his fingers had been the night before. Alex was desperately aware that her clothes offered little protection from the him. She was wearing the thinnest of cotton dresses and was naked beneath, in anticipation of Peter Tourne's needs.

Mario continued to leer at her, and slowly extended a hand. Alex shook her head violently, and started to side step towards the door. As her fingers closed around the door handle Mario lunged forward and grabbed hold of her arms. Her first instinct was to bring her knee up, but to her horror Mario anticipated the move and dodged the blow before it hit home.

His dark eyes flashed with a mixture of anger and amusement.

'You want hurt me?' he said gruffly. Alex wriggled to try and free her hands, pulling desperately to escape him. As she did the door opened behind her and she spun around to see Peter Tourne and Starn framed in the opening. She sighed with relief.

'Oh, thank God,' she whispered. 'He was already waiting when I got here. He—' To her abject surprise Mario didn't release her, in fact if anything his grip tightened.

Peter Tourne smiled thinly. 'I know he was, my dear. He was dutifully obeying my orders, as he always does.' He turned to the driver. 'Tie her up, Mario.'

Alex stared at him in astonishment. 'No,' she pleaded. 'Please, Mr Tourne, tell him to stop – please! You know I'll do exactly what you want!'

As she begged Mario pulled a pair of handcuffs from his jacket pocket and deftly snapped them onto her wrists. Her heart began to race. It seemed the encounter with Mario was part of the education Peter Tourne had in mind for her.

Part of her wanted to laugh; this was silly, just a game – but she wanted them to stop now. She looked from face to face, desperately hoping to find a hint of compassion in the eyes of one of them. Instead she found an unnerving mixture of desire and contempt that knocked every ounce of resistance out of her.

With a slight nod of his head Tourne signalled to Mario, who dragged Alex to the centre of the room. Glancing up she noticed for the first time a hook suspended on a length of chain from the ceiling. Surely it had not been there before? She squirmed as Mario held her with one strong arm while he pulled her hands up and attached the hook to the centre of the chain, which linked her cuffs. He leered constantly, obviously enjoying his work, and then adjusted the chain so that her hands were lifted above her head, her feet just resting on the floor. Alex was trussed like an animal carcass.

Tourne nodded his approval. Mario moved away, and Alex couldn't help but notice his disgusting erection jutting forward through his chinos. Another almost discernible nod from his boss, and Mario rubbed his hands together, and then opened one of the cupboards set in the far wall. From inside he produced a set of leg irons; a long steel bar, with an ankle cuff at each end.

'Please,' Alex begged softly. 'There's no need for all this. I've already promised to do everything you want. Surely you know that? I—' Her ramblings were cut short as Mario grabbed each of her ankles. She shuddered and instinctively tried to draw away from him. He snorted and grabbed her foot, dragging off one of her shoes. He unbalanced her, and the sockets in her shoulders screamed out in complaint. If she fought too much, he would tip her over and then her whole weight would be suspended on her arms. The thought horrified her. Mario lifted one foot higher to snap the ankle cuff into place and as he did he lifted her foot to his mouth and ran his tongue between her toes.

Alex gasped in horror. The sensation turned her stomach to liquid. Spreading her legs wider Mario pushed the bar into position and snapped the second cuff into place. He knelt back on his heels to admire his handiwork. Alex's sense of panic was growing with every passing second.

She was totally at the mercy of the three men – nothing she could do would prevent them from doing whatever they pleased with her. She twisted and tried to meet Peter's eyes. Surely now that his henchman had secured her he himself would take over?

'You have to understand the true nature of obedience, Alex.' Peter Tourne said quietly. 'This is a game we are playing, but you have to understand it is I, not you, who makes the rules.'

His voice shook her to the core. She stared at him. 'Mr Tourne...' she began, uncertain as to what she actually wanted to say.

He held up his hands. 'Speak only when I tell you to. You make the mistake of believing that who you are and what you think is important to us here. In this game the only things you have to offer are a – your body, and b – your total obedience to my every wish.' As he allowed his words to sink in, he nodded again to Mario.

The burly driver stepped closer and pulled a handkerchief from his pocket. Before Alex could protest he blindfolded her.

Suddenly plunged into darkness, Alex felt her terror mingling with the same dark, unnerving wave of expectation that had haunted her since her arrival at KaRoche. Rough hands clawed at her dress, ripping it away like tissue. She mewled in fear as the cool evening air hit her body. Now she was truly defenceless. She strained to try and hear what was going on in the room. Her head span. She was on the edge of hysteria when she felt the touch of a hand. Was it Mario or Tourne or Starn who was exploring her intimately now – pawing and licking her vulnerable breasts and nipples? Her sense of smell gave her the answer she needed; the stench of Mario's beer-soaked and sweating body threatened to overwhelm her. And she knew, as Mario thrust a rough finger into her, that the master and his guest were quietly watching while the servant played.

The sense of humiliation made her flush scarlet. Did Tourne and Starn plan to watch while Mario indulged himself? Did they intend to watch while he forced his thick cock into whichever orifice took his fancy? Tears welled up inside her, soaking the blindfold, while Mario's fingers opened her sex wider and teased at the tight bud of her clitoris.

What stunned Alex more than her fear and her sense of shame was that some rogue part of her mind was breathlessly excited by what was happening. Despite everything, Mario's crude fumbling sent a ricochet of pleasure up through her belly. As he pushed and prodded, making her shriek with fear and secret pleasures, she imagined Peter Tourne's eyes on her, savouring every detail of the erotic scene. Picturing his expression in her mind, she didn't feel Mario's teeth closing on her nipple until too late. She gasped in anguish as he bit her, and then tried to pull away from him, fighting her own mounting desire as much as her tormentor's touch. She heard him snort and step away.

For a moment Alex wondered if Mario would stop now – perhaps her punishment was over. They would leave her tied and alone with her feverish thoughts and fears. Her sense of relief was short-lived. From behind the blindfold she heard the unnerving sound of something cutting through the air, and an instant later a corona of pain exploded in her mind as a lash bit her squarely across the shoulders. She screamed and tried to fight. She twisted and turned against her restraints, oblivious suddenly to the pain in her shoulders. She span so far that the second blow caught her breasts, burning across her already sore nipples like a firebrand. The sensation was so astonishing that she leapt into the air. In her solitude it seemed as if she was defying gravity; almost flying away from the pain.

Before she had time to recover another blow wrapped around her waist, and she knew with blinding certainty that Mario was using an old-fashioned horsewhip. Another blow seared across her shoulders before the pain of the previous one had had a chance to ebb. The sensations threatened to consume her, like a flame speeding along a fuse and leaving a white-hot residue on her flesh and in her mind that refused to be extinguished. Every nerve ending in her body felt as if it was alight. More unnerving, along with the pain, plaited and twisted in with everything else, Alex could still feel terrifying threads of pleasure weaving themselves together. She heard a voice begging and mewling, and was stunned to realise it was her own.

For an instant she wondered if she would go mad. Would the sensations she was feeling catch light and consume her? How was it, that in all the years she'd lived, she'd never been aware of this dark seed growing within her? Out beyond the pain and the pleasure she suddenly understood what was compelling her to accept Peter Tourne's education – it was the act of total surrender. She gasped as the realisation flooded over her, struggling to catch her breath as Mario applied the whip again and again. She had given herself totally to Peter Tourne – an act of trust beyond anything she had ever thought herself capable.

'Let go,' whispered a voice close by. For an instant Alex wondered if it was her own inner voice speaking, and then she realised it was the voice of her master, Peter Tourne. Had he been able to read her mind?

'Let go,' he urged again as the whip bit into her back. She whimpered, finally letting all rational thoughts trickle away as her body was caught up in the maelstrom of pleasure and pain. As Mario struck again all that remained was sensation – as electrifying and all engulfing as a summer storm.

Peter Tourne sensed the moment of surrender, that split second when Alex Sanderson abandoned everything she'd ever known and committed herself to him completely. He had witnessed it many times before, and had an instinctive understanding of when a pupil became his slave. Whatever else happened to Alex Sanderson, she would never be the same again. The seed that had lain dormant for so long would blossom and grow under his expert tutelage.

He signalled to Mario to bring the whipping to an end. A trickle of sweat ran down between Alex's straining breasts. Her body, though trembling, was relaxed now, accepting the whip like a lover's kiss. He smiled and walked over to the blindfolded girl. He gently traced a finger down over her taut nipples. He knew she sensed it was his touch and not Mario's. She whimpered and rubbed herself against him like a cat seeking attention. He motioned to Mario to release the chain so that her arms would drop. She was understandably unsteady. He caught her before she could fall, and guided her down to the floor while Mario worked to free her ankles from the irons. She pressed herself against him, wordlessly seeking his approval. Kneeling over her he guided her face towards his groin.

Although hampered by the intense sting in her back and by the limiting and awkward restrictions of the handcuffs, Alex struggled feverishly to free his aching shaft and pull it into her mouth. She needed the comfort of his closeness. She curled onto her side, drawing him deep between her lips, lapping and licking at his phallus in an act of complete submission. Her fingers cradled his balls, her tongue and mouth eager to suck him dry. He shivered and pressed deeper, relishing the heat and the tightness around him. She moaned in appreciation.

He parted her thighs and stroked the soft naked rise of her sex. Without hesitation she opened her legs wider for him, offering herself up for whatever he wanted to take. She was so wet her juices coated his fingers like a fragrant tide. He smiled and sought out the pleasure bud that nestled like a ripe cherry between the lips of her sex. Her moans of delight vibrated through his shaft, taking him to the very edge of oblivion. He pressed a single finger deep inside her quim, and at once felt her begin to tighten rhythmically around it, her moist heat perfectly echoing the rhythm of her mouth. He had barely touched her, but it had been enough to trigger her orgasm.

'Yesss…' he murmured as he surrendered to the call of his own pleasure, and flooded into her eager and gasping mouth.

Under his expert fingers Alex writhed like a wild animal, giving him every part of herself. It seemed that for an instant their minds met, each sensation replayed and echoed in the other. For that moment master and slave were equal and the same – riders on a storm of ecstasy.

When he'd done with her, Peter Tourne gently pushed her away. She licked her lips as if afraid she'd missed a drop of his precious essence, and then curled back into a ball. Across the room Starn Fettico grinned and began to unfasten his trousers. Tourne shook his head.

'Leave her,' he murmured. 'There'll be plenty of time for that later.' He turned to Mario. 'Take her to one of the cells and leave her chained. This is just the beginning.'

Climbing to his feet, he looked down at the naked English girl, her narrow back crisscrossed with welts, and smiled. It wouldn't take long though, he thought; Alex Sanderson was a natural submissive, even if she hadn't previously realised it herself. She would go far, and he would help her on her way.

Mario unfastened the chain from the handcuffs and hefted the girl up into his arms. His face was a mask.

Tourne stared hard at him. 'Let her rest,' he said, hoping the man would have sense enough to leave the girl alone when he got her to the cell; she'd already given him exactly what he wanted, and had earned herself a rest. He leaned over her and untied the blindfold. Alex's eyes were closed, her face totally expressionless.

Alex's consciousness had retreated into a dark safe corner of her mind, and it took a few minutes to feel she was once again in control. She'd almost felt as if she was watching herself suck Peter Tourne dry. Her body had been working on instinct alone, taking what it craved from the man who would be her master. Now, held tight in Mario's burly arms, she wondered what would follow.

Ridiculously, she felt somehow safe and secure, as if a great weight had been lifted from her. Slowly reason began to reassert itself as Mario carried her across the room to the door beside the bathroom. It was ajar, and inside Alex could just make out a long corridor from behind her half closed lids. It was gloomy and cold. As the chill hit her naked flesh, Alex struggled to suppress a shiver.

Mario walked slowly, though there wasn't the slightest suggestion he might drop her. At the end of the corridor was another open door. Alex stiffened as she glanced inside; it was a cell, barely taller than she was, with a platform along one wall. On the platform was a thin mattress and a rough grey blanket. Beside it was a toilet and a shower. Other than that the room seemed totally bare.

Mario rolled her unceremoniously onto the mattress, caught hold of the handcuffs she was still wearing, and clipped them onto a chain that hung from above. It was arranged so that she would be able to move around the cell, would be able to use the toilet and shower, but would not be able to leave this prison. But what disturbed her more than this alarming form of imprisonment was the expression on Mario's face. He sniffed as he peered down at her, and ran his tongue over his fat lips. He didn't look at her face. Instead his gaze rested on her nakedness, and he casually ran a hand up over her flank.

'You like man to beat you,' he said thickly. 'It make you wet.'

Alex stared at him, struggling to find her voice. 'Mr Tourne said you were to leave me alone,' she said timidly, curling into a tight ball.

Mario snorted. 'He don't care, he not come down here. He just say, 'Mario, fetch the girl. Mario, beat the girl', but he don't come down here. Down here there only me to look after you. If you don't do what I like, then…' he lifted his hands in an all encompassing gesture. 'No food, no water, no blanket… *no nothing!* I make your life very – how you say,' he struggled over the last word, fighting to find sufficient English. *'Difficult!'*

Alex felt her stomach contract. Left under Mario's care her life would be hell. She took a deep breath. 'Mr Tourne will be angry with you,' she said with a confidence she didn't feel.

Mario laughed. 'If you tell him, I make much worse for you. Now, shut up and open legs.'

Alex stayed still. Her jailor's face contorted into a maniacal grin. 'I can make very bad for you, now open legs, you English whore!'

Alex knew resistance was useless, and probably very foolish; it would only succeed in angering him further. She slowly parted her knees.

'Is right,' hissed her tormentor. 'You give Mario pleasure now.' He smiled and spread her legs wider still, driving his fingers deep inside her. She shrieked at his brutality, but his only reaction was to grab hold of her knees and drag her onto her back, scraping the welts across the rough surface of the mattress. He jerked her towards him so that her feet were on the dusty floor, her hips on the edge of the platform, and her tender back on the cold rough concrete. Forcing her legs wider still he stood between them and began to paw at her breasts and quim with one hand, whilst unbuttoning his fly with the other.

Before Alex had time to recover, he plunged his cock home, making her shriek with surprise and fear. He was deaf to her cries and drove on and on, dragging her onto him time and time again. Her back screamed out in agony as it rubbed against the concrete, but nothing she said or cried made any difference. Mario ploughed into her relentlessly, gasping and snorting, and clawing at her nipples until she knew he was close to the point of no return.

Totally disgusted, Alex squeezed her eyes tight to blot out the abhorrent image of his red and contorted features slobbering over her like a madman. She knew he was about to come. At the last second she felt him drag his cock out of her and spurt an arc of semen over her belly. As it splattered onto her skin she felt sick and empty.

Mario wiped his loose mouth with the back of his hand and turned away without a second glance at her.

Alex started to shake, tears coursing down her face. She had to get away from the villa. Whatever Peter Tourne had to offer her it was not worth this. If she stayed she would be at the mercy of any man who wanted her, master or servant, whether it was forbidden or not. The cell door clanged shut and she took a deep breath. Mario's seed clung to her belly in an unnerving puddle. Slowly, steadying herself at every step, she crossed to the shower, the water was icy cold as it hit her, but Alex didn't care. All she wanted was to be clean but she doubted whether water alone would be enough.

Chapter Four

Upstairs in the sitting room, Peter Tourne poured himself and Starn a glass of brandy each. Starn's expression was set, his manner cool and offhand. Tourne knew that by denying his friend the opportunity to make use of Alex Sanderson's vulnerability he had infuriated him, and quite enjoyed the sense of power it gave him. He handed Starn the glass.

'Gena is still waiting for you downstairs,' he said, indicating the door. 'Would you like me to call her up?'

Starn snorted. 'If I'd wanted Gena I wouldn't have bothered to come up here with you. What are you planning to do with Alex Sanderson once you've broken her?'

He shrugged. 'You're tired of Gena, already? I'm surprised I thought she was perfect for you. You want to sell her on? If you do I'm sure I can find a buyer. She's a very beautiful young lady. She would command an excellent price.' He knew it wasn't what Starn meant at all, but enjoyed playing with him.

Starn stared into his brandy balloon.

Tourne continued, 'Armande the Frenchman, Bene, Michael – they would all jump at the chance of owning one of my girls. Would you like me to make a few calls?'

'No,' snapped Starn. 'It's not that I'm tired of Gena you know it isn't. It's just that I thought, as we are friends, you would let me sample your new girl's delights as well. Hell, that greasy slob of a driver of yours gets to have more fun than I do!'

Peter smiled. 'What about this morning? You are so impatient, my friend. You haven't lost the chance to have some fun with her again, it's just that at the moment I feel she will respond more quickly if I alone teach her.'

Starn snorted derisively again. 'You didn't think that earlier when she was here with Gena.'

Peter wondered how he could possibly explain what he had seen in Alex's demeanour that had changed his opinion about her fate. Alex hadn't just been broken she had given herself over entirely to sensation and submission. It was an instinctive thing, part of her nature that Peter recognised as something of great value. Alex Sanderson wouldn't just resign herself to being man's slave; in time, when she came to terms with what she felt, she would learn to relish her new role.

'Of course, Starn, you're quite right. Eventually I will auction her,' he said after a second or two. 'Unless a bidder comes forward in the meantime with a sizeable offer. Just give her a little time more to settle in. In another day or two, when she understands what we expect of her, then of course you can have your fill. Don't let's fall out over one woman, for God's sake – the world is full of them. Here, let me top your glass up.'

Starn seemed appeased. 'An auction? Will you hold it here?'

Tourne shook his head. 'To be honest Alex's arrival at KaRoche has come as a total surprise to me. I haven't had the time to give it a great deal of thought. It might be interesting to let her be sold off with Simon Bay's surplus girls when the time comes. He's staying on the island for the summer. He gave me a ring a week or so ago to say he had a rather good stable at the moment, and suggested I might be interested in taking a look. When Alex is ready we ought, perhaps, to take her over there.'

Starn grinned. 'Simon has a good eye. Perhaps he might even buy your protégé for himself.'

Both men looked at each other knowingly. Simon Bay's girls were famous. A slave master, unrivalled amongst his contemporaries, he was an entrepreneur and businessman

who used his frequent business trips around the wo
acquire girls from everywhere on earth. If Simon Ba
bought Alex for his own use it would be the ultimate
accolade.

Tourne smiled, aping nonchalance. 'It would depend
on what he offered. Now, are you going to call for Gena,
or would you prefer another glass of brandy?'

Starn stood his glass on the bureau. 'I'll go and find
her, and God help her if she doesn't satisfy me. After the
exhibition with your little artist friend, I need more than
just a little light relief!'

Tourne grinned. 'I've had Mario take Alex down to the
cells, perhaps you'd like to take Gena to the Gallery room
and make use of the facilities there? It never hurts to
remind your slave who is in control.'

Starn nodded.

He watched his friend depart, wondering for a few
seconds whether he should go and settle himself in the
hidden room overlooking the gallery to observe what would
undoubtedly be a fine performance by Gena and her
master.

He was disappointed that Starn was so easily distracted
from the exquisite blonde. Originally Gena had come here
to work as a secretary, but he'd known the second he'd
laid eyes on her beauty that her obvious talents would be
wasted behind a desk – over a desk would be a different
matter! He sipped his brandy, closed his eyes, and let his
thoughts drift back to that most enjoyable morning when
he first had the pleasure…

At Gena's interview, after their preliminary discussions,
and as she handed Peter Tourne a letter of recommendation
from her previous employer, he 'accidentally' nudged a
sheaf of papers off the corner of his desk and onto the
floor. Gena instantly and elegantly dropped to all fours to
retrieve them. As she gathered them back into a neat pile,

up and moved around his desk. At once
active reaction was to look up at him. When
net, she blushed, aware that something other
ple interview was taking place. As her colour
and she began get to her feet he lifted a hand.

'I think,' he said in a low voice, 'that you should stay
exactly where you are.'

The blonde girl swallowed hard. 'Stay?' she murmured
innocently. 'Here?'

He nodded. 'You understand precisely what I mean…'
Peter took another sip and allowed his brandy and his
memories to warm him…

He picked up a pair of scissors from his desk and, as if
it was the most natural thing in the world, cut along the
back of Gena's blouse, through her bra strap, down
through her pencil slim skirt and flimsy white panties,
tearing away the fabric as he worked, ruining her
expensive little interview costume. While he worked, Gena
stayed perfectly still, her pale body trembling as the cold
blades brushed her skin.

Finally, naked except for her sandals, she crouched
amongst the ruins of her clothes. She looked exquisite, a
pale creamy-skinned Madonna, cowering, subdued
awaiting whatever her superior had in store for her. For a
few seconds they were both still – master and slave
awaiting each other's pleasure.

When Gena finally looked up to him her dark eyes were
bright with fear and anticipation. She remained crouched
on all fours, her heavy breasts swaying like liquid silk,
breathes coming in short frantic bursts as she waited for
his next move.

Surveying her, Tourne knew that beneath the thin veneer
of sophistication Gena was still a peasant at heart – her
hips were curvaceous and broad, her breasts, now pert
and full, would one day be pendulous and heavy. Between
her pale thighs was a thatch of glistening black hair, at

odds with her bleached blonde curls. She might well have a clutch of diplomas from secretarial college, but her body betrayed the fact that she was born to serve. He indicated she should stand.

Gena clambered to her feet without a word, pushing off the last remnants of her clothes. Tourne ran his hand over her haunches, assessing her body as he would a good horse. She turned instinctively under his fingertips, moving obediently to his unspoken commands. He brushed his fingers over her back and shoulders, letting his hand linger on the curve of her waist.

Already, despite her ripeness, her figure showed signs that it would thicken. For a few years she would serve her master faithfully and later, when she had lost the peach moist richness that suffused her body now, she had the hips to become a breeder, producing a whole new generation of submissive slave girls. He lifted a hand to cup her breasts, fingers working over the pert nipples. She shivered but said nothing. He knew then that Gena was an excellent find. She was naturally quiet and still – an attribute that many men favoured. Her natural demeanour was meek but sensual. She was the ideal submissive companion.

'Would you like to work for me?' Tourne asked, letting a single finger trail down towards her soft, rounded belly.

Perhaps afraid to speak, Gena nodded. He could detect the pulse in her throat fluttering like the wings of a tiny bird. Amongst the trappings of his expensively furnished office her nakedness seemed extreme. Her pale creamy skin was a stunning contrast to the backdrop of dark corporate grey and silver.

'To be honest, I'm not sure you're suitable. My business clients are sophisticates, where you are barely one step away from the vineyard.' He caught hold of one shapely breast, twisting the nipple savagely. He felt her flinch. 'Wouldn't you be happier back down on the farm, barefoot, with some country boy sniffing around you, and a baby sucking on your tits?' He watched her face for a reaction. Her eyes flashed but still she didn't speak. He smiled triumphantly. Walking confidently around her his fingers continued to trace a careful pattern of intimate exploration.

Finally he plucked a long flexible cane from amongst a Japanese arrangement that graced a side table by his desk. He flexed it thoughtfully, eyes never leaving hers. Still Gena did not bolt or cry out.

'Are you still a virgin?' he asked. It would not be unusual for a Greek girl of her age to be unbroken. Country people had always valued virginity as a prize to be held on to until marriage. Blushing, Gena shook her head. It was obvious that even though she was no longer a virgin, she wasn't experienced either.

'Who?' asked Tourne relishing her discomfort.

Gena's colour intensified, but significantly she didn't refuse this complete stranger an answer to such an intimate question. 'My cousin, Giuseppe. Last summer we...' the words dried up as he moved closer to her. 'We only did it the once,' she stammered.

His expression remained impassive. 'Your cousin? You country girls are all the same. How do I know you aren't lying? How do I know you haven't fucked every man you've laid eyes on with those big tits, that arse – how many hands have played around in that wet little cunt of yours? How many cocks have you sucked dry? Or do you prefer it when they fuck you? Or do you prefer other girls?'

Gena's eyes widened in horror. 'Mr Tourne,' she began to protest in astonishment.

'You're no better than a whore!' he snapped. 'And then you come to my office, pretending to be respectable so that you can get a job with my company! What were you thinking of?'

Gena stared at him open-mouthed, too shocked to speak.

Peter Tourne indicated his desk. It was a huge single slab of black marble supported on trestles.

'Bend over,' he said. 'Let me show you how we used to treat the peasant whores on my father's estate.'

A tiny bead of perspiration broke out on Gena's upper lip. The smell of her reluctance and fear were as tangible as her perfume. She didn't move, but he could see her anxiously pondering the distance to the desk, as if she had already taken each step. He lifted his hands in a gesture of dismissal, and as he did so Gena walked slowly towards the austere piece of furniture as though she was taking her last few steps to the guillotine. Her eyes were firmly fixed on the middle distance as she submissively draped herself across the icy marble.

He heard her gasp as the cold stone sucked the heat from her body.

'Open your legs,' he directed. 'Let me see the sweet little honey pot that attracts all those other men.'

Gena complied without a word, revealing the merest glimpse of her quim beneath the shapely contours of her bottom. The muscles in her buttocks were rigid in expectation of what he had in store for her. He stepped behind her and, catching hold of her hips, pulled her off the table a little so that more of the glorious moist pit was exposed and accessible.

First, he thought, he would administer a good sound beating and then, before the pain and humiliation had faded, before the red glow left her flesh, he would slide inside her. She was so mouth-wateringly ripe – there was part of him that adored her peasant fullness and natural subordination.

Stepping away he lifted the cane and brought it down with a resounding crack across her backside. She screamed out in a mixture of surprise and pain, bending into a contorted arc before slumping back onto the black marble. Her breasts spread beneath her, as pale and full as the harvest moon. Back swung the cane and exploded again. She squealed and arched up towards him, but not so violently this time. He hit her again, striking over and over until the rounded orbs of her backside were raw with a tapestry of welts.

Between Gena's thighs he could see her quim was flushed crimson, the moisture clinging like gossamer to the lips of her sex. Stepping closer he undid his flies and guided his raging shaft deep inside her. She squealed again and struggled unconvincingly to unseat him. As she twisted round he locked his fingers in her hair and jerked her back up towards him, his other hand scooping up one of her ample breasts, fingers nipping and twisting her cold, erect nipples.

Gena shrieked madly, writhing under him like a frightened animal, but still he held on, riding her, pulling her back onto his cock again and again, grinding his pelvis against the soft expanse of her glowing arse.

'Please,' she sobbed. 'Please no, I am good girl, Mr Tourne. I am not a whore. Please, please don't do this to me. I am good girl.' But while her mouth said one thing her body told Peter Tourne something totally different. Her quim tightened around him like a clenched fist, pulling him deeper, her hips instinctively pressing against him, driving him towards the point where even his inscrutable exterior threatened to crack and display some emotion.

Gena gasped and sobbed, tears streaming down her face. He took her hand and urged it down to her sex, guiding her fingers to seek out the bud of her own clitoris.

'Touch yourself,' he hissed in her ear. 'Let me show you what it is that all those men want from you.' As he spoke he pressed her fingertips hard against the engorged ridge. She mewled in astonishment, almost convulsing as crystal circles of pleasure formed in her belly, bucking and roaring as he began to circle the little nub, pushing her fingers to and fro until finally her head fell back onto his shoulder and he could feel her fingers moving of their own accord.

With Gena's pleasure building, Tourne began to move in earnest, dragging her back hard, tightening his grip on her hair, his free hand returning to weigh and knead her full breasts. She was moaning and breathing hard, struggling to pleasure them both. He felt the first intoxicating ripples of her quim tightening around his erection as orgasm overtook her, and knew then he was lost too. An incandescent wave flooded through him, driving away all reason as he plunged into her again and again, on and on until he felt he was drowning in a sea of pure pleasure.

When, finally, Peter Tourne slumped onto her back, his body utterly drained, he opened his eyes and smiled. Beside Gena's tousled, sweat-soaked hair, was the letter of recommendation that she'd handed to him only a short time before. One sentence in the main paragraph caught his eye – it read: *I have always found Gena to be an extremely willing and able young woman.* Peter slid out of her and adjusted his trousers. What a shrewd judge of character Gena's previous employer had been.

Now, standing alone in the villa, he wondered whether to go and watch Starn re-enact that first conquest. It might be interesting, but it would never be as magical as that first time when Gena had not known what to expect. He decided, on balance, to refill his glass – after all, he had Alex Sanderson to think about now.

Downstairs in the prison cell behind the gallery, Alex huddled into a foetal ball, trying to block out the sounds of Gena and Starn in the room beyond. Even through the thick walls she could hear Gena's impassioned cries and Starn encouraging her on and on as he laid on the whip.

The blonde's voice seemed to echo from every surface.

Alex closed her eyes, pressed her fingers to her ears, and struggled to fill her mind with the images of the mural she intended to paint on the wall overlooking the pool in Peter Tourne's garden. How likely was it now that she would ever have the chance to fill the cool shadowy space with pictures? However tempting the lessons Peter Tourne had to teach, she was afraid to think of what might happen if she abandoned herself to this madness. If the chance presented itself she would try to escape, even if it meant abandoning her possessions at the villa. Surely someone would help her? Perhaps the old housekeeper, who'd tried to warn her off in the first place, could be persuaded to help her break free.

As Alex tried to settle more comfortably on the thin mattress every muscle in her body ached. It seemed there wasn't a part of her that Peter Tourne or Starn, Gena or Mario had not touched, kissed, beaten or bitten.

Finally, as the light darkened in the cell, Alex slipped into an uneasy sleep, her mind suffused with images of passion and pain. Again and again in her dreams she was torn between the desire to stay and the desire to escape. As she raced through the feverish dreamscape Peter Tourne thwarted her at every turn, and waited for her with a vicious whip in hand.

The sound of footsteps brought Alex back to consciousness with a start. The cell was now grey with early morning light. She felt cold and stiff. When she heard the key turn in her cell door her immediate reaction was to curl back into a ball in case it was Mario coming back for more. The door swung open slowly to reveal the wrinkled features of the housekeeper bearing a breakfast tray. The contents were meagre; a tin jug of water and two bread rolls and an apple, but to Alex they looked like a feast. The woman set the tray on the floor and then eyed Alex thoughtfully, her eyes moving over the girl's nakedness. Her expression was not unsympathetic, and Alex knew she had to take a chance.

'Will you help me?' she pleaded quietly.

The old woman shrugged. 'Is too late for help now. He already work the magic on you.'

Alex felt a ripple of fear run through her as the old woman continued. 'You should go when first I tell you about Mr Tourne. You not listen then, why I listen now?'

Alex struggled to her feet, regretting it instantly as her body groaned in complaint.

The old woman nervously backed away through the open cell door. 'If you give me trouble,' she said, 'I leave you to Mario – and he not always here. He forget to feed you. He *very* bad man.'

Alex stared at her. 'I won't give you any trouble,' she whispered. 'But please, you have to help me. If you go to my room and find my telephone book, look for Laurence Russell's number. Please ring him. He's my friend. He'll come and get me. There's money there, take it all…' as she spoke she heard the sound of approaching footsteps, and the woman's attention was drawn back into the corridor outside the cell.

There was a tirade of words in Greek and then the cell door slammed shut. Alex stiffened as she recognised Mario's voice drowning out the old lady's mumbled protests. In amongst the foreign words she recognised a few English ones – perhaps Mario was adding them for her benefit.

'Not open door!' the driver bellowed at the old woman 'She is mine. Understand? I look after her you not interfere. No one to see her except me. She is mine!'

His words made Alex shudder – if she couldn't speak to the housekeeper and persuade her to help she might never get away. Perhaps, though, she had already said enough. If the old woman rang Laurence she stood a chance of escaping.

While Mario continued to berate the housekeeper outside the cell, Alex, despite the handcuffs, hastily grabbed the apple from the tray and thrust it under the thin mattress. She then took a mouthful of the cool clear water straight from the jug, in case Mario decided to punish her by taking her breakfast away.

Seconds later the cell door slammed open and Mario stood framed in the opening, his face contorted with fury. He strode across the cell and, without warning, hit her hard across the face with his open hand. The power and surprise of the blow made her stagger backwards. Unable to steady herself because of the cumbersome handcuffs, she toppled over onto the floor, banging her head on the corner of the bed as she did.

'You not talk to her!' Mario roared.

Alex's head span, though through the swirling confusion she could see the brute bearing down upon her. For one awful moment she thought he was going to kick her and tensed up, curling into a tight ball, waiting for the blow. Instead he stooped over, grabbed her hair, and yanked her back onto her feet.

'You make me angry!' he spat, throwing her down onto the mattress.Despite his fury his eyes moved hungrily across her naked body. She sensed that for him anger and desire were emotions that were always dangerously close to the surface of a very thin line.

He glanced back at the ruined contents of the tray – the bread was crushed on the stone floor, and the water jug lay in its own puddle.

'You hungry?' he said thickly.

Alex nodded. Perhaps he wasn't such a monster after all.

Grinning, Mario clambered up onto the platform and knelt astride her. She stared up at him in horror as he unzipped his fly, trying to make some kind of contact with the cruel mind behind the bright flashing eyes. She

78

could smell the rank odour of his masculinity even before he pulled out his cock.

'Eat this then,' he snorted grimly, flexing his hips as he thrust his engorged shaft into her mouth it was pointless to try and fight him. Struggling to control the feelings of nausea Alex began to suck, her mind revolted and ashamed as Mario grunted with satisfaction, his fingers seeking out her breasts, his body moving rhythmically against her face. Alex prayed that while Mario was busy abusing her, the old woman had gone to the guest cabin. Mario snorted as the pleasure overwhelmed him, and he pulled her closer. She could feel the tension building in his body and braced herself for his orgasm. Seconds later her mouth was flooded by a wave of thick semen. Alex gagged. She tried to spit his seed out but he clamped her jaw shut tight around him so that she had no option but to swallow.

He closed his eyes and slouched with his chin on his chest, and his whole body in a state of total relaxation. He remained kneeling over Alex with his hands on his thighs, and his shrinking cock being soothed by the natural fluttering of her tongue. She looked up at his bulk and wondered when he would leave her in peace. His cock felt like a slug in her mouth.

At last he slipped from between her lips. He lifted his considerable weight from her aching breasts and clambered off the platform. He grinned down at her. 'I bring you coffee now,' he said, waving towards the discarded tray. 'Hot coffee and more breakfast. You just remember not to speak to old woman – you are mine. I look after you now.'

Alex sniffed miserably, her mouth still thick with the taste of his semen. Glancing up at her gaoler's face she hoped she'd already said enough to the housekeeper. Mario left the cell, slammed the door shut behind him, and turned the key in the lock. Alex stared into the gloom and waited for him to return.

Chapter Five

Peter Tourne sat alone under a parasol on the terrace and ate his breakfast. From his vantage point he could see the fishing boats sailing out of the tiny harbour, and the first of the ferries arriving. Although it was early the sun was already hot. He glanced at his watch. Hearing soft footsteps he looked up into the wrinkled brown face of his housekeeper. She was carrying a jug of coffee. He smiled.

'I thought for a moment you were Miss Sanderson,' he said in English.

The old woman frowned. 'Mario is too rough,' she said flatly in her native Greek. 'He'll hurt her unless you speak to him. Miss Sanderson isn't like Gena, not a local girl. If you're not careful you could get into trouble. She's too delicate to be left to a ruffian like Mario.'

He smiled. 'I understand what you're saying. Would you please ask him to bring Miss Sanderson up here? After all, I commissioned her to paint a mural. There's no need for her to be locked up all day long.'

The old lady nodded and turned away. He watched her leave; Mario wouldn't dare touch Alex out in the open, but locked in the small cell was another matter. What he didn't want his housekeeper to know was that he knew exactly the kind of man Mario was, and that his driver's brutality was a useful addition to every girl's training.

He waited in his study for Alex's arrival. When she stepped into the room he regarded her carefully. He noticed that she didn't lift her head to meet his eyes, which was a good sign. Naked, and with her hands still cuffed, she looked so touchingly vulnerable.

He nodded to Mario.

'I think we can dispense with the cuffs, Mario. After all, Miss Sanderson is an artist, and we can't expect her to work with her hands so crudely bound, now can we? I think I have something here that will do just as well.'

He opened his desk drawer and brought out a narrow leather collar, set with silver studs. Alex looked up towards him for the first time since entering his study. Her face was pale and gaunt. There was a livid red mark on one temple – perhaps the housekeeper was right; Mario was taking his role as gaoler a little too seriously. Tourne had no wish for any of the girls in his care to sustain permanent damage – that would be counterproductive.

He held the collar out to her and turned it in his fingers so she could see what he had in store for her. It had a ring set in it, from which could be hung a chain and handle – like a dog lead. At one end of the collar was a tiny lock fastening that snapped shut and which couldn't be opened without a key. He handed it to Mario. Alex didn't move as the heavy man slid the collar round her throat and snapped the lock shut. When it was snugly in place Mario removed the handcuffs.

Tourne nodded his approval. 'And how is my servant treating you, Alex?' he asked, encouraging her to look at him. Alex glanced up with dark unhappy eyes. He could guess.

Alex shot a quick sideways glance at the swarthy driver, her eyes suddenly flashing with fury and hatred. 'Fine – Mr Tourne,' she said quietly – and wisely.

Peter Tourne smiled. She learned fast. 'Good, then in that case I think it's time you started work.' He looked her up and down. 'I'll have Mario find you something appropriate to wear. The sun is very fierce today and you're so fair skinned.' He paused. 'Fair skins always command a good price at auction.'

He watched Alex stiffen and stare at him.

'At auction?' she repeated, unable to keep the note of astonishment out of her voice.

He nodded. 'What did you think happened to girls like you?' he said softly, seeing the fear moving across her face like water rising. 'When I'm ready I'll sell you on, like Gena, and like a dozen girls I've trained before you. Don't make the mistake of thinking you're special; you're just one of many.' He paused and let the realisation sink in before he continued. 'Fair skin always brings a good price.' He waved to Mario and handed him a leash that matched the collar. 'Get her showered and dressed, and then take her down to the garden so she can begin her work.'

Alex sat in the long cool gallery by the poolside. Around her were the tools of her trade, brought down by the housekeeper and arranged on a small folding table. She had had no chance to speak to the old woman again. Mario had watched them both like a wolf awaiting his chance to pounce.

Alex stroked the boxes of familiar brushes and paint tubes, trying hard to regain some sense of control. It was difficult. A length of chain extended from her collar to a ring set in the floor, which meant she could easily move around but could not escape.

She'd assumed when Peter Tourne had told her she would be found some clothes that he meant something of her own – she had been wrong. Mario had brought her a sheer white cotton shirt, so thin that she might as well have been naked, and a skirt that looked as if it had belonged to the elderly housekeeper. It reached the floor, and was made of rough wool. Barefoot and with no underwear she felt like a peasant servant girl, chained and ready for her master or any other man that passed her way. Every movement made the rough wool brush against her sensitive skin, electrifying her bruises and scratches.

Alex stared down at her drawing pad, wondering how on earth Peter Tourne expected her to work when so much had happened. The ideas forming in her head had nothing to do with art or painting, but of pain and passion and an overwhelming realisation that she had to escape from the clutches of Peter Tourne before it was too late. She could still feel the whip cracking across her back, and still feel Mario's brutal touch...

She picked up her pencil thoughtfully glancing down at the wildly erotic images she'd drawn the day before. Perhaps she could create a moral fairytale – a parable that would warn other girls what Peter Tourne was like. The idea began to take shape. Turning to a new page she began to draw frantically, filling sheet after sheet of paper with rough sketches. Perhaps, if she could do nothing else, she could help warn other girls what fate awaited them in the luxurious villa called KaRoche.

Once the form of the mural began to take shape, Alex became totally immersed in what she was doing. Time passed without her being aware of it. Oblivious now to her surroundings, the only thing that registered were the pictures forming on the page. Almost triumphantly she tore a leaf from her sketchbook and began to transfer it onto the squared paper that would help her scale it up for the long wall. Peter Tourne had promised her that she could create whatever she wanted – she intended to take him at his word.

Alex didn't hear the footsteps approaching from the garden behind her. The first time she registered a presence was when a shadow fell across her sketchpad.

'I've been looking for you,' said a low voice. Alex froze, all thoughts of the mural instantly flooding away as if a dam had burst. She turned slowly and looked up into the grim face of Starn Fettico.

She swallowed hard, knowing she was completely vulnerable. 'Mr Tourne is upstairs, I think,' she offered.

She placed the pencil and pad on the table and sat with defensive expectancy, like a Wild West gambler preparing for an assault by a sore loser; she knew he wasn't looking for his friend.

Starn nodded. 'I know that. It isn't Peter I wanted to see,' he confirmed her fears. 'He's busy this morning.'

Alex felt a growing sense of panic. She watched Starn's eyes move to the contours of her cleavage and breasts, and then fix themselves on the dark peaks of her nipples where they pressed through the thin cotton voile. She shuddered as he looked away, his gaze moving on to trace the silver chain from the ring in the floor to the collar she wore around her neck. Before she could protest he grabbed the chain and jerked it hard, dragging her to her feet. The table at which she had been working tipped dramatically, spilling pencils and paper all over the flagstone floor. The collar slid sharply up under her chin, making her gasp with discomfort.

Starn pulled her closer, ignoring the chaos he'd created. One hand cupped her breast through the thin blouse while he thrust a foot between hers and forced her legs apart. She could feel his hot and stale breath on her cheek – and an ominous lump against her belly.

'Do you like what you're learning?' he hissed. 'Peter tells me you're a natural – but I'm not so sure.'

'Please,' Alex whispered, 'leave me alone. I have work to do for Mr Tourne.' She knew she had to divert his attentions. 'Tonight. Come to my room tonight. I'll be good – I'll do anything you want. Please… you're hurting me.'

'Shut up!' Starn hissed. He jerked the chain again, his hand dropping now so that he could fumble with her skirt, dragging it up to allow him unobstructed access to her tensed body.

'Peter doesn't want me to *have* you yet,' he said thickly, pawing at her thighs. 'He seems to have forgotten that women like you are meant to be used.' He paused. 'He'll sell you on, you be sure of that. He's already making plans to have you auctioned off. I might make a bid myself. You and Gena would be *so* good together.' He grinned, nodding towards her sketches where they lay on the floor. 'I saw you drawing. Are you the princess in the pictures? Gena the peasant bitch and Alex the little English princess. You'd make a superb pair; you with your sexy tongue up inside her cunt, crouched over, lovely cute arse in the air, while I take you from behind. Oh yes, I'd like that.'

Alex shuddered. Without Peter Tourne there to control him, Starn seemed almost as brutal as Mario.

His searching fingers finally found her sex beneath the skirt. 'You'd like that too, wouldn't you?' he grinned as he ran his palm over the close stubble that had re-grown on her quim. He forced his hand experimentally between her legs, cupping the outer lips and teasing a finger inside her.

Alex squirmed and held her breath. She felt him stiffen even more against her belly.

'You're wet already!' he snorted. 'Perhaps Peter was right about you after all – you are made to serve.'

Alex could feel the tension building in the pit of her stomach. The muscles tightened in her shoulders. She had to get away.

Starn probed deeper, his concentration slipping for an instant as he found the goal he'd been seeking. She felt him relax, and suddenly twisted round violently, breaking free from his clutches. She clenched her fists and thumped them down onto his chest, pushing him so hard that he lost his balance and stumbled backwards. With her pulse hammering in her ears she turned to run. In the split second before she took flight, Alex remembered the collar and chain – but it was too late. Starn, breathing heavily, was already ahead of her. Although she didn't see him she felt the chain jerk so violently that it almost choked the breath right out of her. Another violent tug sent her crashing to the floor.

Before she had time to recover Starn pushed her down hard on the cool stone. His fingers closed painfully on her shoulders. His expression was grim, but his eyes flashed with excitement.

'Oh yes!' he panted, dropping down across her chest so that she was pinned down. 'I like it when they fight!'

Alex's survival instinct was taking control. As the adrenaline began to pump she twisted back and forth, struggling to shake Starn off her. Her rational mind knew it was madness; there was nothing she could do with the chain still attached to the collar. It would be far more sensible to submit, but her body had other ideas. Fighting, biting, and writhing she struggled to get away from Starn, and as she did his hands jerked her skirt up. She screamed as she felt his fingers tearing at her thighs, before they plunged into her again. This time it wasn't a curious exploration but a cruel violation. His expression was predatory.

'You have to learn to do as you're told,' he said thickly. 'I want you – so I can have you. It's that simple.'

Alex glared up at him, and then spat in his face. It wasn't something she'd ever done before, and she was almost as surprised as Starn. His reaction was to slap her face hard, making her shriek. Wiping his cheek he clambered off her and jerked her back up to her feet.

Alex was trembling wildly. Her breath came in ragged sobs.

'Leave me alone, you bastard,' she gasped.

'Now, that's pretty unbecoming language for a little English princess. You deserve a good spanking for that.' Starn mocked. 'I'm surprised Peter hasn't taught you the fundamental rule of this wonderful place; you belong to whoever wants you, whenever they want you, however they want you. You have no say in the matter, do you understand?' As he spoke he spun her round to face the wall, and jerked her skirt up.

'Bend over,' he said, in a low and threatening tone. 'And open your legs. I'll show you what we do to slaves who forget their place.'

Alex longed to resist him, and was about to begin fighting again when she heard Peter Tourne's voice above the sound of her thumping heart. Her momentary relief quickly vanished when she realised what he was saying.

'Good morning Starn, I thought I heard your voice.'

There was no hint of rebuke for Starn in his tone; not a word to protect her or defend her.

Starn snorted. 'Your little bitch spat at me.'

'Tut, tut,' said Tourne, turning Alex round to face him. 'I had hoped she would know better.'

She glanced up into his eyes. His expression was impassive, and she felt a sudden chill that cut to the bone.

'I thought she was beginning to understand,' he said, addressing his remark to Starn. 'It seems we have to take more stringent measures to ensure she understands exactly what is excepted of her.'

'Mr Tourne,' she began, with a note of appeal in her voice.

He caught hold of her chin suddenly, his fingers closing like a vice. 'Speak only when spoken to!' he snapped.

Alex looked away, unable to make sense of the complex emotions that coursed through her. Something about Peter Tourne and his cool voice made her stomach contract with fear, and lurch with a dark, eager desire.

He stroked her cheek. 'I really had hoped that you would learn the rules more quickly, Alex. It seems I was mistaken.'

Alex was filled with a sense of foreboding, only his order not to speak made her hold back from begging. She wanted to tell him she did understand – let Starn have her now, she didn't care. She would do whatever he asked.

She did understand!

But Peter Tourne had already turned away and unfastened the end of the chain that secured her to the stone floor.

He didn't jerk the leash, but instead he indicated the door at the far end of the gallery, and Alex obediently and silently moved towards it. Whatever punishment was to follow she had brought upon herself, but the thought did nothing to comfort her as she stepped into the cool and shadowy room. Beside the bathroom in the far wall she could see the door that led down to the cells. Perhaps he would simply lock her up... or perhaps Mario would return.

She stood in the centre of the room without moving an inch, aware of how ridiculous it was to wait so meekly. The chain had been released. She had a hint of an opportunity to escape, and yet she couldn't bring herself to take it. Standing in the doorway Peter Tourne's expression was one of disappointment rather than anger. Did he want her to have more spirit? Did he want to see her attempting to escape? Alex was confused.

Starn's expression by contrast was almost gleeful, as if he'd got some absurd childish delight in getting Alex into trouble.

Tourne took hold of her wrists, and from his pockets produced the handcuffs that Mario had removed earlier. His eyes moved over her body, lingering on her face. She blushed furiously. Snapping the cuffs into place he moved away to where a thick rope was looped around a large cleat on one wall. The rope passed up through a pulley system hanging from the ceiling, and had a large metal hook attached to its dangling end. He unravelled the rope from the cleat and lowered the hook.

Alex almost felt as if she was an observer to her own punishment. She watched, rather than felt, as he slipped the hook through the cuffs and then pulled the rope back up towards the ceiling. With her arms above her head she waited meekly for whatever was to follow. He stepped back and looked her up and down, as still and assured as a big cat hunting game.

The cool room was unnaturally silent. Time seemed to slow until every second was a minute, and still Peter Tourne watched her.

Alex's stomach tightened and the hairs on the back of her neck prickled; this was not the passionate retribution she had expected, but a cool display of superiority that verged on indifference. Would he whip her now? Or would he let Starn loose to do with her as he pleased?

Finally he sighed and turned to Starn. 'Go to my office,' he said in a voice barely above a whisper. 'You know where to find what I want.'

Starn grinned. His obvious delight filled Alex with dread. As soon as he'd left the room Peter Tourne stepped close to Alex.

'You should have obeyed Starn,' he whispered menacingly. 'I thought you understood that I demand total obedience. I'm disappointed with you, Alex. You've let me down.'

Alex's eyes filled with tears, and her view of him became blurred. 'I am sorry, Mr Tourne. I'll try harder next time – I promise…'

Peter Tourne casually stroked her unprotected breasts through the thin voile blouse. Her nipples hardened instantly at his undeniably arousing touch. 'You belong to me,' he whispered. 'Perhaps Starn was wrong in trying to take advantage of you, but even if he was that is none of your concern; you are meant to do whatever he – or anybody else – requires of you. If there had been a fault – a wrong – it would have been his and not yours, had you obeyed him as you should have. Do you understand what I'm saying, Alex?'

Reluctantly Alex nodded. She was nothing more than a possession. Her will was subject to Peter Tourne's. She shivered. He moved away, apparently still unhappy with her. Her breasts felt cold without his touch. Moving across the room he pushed a bell on the wall. Alex closed her eyes, certain that he was summoning Mario. She was right – it only seemed an instant before the swarthy driver appeared.

Peter Tourne barely looked at him. 'Get me the frame,' he said quietly.

Mario's eyes flashed for an instant and then he vanished into the gloomy corridor that led to the cells. After a few minutes he reappeared carrying and dragging something that looked like a single wooden bed frame. A threatening pair of manacles was set at each end, and the body was crisscrossed with slats. Halfway along its length was a broad leather belt, and at one end was a depression, set with two fastenings. Alex realised with a growing sense of trepidation that this depression was there to support her neck and head. She swung round to beg for Peter Tourne's mercy, but his expression – as cold as an ancient glacier – froze the words in her mouth.

He waved Mario closer. The driver manoeuvred the frame into position in the centre of the room, and then set about lowering Alex's aching arms.

Peter Tourne watched Alex with a mixture of pleasure and pride as she allowed herself to be strapped to the wooden frame. He could see the trembling pulse in her chest, and the rise of nervous perspiration between her breasts. He was angry with Starn for disregarding his orders about leaving Alex alone, but even so, Alex had to learn that obedience was everything. The lower manacles secured and held her ankles wide apart. Mario worked slowly and diligently up over her prostrate body, tightening the belt around her waist, snapping the little locks into place on either side of her collar, and then finally taking the handcuffs off and pulling her arms apart and above her head so that he could secure each wrist into the manacles set in the heavy wooden frame.

Alex's eyes flashed with fear, but Peter Tourne knew exactly what had to be done; better now while she was still in doubt about her feelings – it would serve as a proof that she really was his to command.

He nodded to Mario, who slid the final restraint from the back of the frame – a leather hood that covered her head and eyes totally. Framing her nose it strapped securely under her chin, cutting out every shred of light and most sounds. All that would be left when they had done, would be her sensations and her thoughts.

As Mario jerked the tight mask over her face she began to cry out. It was a shriek of fear and uncertainty. Mario looked at his boss, waiting for instructions. On one side of the hood was a flap with a ball gag attached. Another buckle and the girl would be silenced. Peter Tourne considered this, and then shook his head; he wanted to hear her cries. Also, he didn't want to alarm her too much, and if she panicked in such a heightened state of awareness she might choke. Better to leave the gag off on this first occasion.

Starn reappeared carrying a stainless steel box and a similar leather one. Peter Tourne smiled thinly. Beckoning to Mario he stood back while the large man hooked the frame up on the rope and then hauled it up so that Alex and the frame were hanging at an acute angle to the floor. He waited while the man secured the frame so that it was stable.

Alex Sanderson looked divine; an innocent beauty in her thin blouse, her coarse skirt, barefoot and totally at his mercy. He could sense that she was struggling to make out what was happening, and wondered if she had any idea of what he had in mind as her punishment for defying Starn.

He ran a hand over her breasts, and was rewarded by a

91

faint ripple which spread out from under his fingertips. He could almost feel every nerve ending straining to make sense of his touch.

Roughly he pulled her skirt up, exposing her ripe quim. Her lips were open a little, like a ripening bud. Already a light gloss of hair was returning. Mario had already anticipated his boss's needs and hurried across the room with a bowl of water. Tourne smiled and opened the stainless steel box Starn offered him. From inside he took a tube of liquid soap. Gently, almost reverently, he soaped Alex's sex. He felt her stiffen as his fingers worked the lather over her mound. He took the razor from the bowl of hot water, and with skilled hands he removed every last trace of hair. Alex held her breath as the razor sliced through the stubble. When he'd finished he rinsed away the soap.

Before he began the next stage he bent forward and pressed a single kiss to the peach-soft lips, his tongue lingering for a second on the peak of her aroused clitoris. Alex responded instantly with a guttural moan and grind of her hips.

Tourne smiled – she would be *so* good, if only she would trust him; give herself over entirely to his desires. He moved his attention back to her breasts. Fingers catching in the gossamer thin fabric that covered them he ripped it open and, taking a swab offered to him by Mario, began to circle the tight little peaks of her nipples with surgical spirit. He felt her flinch and then snort in disbelief. It seemed she may have guessed what he intended to do – after all, she had seen Gena naked.

With the air of a top surgeon he pulled on a pair of thin latex gloves from the stainless steel box, and then removed the piercing gun. It took him only seconds to slip the pre-sterilised surgical steel nipple ring into place. Taking hold of one of Alex's breasts, nipping it tight so that the nipple protruded like a cherry pip, he positioned the gun with great professionalism before she had time to protest. When the head was flat against her skin he pulled the trigger. There was a faint hiss as the spring released, and then a frantic shriek from Alex as the metal bit home.

'No!' she screamed as the ring slid into place. Her whole body flexed and strained against the leather strap and manacles. Her sobbing echoed off the walls of the little room. When Tourne lay the gun against her other breast the sounds ceased and Alex froze. He could smell her fear, her anger, the sense of humiliation rising from her body. When he'd finished she would be wearing the mark of a slave. Her body would proclaim his possession of her. His fingers closed again around her delicate flesh. The only sounds that broke the tense silence were those of her laboured breathing – followed by the malevolent hiss of the gun.

This time Alex did not shriek or fight, but let out a long low wail of despair that made even the inscrutable Peter Tourne shiver with delight. When the second ring was in place Alex began to tremble. Her shivering was enough to make the sunlight catch and glitter off the two new pieces of body jewellery; they looked magnificent!

Glancing down at the vulnerable folds of her quim, Peter Tourne slipped a long stud into the gun. Today he would pierce each side of her labia and put a stud through each of the holes. Later – when she was ready for sale, he would slide a ring in to join the two; it was a symbolic gesture of closure that marked the completion of any girl's training. When the ring was in place he would be ready to pass her on.

Before he began again he gently ran a finger over one of the nipple rings. He considered it added a strange vulnerability and beauty to the female body; tangible proof of a woman's submission to her master.

Pouring more antiseptic wash onto a ball of cotton he swabbed the thick outer lips of Alex's sex. He felt the tension building again in her body as he parted them, and looked at the pale flower petals within. Occasionally he'd seen girls with the inner lips pierced too, but had always considered that a private matter, something a master did to his own woman, whereas the outer ring could be seen and understood by everyone.

He nuzzled the cold steel head of the piercing gun up under the moist folds of Alex's quim. She whimpered. What little he could see of her face was contorted with fear and apprehension. He calmly squeezed the trigger. A flash of silver traced the path of the steel pin.

Looking up he saw that Starn and Mario had moved closer to observe him at work, their eyes betraying hunger and lust. Though Peter Tourne counted Starn amongst his oldest friends, and considered Mario a good and trustworthy servant, he had little respect for either man.

Starn would never understand the subtle blend of cruelty and kindness, of passion and pain that always brought out the best in a woman. He only ever pursued his own pleasures, and in doing so he never commanded the full obedience, or experienced the full beauty, of a woman's unquestioning adoration that was possible. Mario, he knew, was a brutal and self-seeking bully. Though it served him well to have a man with such drives, he'd always suspected that left to his own devices Mario could brutalise a woman so much that she would be of little use for anything thereafter.

He swabbed the other labia. Already the first had begun to swell, plump flesh rising like new bread around the head of the stud. He rested his hand on Alex's firm smooth belly, stroking her gently to calm her. She was sobbing, but made no further attempts to resist him as he pressed the stainless steel gun into place. He took one final glance at Starn, who licked his lips, salivating at the exhibition. He made a mental note not to sell Alex to his friend, whatever price he offered. Starn had no appreciation of what a fine creature the young English artist was; she needed someone special to help her fulfil the full promise of which she was capable.

He squeezed the trigger that drove the final stud into place. As the pain ricocheted through the girl's body, despite the straps and restraints, she lifted up towards him. For an instant it seemed as if she was offering herself in her entirety into his hands. He smiled – Alex Sanderson was a feast, an exquisite banquet.

Starn was at his friend's shoulder, eyes alight with desire. Tourne could read his mind; he wanted Alex Sanderson and he wanted her now. He sighed and signalled again to Mario. His driver grinned and cranked the rope up so that Alex was now almost vertical.

His friend grinned and stepped closer to Alex, his hand working at the fastenings on her skirt. He dragged it down over her hips, leaving her naked except for the ragged remains of the thin cotton blouse.

'I'll teach her to do as she's told,' he whispered thickly and ran his hands over her newly pierced breasts.

Peter Tourne turned away and picked up the piercing gun. 'Get Mario to put her back in her cell when you've done here,' he said flatly. 'I'll be in my office if you want me.'

Chapter Six

Alex came to feeling as if she'd surfaced from some feverish nightmare. She knew she hadn't been unconscious, but very close to it. Peering around she tried to make sense of her surroundings. She was back in the cell. The little room was cool, dark, and totally silent. The chain glittering above her and joined to the collar around her neck brought back a flood of intense images. The abstract, dreamlike quality of her memories hardened into reality.

As Alex turned towards the door she felt the tension in the sensitive peaks of her breasts. Glancing down she saw the malevolent glitter of the rings and lower still, her sex echoed their subtle gleam, but strangely the pain of the piercing was somehow less disturbing than the memory of the events that had followed.

She knew it had been Starn who'd taken over from Peter Tourne, though how she could be so certain was beyond her. She couldn't remember the mask being taken off, but her mind was full of images of Starn circling her, his hands and fingers working into her most secret places with cool brutality. She could visualise his face, cruel and triumphant, as he drew his fingers over the rings that pierced her nipples – and then there was the kiss of the whip as it had exploded across her buttocks.

Tears threatened as she remembered Starn's voice, as cold and unfeeling as the grave: 'Peter Tourne's gone now. You're all mine. He's so concerned with his ideas about educating that he forgets what you're really here for… pleasure – my pleasure. You won't ever deny me again, you miserable little bitch.'

The whip had curled back like a snake and hit her again. It seemed as if the beating went on without end, one blow running into another and another in a tapestry of breathtaking pain, heat, and noise. And finally, when there was calm, she'd hung on the wooden frame, exhausted, struggling to control her mind, every inch of her body raw and aching – and it was then that she felt hot breath on her thigh, followed by a tongue plunging deep inside her quim. The merest contact against the new metal studs electrified her, sending wave after wave of pleasure and pain through her exhausted body. The next touch of the unseen tongue was across her clitoris, sending a bright glittering paradox through her body as the sensations twisted and tumbled together, cutting though her thoughts like a river in full spate.

Just as she was beginning to be drawn in by the growing heat in her belly, a second pair of hands brushed the cheeks of her backside. Against the raw heat of the beating the touch felt almost icy. Her unseen tormentor pressed a finger into her quim, exploring roughly, dipping into her again and again. She felt the brush of an erect penis on the backs of her thighs, and then gasped as it struggled to ease its way into her.

Afraid that he might hurt her she had moved to try and let him have easier access, only to have the man crouching between her legs grunt furiously and grab at her thighs, holding her still. Behind her the man finally found his mark and slid his cock home. She groaned as he buried himself to the hilt with one swift lunge, his hands slithering round to cup and tease her throbbing breasts.

Alex felt the sense of panic growing and struggled to keep a tight hold of her sanity. Behind her the man – she thought it was most likely Starn – grunted like a pig and forced himself as deep as possible, while the man kneeling in front of her continued his relentless tonguing. She felt to be drowning between the two of them. There was no part of her body that seemed to be her own – every inch was alive with pain or pleasure inflicted by another.

The pulsing erection inside her was close to release she could sense it by the way it jerked and by the rasping breath against her ear. But to her horror – and what frightened her more – was that between her legs the dark fire, kindled by the man's tongue, had taken hold, and a great shadowy flame of pleasure was growing in her belly, as raw and terrifying as a forest fire. The thick animal cries of pleasure that she could hear were her own. She screamed as her unseen lover exploded deep inside her and in the same second the flames engulfed her, driving away all reason, all consciousness, until all that was left was sensation.

Now, alone in her cell, Alex flushed crimson. Humiliation replaced her fear. Unlike Peter Tourne they had taken her coldly, used her without feeling… and yet some part of her had revelled in their abuse. Memories of the intensity of her orgasm made her tremble with pleasure. She huddled under the thin grey blanket, careful to keep the fabric away from the tender wounds, and struggled to find sleep.

The beast Peter Tourne had unleashed in her followed into her dreams, where she relived every stroke of the whip, every touch, every dark compelling sensation.

When Alex woke again it was dark. She stared into the gloom wondering what had disturbed her. A light flickered on in the corridor outside her cell, casting a jaundiced pattern through the bars in the door. Mario's distinctive face peered in through the grating. Alex curled into the corner. The driver grinned as he struggled with the lock.

'Get up. Mr Tourne says you join him for dinner.'

Alex stared at the driver. Dressed only in the remains of the ruined blouse she was hardly ready to eat a civilised meal, or perhaps this was yet another part of Peter

Tourne's education. Mario swung the door wide. Beside him, standing in the shadows, was the housekeeper. She looked at Alex with a hint of pity in her eyes.

'Come with me,' the old lady said in a tiny voice. 'I get you ready.'

Mario unfastened Alex, and then snapped a long leather lead onto her collar. With Alex secured they walked in procession to the bathroom in the room beyond the cells. She tried hard to concentrate her attention on the gentle ministrations of the old lady rather than the dark lustful stare of Mario, who watched the preparations for her dinner invitation with interest. All the time the housekeeper worked the driver gripped the lead tightly, just in case Alex had any foolish ideas about escaping.

The old woman bathed her, washed her hair and helped her to get dry before turning her attention first to her bruises and welts and then to the new rings and studs. With knowing hands she worked cool balm into the tender pierced places. Her touch was so delicate and gentle that Alex thought she might cry.

When she was finished the old lady twisted Alex's stunning auburn curls into a chic knot. Alex wondered fleetingly why it was she didn't feel self-conscious of her nakedness – and then realised with a start that there wasn't a single piece of her body that either Mario or the housekeeper hadn't seen or touched. The old lady held out a hand and beckoned for Alex to follow her back into the main room. It was bare now. Not a sign of the day's activities remained.

After the warmth of the bathroom Alex felt the chill of the night air on her skin. The woman looked her up and down thoughtfully, and then opened a cupboard. From inside she produced a black leather corset set with studs and chains, and held it up to Mario for his approval. The driver grunted and nodded, his gaze still lingering on Alex's naked body.

Alex shivered as the old woman returned to the cupboard and reappeared with a pair of matching ankle boots; a thin silver chain ran between them, effectively hobbling the wearer. Alex remained still, reluctant to dress in the bizarre outfit her train of thought was broken by Mario jerking at the lead.

'Hurry,' he snapped. 'You not keep Mr Tourne waiting. He get angry.'

The old woman wrapped the corset around Alex's shapely body and then began to fasten it. It was secured by a combination of buckles and laces that nipped Alex's skin firmly as the old woman began to adjust them. Alex gasped as the woman cinched it in over her waist. Glancing down she saw that the skilful boning and cut forced her breasts up and forward, laying them out for her master like a restoration banquet. Below her breasts the corset tightened dramatically around her waist before flaring out into shaped points over her hips. The dark leather framed her naked sex, emphasising the pallor and vulnerability of her body. The woman crouched down to help her slip on the stiletto-heeled ankle boots, before kneeling back to admire the overall effect. Once the boots were on she smiled and then nodded to Alex, as if to imply it looked right.

Alex blushed, imagining how she must look. The old woman struggled and creaked back to her feet and went over to the cupboard again; apparently the outfit was not quite complete. She returned with a pair of long black satin gloves and a mask that covered the top half of Alex's face, the eyeholes framed with tiny silver studs. Alex shuddered; in the mask she became anonymous. Stripped of her identity she was transformed into a creature of pure pleasure. As a final touch the old woman reached into the pocket of her apron and produced a lipstick. It was blood red. With steady hands she outlined Alex's full lips, and then stood back to admire her handiwork.

Mario sniffed and then nodded; it seemed he was satisfied with the results. He gave a sharp tug on the lead and Alex had no choice but to follow him. She found it hard to walk in the ridiculous boots; her stride was reduced to tiny steps by the chain and the heels were so high that it was difficult to keep her balance. As if this wasn't enough, the mask restricted her field of vision and the leather corset, tight and unyielding around her cinched body, nipped her flesh making her aware of every weal and ache.

The progress up through the gardens was slow, with Mario tugging impatiently at her lead, making the walk all the more difficult. She caught glimpses of her reflection in the windows as they climbed the steps to the main villa. Her appearance was startling – she looked like a wild erotic ornament; a creature of elicit pleasure. The fragmented reflections, despite everything, increased her sense of expectation, and a tiny flare of excitement formed again in her belly.

Her rational mind struggled with the notion that her ongoing predicament could excite her so intensely. How could this costume and this sense of being nothing more than a possession be so electrifying? Even Mario, her burly minder, somehow added to the growing feelings of arousal. The sea air caressed the naked plains of her body, tightening her pierced nipples into scarlet peaks. Between her legs the same breeze brushed the contours of her sex, teasing back and forth over the creamy folds. Alex shivered; she was wet, she was excited, and yet every shred of her rational mind demanded to know why.

Alex was relieved when they finally stepped into the entrance hall with its bright sparkling fountain. It seemed a lifetime since she had arrived at the villa and first met Peter Tourne. Was it possible that the naively talented artist who had arrived to paint the mural was the same woman that stood there now, dressed as a gift for her master?

The lights were low in the hallway. Candles in glass vases had been set around the poolside. The tumble of greenery around the water reflected the moisture and light, giving the room a magical quality. For some reason Alex was certain that Starn and Gena had left – whatever was to be played out tonight was for her and Peter Tourne alone. As her mind formed his name he appeared from the shadows. She wondered how long he had been standing there watching her. He held out a hand and Mario silently passed him the lead. He looked at it thoughtfully, and then at Alex.

As their eyes met she began to understand her foreign emotions; this enigmatic man had – from the first moment they'd met – instinctively recognised the kind of woman she was. He fully understood the needs and desires even she didn't dare acknowledge existed within her. Did he know her better than she did? For a few seconds they stood facing each other, and in that breathless moment each recognised the true nature of the other: Master and slave, two halves of a complex puzzle that defied all logic and rationale.

'I think we can dispense with the lead tonight,' he said quietly and stepped closer. Instinctively Alex leant into his touch, like a sleek cat seeking the comfort and approval of her owner. Peter Tourne smiled and stroked her neck. She could sense his approval, and felt a disproportionate sense of pleasure. His fingers worked at the fastening on her collar, and then he dropped the lead to the floor. Without a word he turned and made his way up to the dining room. Alex stopped struggling to make sense of what was happening to her, and followed him.

Upstairs the elegant room was lit by candles and the grand table set with just a single place setting. Beside the carver chair at the head of the table was a footstool. Alex had no doubt where her place was meant to be. She would sit at his feet, doing as he willed, obeying his every command. A servant appeared from the shadows and pulled the chair out.

Like Mario, Peter Tourne's houseboy was a local peasant, and Alex immediately sensed his interest in her arrival. His eyes – which rested on her body for no more than a few seconds – gave her a peculiar sense of self-assurance. Stripped of her identity, all she had left to offer was a pure sexuality that was as raw and alluring as a hunger. While the boy busied himself with serving the meal Tourne settled himself at the table and shook out his napkin. Alex curled gracefully onto the stool beside him without a word.

Peter Tourne smiled inwardly as he began his meal, sitting back to allow his houseboy to pour the rich red wine. He wished it was possible for Starn to be there unobserved to watch Alex's unquestioning obedience, but knew it was impossible. Starn had always preferred overt displays of submission, whilst he relished Alex's sweet capitulation. No amount of beating or pain could engender her reaction, unless it was already part of her nature.

He tore the bread on his side plate and offered a piece to his slave girl. She leant forward carmine lips open a fraction to feed from his hand like a tame dog. As her tongue grazed his fingers he could sense the emotion coursing through her veins.

The meal was exquisite, and from each course he saved a little for the girl who awaited his pleasure so willingly. There was a strange erotic charge to the way her lips worked around each morsel, her tongue seeking to retrieve each scrap. If his fingers brushed her cheek she would press against him lightly, her skin warm and inviting beneath his fingertips.

Finally he took his coffee and a liqueur over to the window to look down at the sea below the villa. Glancing over his shoulder he saw Alex waiting for his next command. The leather corset accentuated her subtle curves and the creamy richness of her English complexion. She did not meet his eyes but instead looked down, meek and humble, his command to obey. How much Starn missed with his insensitive fumbling, he thought.

He saw Alex shiver – well aware, no doubt, that he was observing her. As she moved a fraction the candlelight reflected in the silver rings nestled under each nipple and below, between the soft shadowed folds of her thighs he could just see the studs that pierced her labia. She glanced up momentarily, and he beckoned to her. She appeared to slither across the floor, crawling on all fours as if afraid to get up from the stool. As she reached his feet she pressed her face against his thigh. He could feel her breath and smiled. This was all he could have hoped for, and more. He extended a hand and slowly she uncurled and got to her feet.

He nodded towards the table. 'Lay down, my dear,' he said. 'I want to look at you.'

Without a second's hesitation Alex crossed the room and lay down amongst the remains of his meal. He left her there, waiting until he had finished his coffee. When he finally turned to observe her he could see a light sheen of perspiration had risen in the deep valley between her breasts. Her breathing was light and excited. He understood only too well the power of anticipation. He examined her lazily, stroking her sex and running a finger over the swollen places where the studs nestled. As he touched her again she opened her legs to give him greater access and freedom.

He was amused that she should think she could control him so easily. Hadn't he taught her the game was his, and not hers? Between her open thighs he could see the glistening juices clinging to the folds of her quim. She was offering herself up for his pleasure – a touching but unnecessary gesture.

He glanced at the glass of cognac in his free hand, and then with slow deliberation he poured the contents over the sensitive lips of her sex, and as he did so he plunged his fingers deep inside. She groaned as the alcohol seeped over her, startled by the sting and the coldness of it.

'Oh, Alex,' Tourne said as he nipped and pinched at the sensitised peaks of her breasts. 'How clever you think you are. How many times must I tell you, it is I who makes the rules – not you?' He twisted her soft flesh, making her groan again with pleasure, pain, and confusion.

Slowly he backed away, leaving her panting with uncertainty. He was delighted to see she instinctively remained on the table eyes closed, legs still apart, breasts rising and falling deeply. He plucked a candle from its holder, snuffed out the flame, and pressed it into her gloved hands.

'Here we are,' he said softly. 'This is for you. I have no use for your body tonight.'

Alex stiffened, her fingers closing reluctantly around the thick wax shaft. She lay quietly, nibbling her soft lower lip nervously.

'Oh, please don't make me wait,' Tourne whispered. 'Show me what pleasure really can be. Amuse me.'

'Please Mr Tourne...'

'Do as you're told – now!'

Slowly Alex lifted her legs until her booted feet rested on the polished table edge – opening herself as she did. He could sense her fear and humiliation as she guided the candle deep between the sensitive lips of her quim. For an instant the candle withdrew – it glistened with her juices – and then disappeared very, very, slowly as she pushed it all the way home. Her movements were self-conscious and stilted. Her cheeks flushed delightfully, and she nibbled her lip all the more urgently.

Tourne snorted derisively. 'What kind of half-hearted nonsense is this, Alex? Don't be so foolish it wouldn't do to make me angry. Now, I want to see you touch yourself properly. Show me what pleasures your body can offer a man. Show me some passion.' He paused. She was trembling, her fingers still closed tightly around the thick stem. 'Or would you prefer it if I called Mario in to help you?'

He saw her flinch at the mention of his driver, and then suddenly, leaving the obscene wax stem embedded in her succulent sex, she moved one hand to her clitoris where her fingers rubbed vigorously and the other lifted to cup and squeeze her breasts. He hardly needed to see any more of her performance – beautifully arousing as it was; her unquestioning obedience was the goal he sought.

As he turned away from the gorgeous scene he noticed a flicker of movement from the corner of his eye, and realised that he hadn't dismissed his houseboy; he'd been so intent on Alex that he'd forgotten the boy was there.

A thoughtful and mischievous smile slowly lifted the corners of his mouth. He moved smoothly back to where Alex lay quietly panting, shook loose a crisply starched napkin, and blindfolded her with it, whispering assurances as he worked.

When satisfied that she could see nothing, he nodded towards the shadows, his gesture an explicit invitation. The boy's bright eyes stared back at him, unconvinced.

Tourne waved him closer and whispered in Greek, 'Do what you want with her. Whatever you like. While she is on this table she is yours.'

Alex lifted her head from the table and strained to hear. 'Mr Tourne, what are you doing?' she asked timidly. 'Is somebody with you?'

'Sssshhh my dear. Of course not – it's only me here. You look so wonderful, well, I don't think I can resist you after all. It would be such a waste...'

The boy still looked a little uncertain, but bowed his respectful gratitude. His face was an amusing mixture of anxiety and enthusiasm as he dragged his thin cotton shirt off. Watching him, Peter Tourne realised the boy was barely out of puberty – seventeen or eighteen at the most. Underneath his shirt he was as willowy as a reed, with a straggling triangle of dark hair that extended from between his nipples on his undeveloped chest to the waistband of his drawstring trousers.

Peter Tourne watched the boy gazing longingly down, clearly unable to believe his luck at the beautiful English girl spread before him. He smiled with amusement at the youthful erection that strained and threatened to split the front of his trousers. Of course, the lad had seen everything that had gone before, and it would be impossible for him not to be excited. His anticipation and excitement were as tangible as Alex's.

As Peter Tourne watched like a teacher monitoring the capabilities of his favourite student, the boy's hands worked clumsily down over Alex's slim hips. He slipped the candle out, replacing it first with his finger, and then his tongue. At first his caresses were experimental and tentative, as if he expected his employer to call his explorations to a halt at any time. As he slowly realised this wasn't going to happen, he grew more confident, and began to relax and enjoy himself. Tourne warmed to the boy's clumsy eagerness and tried to remember his name, but nothing formed in his mind.

Much to his delight, the boy grew more rough with poor Alex as he grew more confident, although his abrasive fumbling came about more through ignorance than design. He turned Alex this way and that, exploring every inch of her vulnerability as if she was a new toy.

The surprised confusion was etched on Alex's face; these were not the ministrations of one so experienced and refined as her host and patron. 'Mr Tourne...' her whisper was barely audible above the eager sucking of the boy. 'Mr Tourne... please.'

'Sssshhh…' Peter Tourne soothed again, and Alex moaned and stiffened as the boy accidentally found the spot.

Peter Tourne doubted the boy had ever had a woman before, and if he had it had never been like this. Perhaps the boy had shared some guilty fumbling with a village girl in a dark alley, but certainly never had he had one totally at his mercy – his to command. Tourne grinned, imagining the houseboy having his face slapped by a peasant girl as their wills clashed over what part of her he might be allowed to touch or kiss. With Alex he would have no such trouble – she had relinquished herself completely to their control. The boy groaned hungrily, biting and nipping with his sharp white teeth at the soft places between her thighs. She squirmed and twisted exquisitely from side to side, moaning and rolling her head as his explorations grew more and more urgent.

Suddenly he pulled away, eyes alight as his hands continued to nip and squeeze at her submissive flesh. His lips were glossy with her pleasure. He scrambled up onto the table. He straddled her waist, jerked down his trousers, and lay his bursting cock into Alex's perspiring cleavage. He cupped and moulded her breasts around his erection, and thrust his narrow hips ever more urgently, until with an excited shudder he ejaculated over her throat and breasts. His seed exploded over her like an arc of milky stars.

Peter Tourne smiled, thinking that the impromptu exhibition was over, and then realised he was wrong.

The boy, sweating heavily, crouched lower, his cock still jutting forward and glistening with his own juices. He began to lap hungrily at Alex's face and throat, and then sucked and chewed her budding, sperm-coated nipples. Easing himself further down the table his fingers returned to her sex and, pushing her fingers aside, he began to drag and paw at her clitoris.

Alex groaned softly, relinquishing her body to the unseen stimulations. The boy grinned as she continued to writhe under his touch. His attentions turned to the candle which still lay between her legs on the table. He picked it up and buried it into her with one smooth movement. Alex whimpered, and her whole body convulsed. Her back arched and lifted from the table as the boy's fingers returned to her pleasure bud. His tongue lapped and circled the pierced peaks of her breasts. Peter could sense her impending orgasm and was stunned that the boy could put on such a spectacular show.

Alex expelled a long low mewl of utter pleasure and slumped motionless on the expensive tabletop. The boy finally collapsed onto her exhausted body, and lay with his contented face between her magnificent breasts. After a few minutes, suddenly remembering where he was, he quickly scrambled to his feet, and dragged his trousers up to hide his withering embarrassment from his employer's perceptive gaze.

Glancing furtively at the man by his side, the boy blushed furiously. Peter Tourne shook his head and mimed a show of applause.

'You've done very well,' he whispered. 'What's your name?'

The boy's colour intensified. 'Raymond, Sir,' he stammered, unable to meet his elder's eye.

Peter Tourne nodded. 'Good. Fetch some fresh coffee, Raymond. I'll be out on the terrace. You may tidy up in here later.'

The boy nodded and hurried away.

When they were alone Peter Tourne looked down victoriously at Alex.

'Get up. Come here,' he said in a low, even voice. Alex slithered from the table, her body slick with sweat and the remains of the boys' excesses. The candle was still buried inside her. Her face was flushed.

Peter Tourne ran his hands over her breasts and then down to her belly, his fingers fixing tight on the slippery wax. She gasped as he pulled it free. Slowly he trailed the wet shaft over her breasts where her soft flesh was still smeared with the boy's glistening seed and saliva.

'Tell me Alex, whose game are we playing?' he asked, catching hold of her chin and tilting her face up towards him. 'Whose rules do we abide by?'

Her eyes were glassy. 'Yours, Mr Tourne,' she murmured.

'Good. You have to understand that above all else.' He rolled the candle thoughtfully between his fingers and then ran it across her lips. She shuddered. Her carmine lipstick left a smear on the white shaft.

'Open your mouth,' he whispered.

Alex swallowed hard, quite obviously fighting her revulsion, but slowly her lips parted and he drew the candle back again. This time her tongue, moist and pink, trailed along the glistening cylinder. He angled it and pushed the tip against her pouting lips. They peeled open, and he slowly but firmly fed the inanimate object into her hot wet mouth before turning to pull the bell that would summon Mario.

Alex open her eyes and stared at him with a mixture of arousal and surprise as the candle was slipped from her mouth. It was obvious he was dismissing her.

'But, I thought—'

Her host's face hardened. 'I have already told you – you are not expected to think, or to talk. Is it so hard for you to understand?'

Alex looked down at the floor. Because he'd invited her to join him for dinner she'd assumed her reward would be to make love to him. Certainly she had not expected to be abused by him as she had been on the table, or to be manhandled again by his servant. She wondered if he would punish her now for her disobedience – but to her regret he turned away. Such exquisite torture, she thought miserably.

Mario opened the door. His boss didn't even speak. Mario had the lead in his hand and Alex knew then that whatever attentions were to be metered out it wouldn't be Peter Tourne who provided them. She shivered; Mario's expression suggested he'd been waiting for this moment. Alex looked desperately at her host as he casually dismissed them both with a wave of his hand and then headed out towards the terrace.

Mario clipped the lead back onto her collar and gave it a sharp tug to let her know that he was now back in control. Alex nibbled her lip anxiously.

The driver rubbed the back of his hand across his wet lips and then greedily stroked one of Alex's breasts. He grinned and jerked the lead again. This time Alex followed him – she had no choice. Glancing back just as Mario led her through the door, she saw Peter Tourne out on the moonlit terrace – he was staring out to sea, oblivious now of her presence.

Chapter Seven

After that night with the houseboy, days at the villa KaRoche began to take on a regular pattern for Alex. Each morning Mario would unchain her and lead her out from her cell to the long gallery beside the pool, where she would work on the mural. At first Alex thought it would be impossible to paint under such circumstances, but soon discovered creating the mural was the only vestige of normality that remained, like a touchstone, in her new and strange life.

The way she was dressed was dependent upon Mario's lecherous whims. Sometimes he left her naked, other times he dressed her as a peasant in cotton blouse and skirt, or sometimes he strapped her into a tight leather concoction.

In the heat of the afternoons she was allowed to rest, chained back in her cell. The hours of siesta were always fitful and uneasy; if Mario was not required to drive his boss anywhere or had no other work in the villa he would visit her. Sometimes his visits were purely for sexual relief, on others, if the day had gone badly, he came to take his frustration out on her body with a whip or a leather belt. She dreaded the sound of his footsteps outside the cell door.

In the evening Mario and the housekeeper would appear to dress her for Peter Tourne's pleasure. She would be perfumed and painted, and then dressed according to his instructions; sometimes in exotic ball gowns, sometimes in an elegant evening dress – most often though it seemed he preferred her in a boned leather basque or corsets, her features obscured by a masquerade mask.

Upstairs in the dining room Tourne would feed her by

hand as she knelt at his feet. On some nights he required nothing more than her silent companionship. On others she was expected to exchange social niceties or embark on long conversations about art or literature. Part of the game he played with her was that she was supposed to guess which it was he required. If she made a mistake and was unable to guess, her punishment was to be handed over to the houseboy, whose taste for oral sex and ejaculating on her exposed flesh seemed endless. As Tourne ate his dinner she was always aware of the boy waiting eagerly in the shadows – waiting for his turn to make use of her body. Whenever Tourne beckoned the boy over his youthful eyes would sparkle intensely. Alex had felt totally humiliated when she'd learned the truth about that first night on the table, and the humiliation lessened little with each subsequent occasion she was given to the boy. Peter Tourne always preferred his servant to make love to her – if that was indeed what it was – on the table, so that he could enjoy their exhibition. Sometimes he would offer words of encouragement to the youth, guiding him and educating him in the ways of taking her. When the youth had had his fill Tourne would wave them both away and Mario would take her back to the cell to begin the ordeal afresh.

Though it seemed impossible, Alex began to settle down to the peculiar rhythm of life at the villa KaRoche. Within a fortnight her life in London was but a distant memory, and all the while the mural, the finest thing she had ever painted, took shape along the gallery walls, recording forever a coded warning of the events that had overtaken her at the villa.

Her plan for escape rapidly became a dream to sustain her in the long dark nights, chained to the bed, waiting for a footfall in the corridor that would announce one of Mario's late night visits.

Starn didn't reappear at the villa for some time. At first

she thought it was Tourne's way of punishing him for trying to take advantage of her while she'd been painting in the gallery, but overhearing a telephone conversation while she was at dinner with her host, she realised that it was because Starn and Gena were away on a business trip in London. Knowing that Starn was staying in the city in which she lived made her wistful. Would she ever be allowed to go back to the life she had known?

As the days passed, it was obvious to Alex that the elderly housekeeper couldn't have rung her agent, Laurence. If the old woman had done as she'd asked, Laurence would surely have come to rescue her by now.

Sitting at Peter Tourne's feet in the dining room one night she wondered fleetingly if Laurence had contacted him since that first phone call. Normally she would have expected her agent to have rung her at least once or twice a week while she was working on a commission, to see how the work was progressing. It seemed that nothing at KaRoche was as normal. She wondered what excuse Tourne had cooked up to explain why she never came to the phone.

'You seem distracted this evening, my dear,' he said, running his hand down over the curve of her shoulder.

Alex blushed and looked up. 'I'm sorry,' she whispered.

Tonight she was dressed in an elegant white shift dress and high gold sandals. Under different circumstances she might easily have passed for a society beauty dining with her lover.

Tourne smiled indulgently. 'I went to see how the mural was progressing this afternoon. It's very good. I am extremely pleased with what you've created for me.'

Alex nodded; she'd learnt it wasn't wise to be too forthcoming. He got to his feet and poured them both a glass of wine.

'How much longer do you think it will be before it's finished?'

Alex stiffened; finishing the mural was something she hadn't given too much thought. When the mural was complete would he let her go home, or would he sell her on as Starn Fettico had predicted? She glanced up at him, trying to suppress the strange mix of hope and fear that formed in her belly. His expression revealed nothing.

'A few more days,' she said carefully. 'Perhaps a week, at the most.'

'Good,' he said. 'Starn and Gena are due back from England tomorrow. I intend giving a dinner party to welcome them.'

Alex wondered whether he meant to include her too, but decided to say nothing.

He turned his glass thoughtfully in his fingers. Alex couldn't help but notice the houseboy hovering hopefully in the shadows. He was watching her with interest, his stare burning with intensity. As their eyes met he licked his lips and lewdly rubbed the already considerable swelling in his trousers. Alex shivered. She knew he was hoping she would make some small mistake that would fire his employer's displeasure.

As she turned away she realised to her horror that Peter Tourne had been speaking '...We've been friends for years. Like you he is English. I'll be interested to see what he makes of your progress.'

Alex struggled desperately to reconstruct the words she hadn't paid any attention to, but fortunately her host didn't seem to have noticed her rude lapse of concentration. He beckoned to her.

'Now, stand up, my dear. I'd just like to assess your progress.'

She did as he asked without thinking.

'Good. Take off your dress.'

Alex reached round to find the zip. He shook his head in exasperation and clicked his fingers toward the houseboy. 'Help her with the dress.'

Alex felt the youth's hands on her back his breath was warm and moist on her skin. Was Peter Tourne giving her to this enthusiastic but clumsy boy yet again? What had she done wrong? The boy struggled to unfasten the zip and then pulled the thin fabric down off her shoulders. The delicate dress slithered to the floor like liquid. Beneath it Alex was naked. The boy didn't move away – Alex could almost feel his excitement scorching her bare flesh.

Peter Tourne studied her beauty thoughtfully. 'Turn around,' he instructed her with quiet confidence.

As Alex obeyed she lowered her gaze to the floor; she couldn't bear to witness her own humiliation in the victorious expression of the young lad. She knew he was taking advantage of her closeness to drink in every inch of her nakedness.

Tourne murmured his approval. 'The bruises have gone,' he said, almost to himself. 'And there are no weal marks. Good. I'm sure you'll meet with Simon's approval.'

Alex completed her slow turn. As her compliance had grown Mario had been less vehement in his beatings. She'd quickly learnt, however repellent his desires, it was far better to do as she was told than risk his fury. As a result, he'd been less quick to use the whip or belt on her.

Tourne leaned forward in his chair, and then began a more thorough examination of her. It seemed he was particularly interested in the rings that pierced her nipples and the studs that pierced her labia. Though far from healed, they were no longer sore or inflamed.

'They've taken very well,' he murmured as he ran a finger over them. Alex shivered – the nipple rings in particular made her feel totally vulnerable. 'You are very nearly ready, my dear.'

Alex's mind raced. Ready? Ready for what?

'My dear friend Simon has expressed an interest in you. He will be here tomorrow night, and then, when the mural is complete, and if he thinks you are suitable, you will join his stable for auction.'

Alex's stomach churned sharply while her urbane host turned her to the left and to the right, holding her at arms length, making a cold appraisal of what he saw as though he were an antiques dealer assessing a fine piece of porcelain.

He continued: 'I'll make certain Mario doesn't mark you before tomorrow tonight. Simon isn't very keen on bruised fruit. You're a little small for his tastes – but beautifully proportioned, and *so, so* succulent.' He cupped and squeezed her breasts as if he were weighing apples. She blushed. He stroked her belly with a flat palm, and then slid a hand down between her thighs. A single finger probed and then opened her sex. 'And still nice and tight here,' he continued his commentary, 'that's good.' He moved his attention to the studs that nestle in the plump outer lips of her quim. There was no emotion in his touch; it was simply a cold assessment of her flesh. 'I'll change these for my family mark once Simon has given his approval. Turn around again, and bend over.'

Alex flushed crimson. The houseboy, as if anticipating his master's requirements, gripped her shoulders to support and ease her forward until her face was almost level with his groin. She could make out the clear swelling before her eyes, and despite herself she was gripped by an almost overwhelming desire to open his trousers and swallow the young cock deep into her throat. Her mouth was parched. It wasn't the houseboy that interested her – it was the near virginal erection hidden within that stretched material.

Suddenly she gasped, and her attention was drawn to Peter Tourne's exploratory fingers. He spread the cheeks of her bottom and ran an inquisitive finger over her anus. Alex shivered; it was the focus Mario's particular pleasure, and the memories of the driver plunging into those most secret places of her body made her stomach churn anew.

She felt something cold and oily trickle down the crease of her backside, and then felt a rush of humiliation as he worked a finger into the tight and dark closure. Her whole body tensed. Tourne grunted as he tried to breach the tight band of muscle.

'Still very tight here too. Relax and pant, my dear, I need to get inside you.'

Alex felt the houseboy's hands tighten on her shoulders. Her shame excited him even more. She gasped as the finger pressed insistently at her entrance. She struggled to control her breathing, so that the tense band of muscle would relax and allow him entry without causing her unnecessary discomfort. Suddenly she emitted a long low groan as she opened and the digit slid home.

Without warning the finger left her as quickly as it had violated her, and the satisfied Peter Tourne moved away, leaving Alex feeling embarrassed and exposed. She was about to straighten up when his voice stopped her.

'Don't move. Stay as you are.'

Alex took a deep breath, wondering what would follow. It didn't take long for the answer to arrive. From the corner of her eye she watched Peter Tourne cross the room and open the door. Mario was already waiting outside. He grinned salaciously when he saw Alex bent over, supported by the houseboy.

Peter Tourne told his driver to enter, and then settled himself in a comfortable armchair. Alex couldn't understand what was said between the two men, but she guessed that her host intended to observe and enjoy whatever was to follow. She watched him top up his brandy balloon from the drinks trolley by his side, and then wait for the show to begin.

Between them, Mario and the houseboy manhandled Alex over to a stool and lay her across it. The corpulent driver knelt behind her, and the houseboy unleashed his raging virility.

A charming little *ménage à trois*, thought Peter Tourne with pleasure. He knew that if he indulged Mario's lusts now it would help ensure Alex arrived at tomorrow night's dinner party unmarked.

Mario grinned lustily down at the houseboy's youthful cock, closed his fingers around it with surprising tenderness for such a big man, cupped and raised Alex's chin with his free hand, and fed the straining erection into her mouth. The boy gasped with delight and threw back his head. Mario undid his young accomplice's shirt. His thick fingers worked at his plump purple nipples. He leant forward and planted a delicate kiss on each, his tongue working around the buds.

Peter Tourne wasn't repulsed by the display of affection between the two males; he was enchanted; he had never observed this side of his driver's nature before. If indeed Mario did prefer the muscular charms of the peasant boy it would explain his preference for buggery.

Alex's delicate English rosebud mouth closed around the houseboy's shaft. Her red lips were stretched, and her eyes were shut tight. Mario shuffled behind her, struggled to free his own bursting cock, and then buried himself to the hilt in her unprotected quim. Crouched between them she was rapidly becoming just a vessel for their mutual desire.

Peter Tourne suppressed a smile as Mario began to plunge in and out of her; it seemed that in front of his master, Mario was conforming to a more usual course of pleasure. Perhaps he was afraid he would incur disapproval if he drove home into his preferred orifice.

Alex let out a thick guttural grunt as Mario began to move in earnest. He slid his rough hands up under her ribcage, turning his attentions to her nipples. His fingers twisted and teased at the engorged peaks, making Alex want to cry out – although the houseboys' cock muffled her cries.

Mario's attentions returned to his accomplice, whose expression was one of absolute ecstasy. Seemingly oblivious to the girl squashed and huddled between them, Mario pulled him closer and planted a long kiss on his gasping mouth. The houseboy groaned and held Mario to him. Alex, humbled and reduced to a mere vehicle for the two males' pleasure, was completely forgotten as they grunted and rutted enthusiastically towards release.

As Mario's lips worked against his, the houseboy groaned again and flexed his hips, driving his cock deeper into Alex's waiting mouth. Mario snorted, almost as if he could feel the boy's excitement directly, and renewing his rhythmic thrusts in and out of Alex, began to gasp and moan as orgasm overtook them both. The houseboy's eyes opened to reveal a strange mixture of pleasure and fear, and then he convulsed. His seed exploded into Alex's mouth and seeped from the corners of her lips. Mario shrieked in delight, clawing the boy closer, sweat pouring down his face as the convulsions and contractions of his own climax closed over him.

When their passion was spent, Peter Tourne got to his feet and waved his driver and houseboy aside. Alex, still crouched over the stool, was wet with their perspiration. He helped her to her feet. Mario's seed trickled from her sex, and a smear of the houseboy's semen clung to her chin.

Peter Tourne smiled warmly. 'You are ready,' he said softly, and handed her back to Mario.

Returned to the darkness of her cell and chained for the night, Alex lay staring up into the blackness. She could still taste the houseboy's excitement in her mouth. Her body's raw desire for satisfaction dispelled even her dreams of escape.

The two servants had been oblivious to her own needs; they had used her, and wanted nothing but her body. That knowledge – dark and compelling – made her ache with a strange sense of pleasure. Peter Tourne was right; she was ready. There was no possibility of going back or unlearning the lessons he had taught her.

She slid a finger between the lips of her quim. Mario's seed coated her fingers, lubricating her caresses as she stroked the soft folds of her sex. Need rose up through her belly like an angry roar. She instantly found the tiny bead that was the seat of all pleasure. Circling the hood with a deft knowing finger she drove another deep inside her quim. The need for release was so close to the surface that the first brush was enough to light fantastic fires in her mind.

As the pleasure began to build Alex imagined Peter Tourne's face; imagined him watching as the two servants had taken her; imagined their bodies penetrating her depths – and instantly she was lost. Deep inside her sex began to contract, sucking her fingers down as orgasm drove away everything but the intense image of Peter Tourne's dark flashing eyes.

When Alex rose and showered the next day the villa KaRoche was already humming with activity. Mario brought her breakfast early, but was so preoccupied that he barely looked at her. Later, while Alex worked in the gallery, the sound of voices from the main villa filtered down to her. She could hear vehicles arriving, the sounds of male voices, and muffled banging and thumping.

Mario had barely seemed interested in the ritual of deciding what she was to wear for the day; she had ended up dressed quite comfortably in a thin summer dress and sandals. Had it not been for the collar and chain she could easily have passed for a houseguest. Alex guessed that this was Mario's intention; should a deliveryman inadvertently find his way into the gallery it wouldn't do to find a woman, naked except for a leather basque, chained to the wall.

She worked without interruption all morning, and instead of Mario arriving at lunchtime to take her back to the cell, the housekeeper arrived with a tray. The old lady's expression was tight and preoccupied. She avoided Alex's eye as she slid her lunch onto the table alongside her paints. It seemed that the dinner party had taken precedence over everything else. Alex really didn't mind. It made a pleasant change to sit in the shade by the pool and eat her food.

After she'd eaten Mario arrived, dressed in a clean and tailored uniform, and without comment he took her back to the silence of the cells. His face contorted into a grimace as he chained her.

'He say not to touch you,' he said with obvious frustration. His expression hardened. 'Not to touch, pah!'

Alex felt a sense of triumph; it appeared that Peter Tourne's will did extend to events in the cells after all. Her delight was short lived as Mario unbuckled the belt that held up his tailored trousers. 'He means I should not mark you.'

Alex stiffened. 'I'll tell Mr Tourne—' she began, but instantly regretted it. Mario's eyes flashed with fury. Drawing back his hand he slapped her face with the open palm.

'You tell him nothing!' he snapped, and slapped her again. As she stumbled he stooped and grabbed her calves with surprising agility, and flipped her onto her back on the platform that served as a bed. She shrieked in surprise at his swift assault. Mario jerked her legs apart and moved forward sharply so that her feet rested on his shoulders. 'You make big mistake. Mario can do things to you that leave no marks.'

Alex flinched as his fingers tore at her dress – but as he pulled it aside she knew it wasn't her sex that drew him, but the dark closure behind. He spat into his hand and stabbed a finger roughly inside her anus; with hardly any lubrication her body screamed out in protest.

'Tonight,' he hissed between gritted teeth as his fat finger plunged in and out, 'when Peter Tourne and guests have finish with you, I and the boy will be down to give what you deserve! No one will hear you cry – all people be too drunk to care!'

Alex shivered. 'N-no, Mario, p-please,' she stammered. 'There's no need to be rough with me. I'll be nice to you, and your boy!'

Mario snorted and spat into his hand again. Dragging his finger out of her he unceremoniously flipped her onto her belly and spread his saliva over the tender puckering. With her face forced down into the thin blankets she tensed as she felt his cock brush her thighs.

An instant later he breached the tender skin. She held her breath – she wasn't ready. Terrified that he might tear her she willed her body to relax. Mario was oblivious to her concerns. Alex screamed as he forced himself deeper. A hand clawed round and over her face, covering her mouth.

'Quiet, bitch!' Mario snorted. Alex clenched her fists and bit down on his hand, trying to find a way to combat the pain. Behind her she heard Mario laugh. 'You not hurt me,' he sneered, 'and if you do, you pay later!'

Upstairs in the villa preparations for the evening's dinner party were well underway. Peter Tourne kept only a handful of staff at the villa: Mario, his housekeeper, and a procession of local boys to wait on table and tidy the garden. For any formal or important occasion he would hire in the staff he needed and arrange for the meal to be catered by an exclusive catering company – his housekeeper's cooking, though adequate for his own private tastes, was more often than not little more than simple peasant fayre.

For Starn and Gena's reappearance and the visit of Simon

Bay, he wanted something more spectacular. Flowers had already arrived from the mainland, a chef and his retinue were busy working in his kitchen, and various lackeys were preparing the dining room.

Tourne glanced at his watch. He had no particular need or desire to impress Starn – but Simon Bay was a different matter. In his office he had a gown that had arrived on the ferry, delivered by courier that morning, for Alex. He wanted Simon to be impressed by his latest pupil. It would be extremely convenient if Simon could be persuaded to allow Alex to join his stable for his annual slave auction.

Tonight he would oversee Alex's preparation's himself. He sighed – in a way he would be sad to see her go, but for him it was the challenge of the initiation that gave him the greatest delight. Once a girl was broken he would rapidly tire of her company. He much preferred it if they left KaRoche before they lost their appeal. It would be sad if that happened with Alex. A month at his villa should be enough – after that he would let Simon Bay do what he could with her.

As the florist carried a huge display of lilies into the hall, Peter Tourne's mobile phone rang.

'Tourne.'

'Hello, Peter,' a familiar voice at the other end of the line laughed. *'It's Laurence here. I've just rung to see how Alex is getting on.'*

Tourne glanced over his shoulder at the milling servants. 'One second,' he said in an undertone. 'I'll just take your call upstairs to my office.'

Laurence laughed again. *'No chance I could have a word with her?'*

Tourne sighed. 'My dear friend, it's siesta time here.'

'Ah yes, how foolish of me to forget.'

Peter Tourne, cradling the mobile phone, climbed the stairs to his office and closed the door.

Chapter Eight

After Mario finally left Alex's cell the day seemed to pass slowly. Alex dozed spasmodically, her dreams suffused by images of Mario, superimposed upon Starn, the willowy houseboy, and last of all Peter Tourne – who, in the frantically erotic dreamscape, watched Alex's every move, his eyes alight with vicarious pleasure.

She had assumed that at some time during her imprisonment he would make love to her, but it appeared, since that first night when he'd shown her the delights of the gallery, that his real pleasure lay in voyeurism.

Tonight he would introduce her to his friend, Simon Bay. He had no intention of keeping her at KaRoche once the mural was complete – and she knew without a doubt that the plans that had formed in her mind for escape had to be put into action now. She had no desire to be the plaything of yet another unknown man. She closed her eyes, trying to imagine what it might be like to be auctioned off to the highest bidder. Her fear and anger were balanced by a darkly erotic counterpoint; there was a strangely erotic frisson in the idea of being bought and sold like a common slave, tied and naked for the eyes of her would be masters.

As evening fell Alex heard the sound of approaching footsteps and stretched, readying herself for the arrival of Mario and the housekeeper. She wondered what they had brought for her to wear; Mr Tourne's tastes were eclectic to say the very least. She was surprised when the door swung open and Peter Tourne himself stood framed by the shadows. He was dressed in an elegant dinner suit, his hair slicked back and tied into a knot at the nape of his neck. The darkness gave his lean features a predatory, wolfish cast.

Behind him, Mario and the housekeeper waited expectantly. For a few seconds the atmosphere in the cell seemed tight with anticipation. He held out his hand towards Alex, and she was stunned to realised that the feeling she experienced in the wake of the simple gesture was akin to love. Something caught in her throat, tears bubbled, unbidden, behind her eyes. She wanted to beg him to let her stay at KaRoche, to let her serve him and him alone. The words that formed in her heart wouldn't form in her mouth. The moment of intense emotion passed and Mario silently unclipped her leash and led her to the room beyond the cells.

Someone had set a tin bath in the centre of the gallery, and beside it stood a large solid table. Lamplight threw the objects into sharp relief. Alex felt as if she was about to step onto a stage.

Peter Tourne settled himself against the wall in the shadows and watched while his servants prepared her for her introduction to Simon Bay. Despite everything the sense of theatre remained, as if she was taking part in a strange ritual. The old woman soaped and shaved her quim. Mario washed her hair then lathered her breasts and back. The two of them worked in complete silence as if they had performed the same rite a thousand times before. The only sound in the room was the water lapping over the side of the tub and splashing onto the flagstone floor.

With every passing second Alex felt more and more like a prize possession being prepared and polished for a final exhibition. None of the others in the room seemed to care who she was – it was her body they were preparing, not her mind. Waves of panic closed over her just like the water that washed over her ripe breasts and slim hips. Finally the old woman helped her out of the tub, dried her with fluffy towels, and then guided her to the table.

Mario took her wrists and lifted her onto the cool wooden surface, urging her down onto her back. The tabletop was set with manacles that snapped around her wrists with an unnerving finality.

Her ankles were next.

Spread-eagled and naked Alex held her breath as Tourne approached and ran a proprietorial hand over her breasts. He cupped and stroked them thoughtfully. Mario appeared at his shoulder carrying a small stainless steel box. Alex stiffened, knowing with an uncanny certainty that the box held the tools that had pierced her.

She hoped he would look at her, his expression giving her the reassurance she needed, but instead he seemed intent on the contents of the box. From inside he produced a fine silver chain and a pair of pliers. She flinched as he cupped first one breast and then the other. With a cool professional touch he slipped the chain though the nipple rings, and used the pliers to close the links at each end to link the two rings together.

Next he moved down to the studs that pierced her labia. Alex winced as he forced the studs up. Mario handed him something from the metal box. Alex strained to watch the journey of the object he was now holding. He was replacing the studs with a single heavy silver ring. A small ornate medallion bearing a tiny coat of arms hung from it. It was a sign of her origins, a mark of ownership. Alex closed her eyes. The first and last time she had seen a ring like it was when she had been making love to Gena. She shivered. The ring slipping through the lips of her sex seemed like a gesture of finality. The mental anguish she felt was far greater than the physical pain of the studs being removed.

When satisfied with his work he turned away and Mario unlocked the manacles holding her ankles and wrists. Alex watched the housekeeper approaching with her outfit; a long sheath dress of gold voile. The fabric was so sheer it looked like gossamer. The old woman slipped it over Alex's head, gently lifting it over the chain that now linked her breasts. Mario added a pair of high golden sandals while the housekeeper set about dressing Alex's tumble of titian curls. Tourne watched without a word until the old woman added the customary slash of scarlet lipstick.

'Do her nipples too,' he said. The old woman undid the high neck of Alex's dress, carefully folded it down, and traced her nipples with the scarlet stick. They hardened instantly under the housekeeper's deft touch. The old woman pulled the dress back into place.

Tourne nodded his approval. Alex reddened; the approval was not for her but for the servants who had transformed her. Helping her to her feet, the housekeeper turned Alex round so that he could admire their handiwork further. As Alex turned she gasped; for the first time since she'd been held prisoner here she was confronted by a full-length mirror, which had been brought into the room without her noticing. What she saw made her freeze.

The exquisite gold evening dress fitted her like a second skin. Intricate gold embroidery emphasised her slender yet shapely form, revealing tantalising glimpses of her breasts and sex. Her tinted nipples pressed in dark invitation against the fabric, the silver chain and rings adding a strange glittering counterpoint to her creamy flesh.

The housekeeper had spun Alex's long hair out into a halo of curls, and subtle make-up made the most of her fine bone structure. Under any other circumstances her appearance would have been a thing of simple beauty – but instead Alex was aware that the outfit subtly proclaimed her submission; the fine studded leather collar still encircled her neck, and the silver chain hung down invitingly between her breasts. Any man alive seeing her dressed in the beautiful gold confection would instantly know she was nothing more than the slave of a very wealthy master; a pretty bauble created for pure pleasure.

Peter Tourne appeared in the mirror beside her. His eyes moved over her reflection, appraising what he saw with a detached look. After a few seconds he offered his arm to her, and Alex felt powerless to resist him. It seemed he was ready to present her to his guests.

Outside the night was already dark and starry. The confident man and the beautiful girl walked in silence to the villa. She longed for him to say something – to offer her some words of comfort or support, but instead his eyes remained firmly fixed on the steps ahead.

Inside the main hallway a uniformed lackey handed them a glass of champagne each. Peter Tourne turned towards the front door, awaiting the arrival of his friends. Beside him Alex trembled as she heard the soft purr of a car engine and the crunch of tyres on the drive.

Starn Fettico appeared first, dressed in a white dinner jacket. Tourne grinned as Starn crossed the room.

'Starn,' he said warmly. 'How good to see you again. How was London?'

Starn grunted and embraced his friend. 'Wet, cold – a perfect English summer.' He eyed Alex, who instinctively looked down at the floor. 'I see you've nearly done with her then?'

Tourne shrugged. 'Almost. I've invited Simon Bay to join us tonight. I hope you don't mind, I want him to take a look at her. Where's Gena?'

Starn took a glass of champagne from the proffered tray. 'I met Jack Casman whilst in Bonn. He offered me a good price...' the Greek shrugged dismissively. 'What can I say?'

Alex stiffened as she realised what Starn was saying. Gena had been sold off like an unwanted puppy.

Tourne nodded. 'So, you're in the market for a new companion too now? How is Jack?'

Alex's mind was reeling. There wasn't a shred of emotion in Peter Tourne's voice – not the slightest hint of concern for the fate of the beautiful blonde he'd trained.

'He's fine,' Starn had continued. 'Actually, I picked up something that might be of interest to you.' He turned and waved to his own driver who was standing in the open doorway. 'Jack took me to a little club near his mansion – Carmino's – perhaps you've been there? They deal mostly in imports. I would suggest the next time you're in Germany you take a look. They had some interesting things on offer there...'

His voice faded into the background as Alex's eyes were drawn to the doorway. The driver had reappeared, his gloved hand holding two leather leads, attached to which were two girls. Alex stared in astonishment. At first they seemed but mere children, but as they stepped into the light Alex realised they were in fact two exquisitely beautiful young women, perhaps seventeen or eighteen years of age.

Identical twins. They appeared to be Eurasian, with waist length oil-black hair and huge brown eyes. They were naked except for sheer white silk shifts that came down to and swayed around the tops of their thighs. The fabric was so finely woven it revealed every intimate curve. The girls' breasts were small but firm and thrusting, and topped with pert mauve nipples, and their genitals were hairless and oiled. The two of them stared around the opulent interior of the villa, and then giggled nervously. They seemed to bloom like perfectly ripened fruit.

Starn smiled indulgently at his latest purchases. 'Bring them inside,' he said to his driver.

Tourne whistled appreciatively. 'Very nice... very nice indeed.'

Starn sipped his champagne. 'They cost me a mint. A matching pair, fresh from their village – certified virgins. They'd been in Bonn for only three days when I saw them. Barely long enough to have a medical check and arrange some paperwork.'

Starn took a cigar from his top pocket and lit it. The twins meanwhile stood very still, holding hands, obviously apprehensive, watching their new master for some kind of signal. He beckoned them further into the room, and they scurried over to him. Starn relieved his driver of the leads and the girls immediately sank down and knelt either side of him on the cold tiled floor.

Peter Tourne smiled. 'A very nice find. Are they broken yet?'

Starn grinned and took a long pull on his cigar. 'What do you think? It felt just like Christmas, they were so ready for it.'

Alex stared down at the twins. They were naturally subservient. Everything about their body language implied their unquestioning obedience. They looked so sweet and vulnerable. Alex hoped Starn had been kind to them, but doubted it. One girl nuzzled Starn's thigh, seeking attention and favour. Starn appeared oblivious to her. As she moved her glossy hair fell forward, and Alex could see a fine red weal across her shoulder. It seemed almost an obscenity to mark her silky gold tinted skin.

Alex's attention was broken by the sound of Tourne greeting someone else. She looked up and the breath caught in her throat.

'Simon! How wonderful to see you again. I'm so glad you could make it,' the suave host said with genuine warmth as he stepped forward to embrace his guest of honour. 'We were just admiring Starn's latest acquisitions. You remember Starn, don't you?'

Simon Bay – the man invited to come and examine Alex – stepped into the room flanked by two dark skinned women of Amazonian proportions. The girls were both over six feet tall. With spiked shoes that added at least four inches to their natural height they appeared quite awesome. Their voluptuous curves where strapped into fabulously cut leather body harnesses, but, for all their astonishing beauty, it was Simon Bay who captured Alex's attention.

She stared at him in open-mouthed disbelief, recognising his aristocratic features instantly. This wasn't the anonymous slave master she'd been expecting, but a face from the gossip columns – a member of one of the richest and most well known families in England, who's photograph she'd seen time and again in the society pages, squiring some titled beauty or other to a gala, or a ball, or a first night.

He was dressed in a long Edwardian style jacket. His mouth was cruel, and his eyes flashed like a bird of prey as he met her gaze and unashamedly took in the contours of her luscious body. Alex dropped her gaze, feeling her cheeks colour furiously. It seemed the guest of honour hid his real name, but not his nature, behind a pseudonym.

As Tourne, Starn and Simon Bay exchanged social pleasantries, Alex could feel the latter's hungry eyes crawling over every inch of her.

'So,' said Bay, accepting the glass offered to him without interrupting his blatant inspection. 'This is your latest pupil, Peter?'

Tourne nodded. He'd sensed his friend's interest as soon as he'd walked into the room. Good manners had required he show him Starn's new girls first, but he knew that Simon's preference was for European or black slaves; they offered a real challenge.

Simon Bay pensively turned the glass in his long slim fingers. 'Physically she's not quite to my taste,' he said flatly as he slowly began to circle Alex as though stalking his prey.

Tourne nodded. He'd expected as much. Simon liked muscular, heavy breasted women.

Simon Bay teased out a lock of Alex's hair and twisted

132

it thoughtfully around his fingers. 'That isn't to say I couldn't sell her for you. She looks presentable. Interesting colouring. There'd be no need for a master to hide this one away.' As he spoke he glanced at Starn's matching pair of fillies as if to make his point. 'I'd need to have my doctor look her over – put her through her paces.'

He stopped his circling and stood close behind Alex, looking over her shoulder and admiring the slow swell of her breasts. He gripped the hem of her dress and began to pull it up. His thin hand slid between her smooth thighs, making her catch her breath and shiver. His face registered disapproval. 'She's dry.'

Tourne sighed. 'My servants just bathed her.'

Simon Bay shrugged. 'I always prefer them unwashed. Their scent is part of the appeal for my clients.' He pulled his hand away and looked round. 'Have you some oil, and a towel?'

Tourne nodded towards one of the lackeys, cursing himself for not being prepared; a girl sold by Simon Bay had great cache.

Beside him Starn grinned and lifted the leads on his two Eurasian girls. 'Perhaps you'd like to look over my new stock too? I can guarantee they're good and wet. And I'd appreciate your opinion, though they're not for sale.'

Simon Bay nodded. 'Of course, my dear chap. I've always liked twins, though they can be harder to manage. Don't be tempted to split them up – together they're worth at least four times their value as individuals.'

The servant reappeared and Simon Bay slowly poured the olive oil over his fingers. Peter Tourne glanced monetarily at Alex, willing her to behave as he knew she could. She looked at him, her eyes glassy with unshed tears. He nodded his approval and silent support. Without a word she opened her legs, bending forward a little so that Simon Bay could begin his examination without hindrance. She bit her lip as his fingers explored her most intimate parts. He mumbled his approval as his finger slipped comfortably into her quim.

'Nice and tight here. Shame she's so dry, it really spoils the overall effect. She's supposed to be ready whenever she's required.' His finger slipped out and he sniffed it speculatively like an expert wine taster. 'Subtle bouquet,' he mumbled again. 'But difficult to judge when she's so clean.' He oiled his fingers again.

Peter Tourne watched Alex stiffen, and knew from the exquisitely confused expression on her face that his distinguished guest's hand had slid between her buttocks; he knew where Simon Bay would inspect next. As a persistent finger pressed home Alex let out a soft mewl of discomfort.

'Perhaps a little too tight here,' Simon Bay said casually as though commenting on a piece of clothing, 'though she is very tense. If I take her on I'd have to insert a stretcher. A lot of my clients would be reluctant to purchase her if she couldn't take them anally as well.'

Tourne nodded his understanding as Simon Bay wiped his hands on a towel the servant held out for him. He circled Alex again and stroked her breasts through the sheer dress. Her nipples hardened at once under his knowing touch.

He nodded thoughtfully. 'All in all, not too bad, Peter. I'd certainly be happy to put her on the auction list – providing you can let me have her for a few days before hand. Not that you've done a bad job, old chap – she's a fine specimen, but she still requires a little more work. A little... fine tuning, so to speak.'

'I see.'

'Don't look so worried old man, I'm certain she'll make a decent price for you.' He grinned. 'When can you deliver her?'

Tourne's delight at his friend's words was tinged with a sense of regret. He suddenly experienced strange feelings towards Alex. 'A week, she has to finish the mural I told you about.'

Simon Bay nodded. 'Ah yes… By the way,' he said as he took his glass of champagne and instantly changed the subject with a bizarre air of normality. 'Did you hear that Monique is coming to my party tomorrow night. She's calling in on her way back to the States. I've already invited her to fly back to my place for the auction…'

The conversation moved away from Alex and on to wider things. Peter Tourne glanced back as his friend warmly threw an arm around his shoulder and invited him to look over his new body slaves – a single tear was trickling down Alex's exquisitely made-up features.

The dinner party was a great success. Wine – served by Alex and Starn's new Eurasian girls – flowed like water. Simon Bay's intimidating slave women stood sentinel by the double doors of the dining room, their faces impassive, and their eyes flashing as the men indulged in a magnificent meal.

Alex couldn't reconcile the feeling of pain she felt as Peter Tourne played host to his two guests. He seemed oblivious to her now that Simon Bay had given his seal of approval. Her mind was wandering as she refilled their wine glasses for what must have been the sixth or seventh time, and – while not concentrating – the neck of the decanter caught the top of one of the glasses and tipped the contents over the table. Instantly the conversation ceased.

Nervously Alex began to dab at the spreading scarlet pool with a napkin, feeling a tiny flurry of fear in her stomach; it almost seemed the men had been waiting for her to make some kind of mistake. Simon Bay looked at Peter Tourne, and then beckoned Alex nearer. Drunkenly he slid his hands up under her skirt, and teased the lips of her quim.

'Not so dry now, eh?' he purred with amusement.

Alex swallowed hard and looked at Tourne.

'I'm very sorry about the wine,' she began.

Simon Bay grimaced theatrically. 'She speaks too readily. Haven't you taught her that slaves are expected to be quiet?' he said to Tourne. His fingers pawed further. 'In some places they'd cut out her tongue if she refused to obey.' He grinned crookedly. 'Always seems such a shame; a tongue can be used for so many lovely things besides talking.' The wine had made him rough. Alex flinched as he clumsily prodded a finger up inside her. He sniggered and burped quietly. 'Maybe your protégé is not as obliging as you would have me believe, Peter. It's her European upbringing. One of my handsome coloured girls, or either of those pretty little twins of Starn's, would have their legs open the instant you touched them, eager to satisfy their master.'

Peter Tourne, his cheeks similarly flushed with wine, snorted 'that's what makes her special, Simon we both know that. She is yours to command – do what you like with her, you'll see she's better than all of them put together.'

Simon Bay sniggered again and jabbed another finger into Alex. 'She's still too dry.' His fingers slipped out and he turned her to face him. 'My good friend Peter tells me you're willing to please.'

She nodded warily; she knew there was little else she could do.

'Very good,' Simon Bay blinked slowly as if it took a great deal of effort, and then slurped his wine. 'Then lift up your dress.'

As Alex obeyed, Simon Bay – his eyes firmly set on the pierced lips of her quim – lifted a hand and beckoned to the Negro girls who flanked the door. He looked up into Alex's eyes as the coloured girls approached. 'They will make you wet for me,' he said softly. 'Open your legs.'

The heavily built women moved with deceptive grace and silence. Before Alex could compose herself one girl dropped onto all fours between her and Simon Bay and ran her snakelike tongue across the lips of Alex's naked sex. Alex gasped with a mixture of shock and surprise. A moment later the second woman closed behind her and reached round the stunned girl to cup her breasts. Her alien sex brushed Alex's back.

For an instant it felt to Alex as though they would overwhelm and consume her. Between her legs the tongue flicked back and forth across her pleasure bud, while the pinching fingers sent wonderful sensations through her nipples and breasts. She struggled to catch her breath.

Starn snorted and refilled his wine glass.

Simon Bay looked across at him through slightly blurred eyes. 'You have something to say, Mr Fettico?'

Starn leered drunkenly. 'If it were me,' he waved a finger unsteadily in the air, 'I'd punish her for being so bloody clumsy, not let your trained tigers lose on her. She's bloody enjoying herself. She should be whipped!'

Simon Bay nodded. 'Patience, Mr Fettico, patience.'

As the men spoke Alex felt a flash of pleasure lighting in her belly. The black women knew exactly where to touch her. A long tongue slithered over the engorged ridge of her clitoris, caressing the silver ring on its journey through her labia, while strong hands glided up over her thighs. Simon Bay would have had no worries now; Alex could already feel the wetness forming deep inside her. The two women encouraged her to let them take her weight. She leant further and further back against the giantess behind, opening her legs so that the woman crouched between her legs could have greater freedom to kiss and caress her. Long fingers pressed deep inside, exploring the moistening contours with surprising tenderness.

Alex felt the tension in her spine begin to fade. The instant she began to relax her unlikely seducers seemed

137

to sense the change. The woman behind grabbed her ribs. The woman at her feet grabbed her thighs, and they unceremoniously picked her up and threw her face down onto the table amongst the remnants of the dinner. Alex shrieked. A strong pair of hands grabbed at her legs and jerked the beautiful evening dress up around her waist. Alex began to struggle, but she hadn't bargained on the tenacity and strength of Simon Bay's two black slaves. One of them mounted the table with feline agility, held Alex's arms before she had time to respond, and pinned her down against the wine soaked cloth. To Alex's utter horror she could feel the seeds of arousal that had formed in her sex now glowing white hot – screaming for release. She swooned under the treatment of the two women.

She heard Simon Bay laugh arrogantly. 'Perhaps this is more to your taste, Mr Fettico?'

A few moments later something hissed through the air and a lightening strike exploded across her naked buttocks. Alex screamed in astonishment. The woman tightened the grip on her shoulders, and Alex realised that in a strange way that touch was meant to reassure. An instant later the whip struck again. This time the blow was harder. The sensation was so intense that every cell in her body seemed to register it; the sensation swept through her like a volcanic blast, driving away every thought, every shred of consciousness that could not be registered as feeling.

Blow after blow detonated across her naked back and buttocks until she couldn't tell where one stroke ended and another began. She thought she might lose consciousness, her mind driven into a corner by the pain, and worse still, the terrifying knowledge that the same pain and feeling of humiliation fed the dark creature Peter Tourne had created in her.

Suddenly the hands on her shoulders rolled her over onto her back. They manoeuvred her effortlessly until her sore bottom was perched on the edge of the table and her legs dangled towards the floor. She closed her eyes, unable to face the gaze of the assembled diners and their slaves. All she could hear was the ragged sounds of her own breath, and then she smelt something that made her gasp. She knew immediately what it was, and then she felt the brush of warm flesh against her cheek and lips. Someone was straddling her shoulders. She opened her eyes and saw the gaping quim of one of the slaves. The musky smell of the woman's sex was almost overwhelming. Before Alex had time to protest or resist a hand lifted her head up towards the folds of dark wet flesh.

Alex trembled as she breathed in the unmistakable scent. Her body seemed to be covered in a blanket of the female perfume; the odour flooded her every sense. To her horror her mouth began to water. In the instant before Alex pressed a tentative kiss to the woman's body, another tongue opened her own quim and slid effortlessly over the swollen bud of her clitoris.

Alex mewled, the noise buffeted and echoed against the closeness of the woman crouched above her.

Peter Tourne was absorbed by the tableau being enacted in front of him. The two amazons looked as if they were eating Alex alive. They crouched hungrily over her prone body, both facing her feet. The one whom Alex was tonguing had her finger's buried deep in her companion's sopping sex, who was in turn lapping enthusiastically at Alex's unprotected quim. Beneath them their victim was gasping and twisting wildly from side to side, her whole body and mind caught up in the intensity of the moment.

Simon Bay, standing now between Alex's open legs, looked on in triumph. The English girl's cries were getting more and more instinctive as pleasure and passion unseated pain and reason. He dropped the riding crop he'd used on her, opened his trousers, and unceremoniously drove his cock into her dripping sex. Alex arched herself to take him, while his slave's long pink tongue lapped at his shaft as it slid home.

On the far side of the table Starn Fettico grinned slyly. Moving closer, ignoring both his slave girls, he too unfastened his trousers. His cock jutted forward like a scimitar. As the coloured girl squatting over Alex's face moved, her quim opened and closed like a gaping scarlet mouth. Starn gripped her broad hips and pulled her a little closer. Climbing onto the table he guided his shaft into the hot wet depths of her body, his hands sliding along her sweating torso to cup her pendulous breasts.

Peter Tourne saw Alex hesitate for a moment as the coloured girl above her wriggled back a fraction to allow Starn Fettico to drive deeper. He imagined the thoughts and sensations going through her mind as she felt the contours of Starn's knarled cock sliding over her tongue, the brush of his balls against her forehead and closed eyes, and the smell of his body; he could imagine it all.

Alex suddenly let out a long guttural screech of pleasure, and her whole body stiffened and convulsed as the first waves of orgasm ripped through her. As she began to writhe those around her were caught up in its wake. Like a house of cards the lovers began to quake and fall way – all sated, all pleasured.

Peter Tourne smiled, topped up his brandy balloon, and settled himself back in his chair; Alex Sanderson had surpassed anything he could have expected of her. He was certain that Simon Bay would feel the same way.

When she emerged from between the coloured woman's thighs, Alex's face was flushed, her lips slick with the juices of the dark beauty, her sex pink and moist from the attentions of the other slave and Simon Bay's orgasm. She blushed furiously as she realised Peter Tourne had been watching her. He extended his hand and she took it without a word. He pulled her close and kissed her, relishing the taste on her lips. She looked around nervously as the others began to tidy themselves.

'Can I go to the bathroom?' she whispered, her colour intensifying as she spoke.

He nodded. 'Don't be long,' he said softly. 'I'll be waiting for you.'

When she'd gone he went over to the ice bucket and poured three glasses of champagne – after all, he had something to celebrate.

Chapter Nine

Alex hurried from the dining room, still trembling from the events that had taken place under the cool eyes of Peter Tourne. She was certain she'd passed the test that he'd set her. Her whole body hummed from the intensity of her orgasm. She glanced left and right, struggling to regain her composure and get her bearings. There was a cloakroom in the main hallway. She scurried downstairs – a trickle of semen already running onto her thighs.

As she passed Peter Tourne's office she realised that the door was open – and in the lamplight she saw the phone on his desk. An idea took shape in an instant, and before she really had time to consider any possible consequences she hurried inside, picked up the receiver and tapped in a London number.

To her immense relief Laurence Russell picked up the phone on the second ring. She sighed and thanked God that her agent was a famous workaholic who seldom left his office before midnight. Glancing anxiously over her shoulder she whispered, 'Hello?'

Laurence coughed. *'Hello? Who's that? Is that you Alex? Where the hell have you been? I've been worried about you.'*

Alex felt a lump form in her throat at the sound of his familiar voice. 'Laurence,' she said unsteadily. 'Please listen to me. I haven't got the time to explain. You have to come and get me. I'm still at the villa KaRoche.'

'What's the matter? Can you speak up? I can barely hear you, Alex. Is there a problem at the villa? You sound different.'

Alex looked up, catching sight of her reflection in the

enormous picture window that overlooked the sea. Her skin was glowing her eyes alight with the after-effects of pleasure. The lamp on the desk reflected in the chain that linked her nipples – She most certainly was different.

'I can't talk to you now,' she whispered hurriedly. Where would she begin even if she had the time to explain? 'Please, Laurence, just come and get me. Something has happened.'

'All right,' comforted Laurence. *'But I—'*

Alex jumped and squealed as a pair of hands grabbed the receiver from her fingers and slammed it back into the cradle. She spun round, her expression taut with fear. Mario leered at her.

'Who do you ring?' he snapped, gesticulating towards the phone.

Alex felt her colour drain. 'No one,' she said, backing away from the desk. 'I couldn't get through, that was… that was… the operator.' Alex cringed at her own feeble answer.

Mario's face contorted into a sickening grin. 'I tell Mr Tourne,' he said flatly.

'No!' snapped Alex, holding her hands up to keep a distance between them. 'Please don't, Mario. I'll do anything you want – anything. Please – just don't tell Mr Tourne.'

Mario looked her up and down. His fingers snaked forward to cup her sex. He snorted, rubbing the fabric of her dress up into her quim. 'You're very wet – how you say, *very horny.*' He sniggered. 'They all fuck you, already? You save a little for later. I and the boy – we want our share.'

Alex reddened as the driver pulled his hand away and sniffed his fingers.

'What's going on in here?' Peter Tourne's voice from out in the hall made Alex jump again. Mario grinned at her, and then turned to face his employer.

'I catch her here,' he said nodding towards the phone. 'She going to ring someone.'

Tourne stared past him at Alex. 'Is this true?' His expression was stony.

Alex knew that Mario had already lied for her and that she was now beholden to the brutal driver.

'Well?' snapped Tourne. 'It is true, Alex?'

Looking down, Alex struggled to conceal her guilt, and nodded miserably.

'Yes,' she mumbled. She could sense his displeasure. When she finally looked at him she realised he was more disappointed than angry.

'How could you defy me, Alex? I instruct you. I show you your true nature. I invite one of the world's most respected masters to come and examine you,' he stopped and shook his head. 'And yet you still try to escape?'

'Oh, Mr Tourne,' Alex said softly. The tears that had threatened earlier when she'd spoken to Laurence Russell trickled down her face. 'I don't know. I don't know what I want. I don't understand what's happening to me.' She paused. 'I'm afraid of what you make me feel.' It was true. She was afraid of losing herself in the maelstrom of emotions that Peter Tourne had shown her; afraid that in submitting to her darkest instincts she would lose everything.

Peter Tourne sighed and touched her face. 'Afraid? Oh Alex, what is there to be afraid of? Haven't I told you this is a game – a complex charade that feeds the pleasures of those who lead and those who follow.' He paused. 'Trust me, Alex. Let go and relish the pleasure.'

Alex pouted. 'But you're going to sell me. That's why Mr Bay is here tonight, isn't it?'

He nodded. 'That is true. Another games master, another game.'

'But I don't want to be a slave.'

He smiled wryly. 'Are you so certain of that?'

She felt a flicker of panic. 'But what if— ?'

'When you tire of the game all you have to do is walk away. But I don't think you will; you like what I've shown you too much. Something you have to understand is that I'm your master because we have an unspoken agreement that allows me to dominate you. To teach you. To show you all that can be shared. You just have to trust me, Alex.'

She stared at him, trying to grasp what he was saying, but sensing that he was right. Didn't her whole body glow whenever she obeyed him? Hadn't the greatest moments of sexual satisfaction she'd ever experienced come when she gave up her whole mind and body into the hands of this man? Didn't she relish the fact that he took what he wanted from her without question?

Tourne stroked her hair with surprising affection. 'Simon is prepared to sell you at his auction. He's invited us to his villa for a party tomorrow.' He looked at her thoughtfully. 'At the end of the week I'll hand you over to him. You have a day, perhaps two, to finish the mural.'

Alex felt sick. 'Another games master?' she whispered.

He nodded, indicating the phone on his desk. 'Or if you prefer you can walk away now. The choice is yours.'

Alex struggled to make sense of the tumult of feelings that bubbled inside her.

Mario, still standing at his employer's shoulder, leered at her. Voices from outside the office broke the tension, and Tourne turned away to greet Simon Bay and his entourage.

The guest of honour again looked Alex up and down before he spoke, though his remarks were directed towards his host.

'I wondered where you'd got to, my friend. Your houseboy is ready to serve more coffee and liqueurs, and your friend Starn is anxious to show off his latest toys.'

Tourne nodded. 'I'll be there in a second or two Simon.'

Simon Bay's eyes hadn't left Alex. 'Trouble?' he asked. Tourne shook his head. 'Not really, is there, Alex?'

She had to make a decision. Swallowing hard, she shook her head. 'No,' she stammered. 'There's no trouble.'

Simon Bay slapped his friend on the back. 'Oh come on, Peter. Why don't you let me take her with me tonight? It'd solve everything. Let me have her for a day or two extra.'

Tourne held out a hand to guide his illustrious guest back upstairs. 'No, thank you, Simon. It's a very generous offer, but she has to finish the mural first.'

As they left he turned back to look at Alex. 'When you've been to the bathroom come back upstairs and join us. Don't be long.'

Alex nodded. Mario grinned. She knew that the sophisticated game of passion Peter Tourne had taught her was lost on Mario – and she now owed him.

She hurried to the downstairs bathroom and turned the taps on full. Splashing her face with cold water helped restore a sense of balance. When she returned to the dining room Starn's latest acquisitions were staging a lesbian exhibition. Despite their writhing and moans Simon Bay looked thoroughly bored. The beautiful little Asian girls were self-conscious and ill at ease as they went through the stilted routine Starn had obviously taught them. Despite their beautiful bodies and sinuous curves, it was far from stimulating.

Alex took her place at Tourne's feet and rested her head in his lap while the girls stroked and whispered their way through a mockery of true eroticism. Starn however was delighted, and had no hesitation in joining them, making love to one while tonguing another. Finally, breathlessly, at the point of orgasm he sunk his teeth into one of them. For the first time Alex felt the shriek of pain that followed was close to the reality of sensations that Peter Tourne had so cunningly taught her.

Her eyes felt heavy, and she was surprised when the next thing she saw with any clarity was his face not more than an inch or two away from hers.

'They've all gone home,' he whispered. 'It's time you were in bed.'

With a yawn she uncurled and stretched her knotted limbs. She rubbed her eyes and looked around for Mario. He was nowhere to be seen. No doubt he was lurking somewhere outside, waiting to extract the price for his silence once they had reached her cell. To her surprise Peter Tourne extended his hand and helped her to rise.

'Come with me,' he said softly.

Tenderness was the last thing Alex expected.

Silently he led her into a part of the villa she'd never seen before. At the top of what seemed like an endless flight of stone stairs, double doors opened onto an enormous vaulted chamber. The room was lit by candlelight and appeared to have been carved out of the hillside the centre of the room was dominated by a huge bed. He turned to her as they stepped inside.

'Until you leave here you are my slave, and mine alone.'

Alex nodded and followed him into a marble lined bathroom. Set in the floor was a bath already filled with steamy aromatic water. With trembling hands Alex set about undressing the man who had initiated her into the dark game. As her fingers struggled with his clothes she realised that in all the time she had spent at KaRoche she had never seen him naked. The thought made her stomach flutter with anticipation. She wondered if there was some way she could convince him that she ought to stay with him at the villa. She could be everything he wanted.

Every touch was an act of worship – she unbuttoned his shirt, slipped off his jacket, undid his dress tie, all the time aware that he was watching her. As she pushed his shirt back off his broad shoulders she pressed a kiss to his dark hair trimmed nipples, her tongue paying homage to him, like a supplicant at an ancient altar. She knelt down to unfasten his trousers, eyes chastely lowered to the floor.

Tonight she was Peter Tourne's handmaiden, his body slave, and every cell of her mind and body relished her submission. His cock was magnificent; broad and curved it sprung into her fingers like a sword. She ran her tongue along it, pausing to kiss the engorged scarlet crown. He moaned softly, stroking her hair as she lapped and caressed his shaft. Lifting her hands to cradle his balls she drew him deep into her mouth. She felt the tension growing in his body, and smiled.

'No, not yet,' he said in a husky whisper. 'I want you to bathe me.'

Denied her prize, Alex nodded and moved aside, reluctantly letting go of him.

His body was quite beautiful; slim and muscular, his skin had a soft golden glow to it that made her mouth water. There was nothing she wanted more than to service him, to feel him deep inside her, to give him whatever pleasure he demanded. She trembled, ripples of desire forming and reforming in her belly.

He smiled at her and stepped down into the water. Alex slipped off her evening dress and hurried to join him. With gentle hands she soaped every inch of his glorious body; every touch, every single gesture confirming his status as her lord. He closed his eyes and lay back in the warm water. Alex felt almost overwhelmed by her tenderness towards him. The feelings were so intense she thought she might cry.

When they were done, he allowed her to wrap him in a thick towelling gown and pour him a glass of wine from the tray arranged on the sideboard in the bedroom. Alex noticed that beside the tray was a finely tooled leather strap with a split end. She bit her lip, momentarily touching the cool leather before carrying the wine to him, eyes humbly downcast.

Naked and still wet from the bath she curled at his feet, awaiting his instructions. Tourne set the glass down on the arm of his chair.

'You've forgotten something,' he said.

Alex shivered; she knew what he meant. Struggling to control her racing thoughts she rose and brought him the leather strap. He took it from her and ran it thoughtfully between his fingers, his eyes working up and down her naked body. She felt the anticipation in her belly growing under his undisguised examination. Her body was already crisscrossed with the weals from the beating given by Simon Bay – but what filled her mind was not the painful marks, but the ever growing sense of expectation. She tensed as he got to his feet and swung the strap back.

'Come here,' he ordered, indicating the rug in front of him. She stepped closer. 'Put your hands on top of your head.'

She did as he said – and closed her eyes.

The first blow hit squarely across the tensed peaks of her breasts. She shrieked, astonished that he could still be so cruel. The second blow hit her across the belly, lifting a broad red plain of tender flesh. The pain from the strap was different from the whip; the sensation was more diffused, dissipating through her like molten magma. The third stroke caught her sex, exploding across the ring that pierced her labia.

Her mind flared – hadn't she already proved she was his slave? Hadn't she already given herself to him completely? Why did he still have to punish her? The answer was as obvious as the question; it was all part of the game. She was his to do with as he pleased, and if she wanted to partake in the pleasure of submission she must never forget that truth.

The fourth and fifth strokes hit her low on the buttocks, making her gasp.

'Open your eyes,' Tourne said.

149

Alex stared up at him. His eyes flashed with desire and pent-up emotion. He threw the strap to the floor, crossed the room, and lay on the bed. She hesitated, wondering what he wanted next. He glared up at her.

'Come over here and give yourself to me, Alex. Show me what a good slave you have become. Show me that you understand the rules of the game.'

She swallowed hard. In some ways, after the beating, she knew this would be the ultimate test; to come willingly to her tormentor, and to surrender unquestioningly to his desire. She walked towards him as gracefully as her trepidation would allow; aware that with every step she was getting closer and closer to losing herself forever in his passion. His eyes remained dark and devoid of emotion.

Slowly she climbed onto the bed and straddled his calves, touching herself as she did. She could feeling the moisture forming in the innermost recesses of her sex.

Tourne glanced down at her fingers. 'Are you wet?'

Alex nodded.

He smiled. 'Good. Now show me what you've learnt. Give me the undivided devotion and pleasure I deserve.'

Trembling, Alex crouched over him, crawling up over his warm muscular body, fluttering kisses over every inch of his frame. Her tongue lapped at his balls, caressing and stroking the intimidating curve of his shaft. Her lips closed around its head. She ran her tongue around its edge, then across to kiss the single moist eye. Whatever else happened to her, Peter Tourne was her first master and every thought that formed in her head was concentrated on giving him pleasure.

Eagerly she drew him deeper, sucking and lapping, willing his approval. When she sensed he was ready she moved over him, replacing lips and tongue with her hands as she lifted herself up to guide him into her. As his cock parted her delicate inner lips, as she felt the sheer strength of his need, their eyes met. He looked into her mind. His gaze was suffused with tenderness.

Without hesitation she impaled herself on him, drawing him deep into her throbbing quim. For the first time she saw a look of pure uncomplicated joy on Peter Tourne's face. She began to move up and down, giving herself to him entirely, her feverish grinding taking them both to the edges of madness. He groaned. Unable to hold back any longer he thrust into her. His face contorted and his movements became wild and instinctive. Alex cried out, feeling the rush of an ancient passion that exploded inside her mind and her body, as they fell into the abyss of orgasm. Down and down they both tumbled, twisting and turning, gasping for breath, until finally it was over and they were still.

Peter Tourne pulled her close to him, his lips brushing her forehead. She sighed – exhausted and completely spent. She was pleased with herself. She curled up under his arm and slipped effortlessly into comfortable sleep.

The next day was the strangest Alex had spent at the villa KaRoche – strange because of its normality. She woke up still beside Peter in his bed, got dressed in her own clothes which were brought to her by the housekeeper, and then after a breakfast they shared on the terrace she went to work on the mural. Peter spent the morning with her, sitting in a garden chair and reading. He even joined her makeshift picnic lunch.

He was a wonderful companion. For once he was more lover than master, but even so Alex could still feel the subtle strength of his power as they chatted and laughed. He was still her master despite appearances, of that she had little doubt. Finally, as the long hot afternoon began, he dismissed her.

'Go back to the guest cabin and rest,' he said softly. 'Tonight, at Simon's party, another phase of your education begins.'

Back in the guest cabin Alex stared at her possessions. Everything was exactly as she'd left it. It seemed so long since she'd unpacked her clothes and arranged her toiletries in the bathroom. She glanced up at the open door, imagining that Gena would appear at any second. She stared sadly at the void – was Peter letting her have one day of freedom before handed her over to Simon Bay? He'd told her it would be at the end of the week, but the way he now looked at her and the gentleness with which he was treating her made her suspect that he might have changed his mind.

Outside in the raw heat of the day the cicadas were buzzing. The fragrances of the exotic flowers wafted on the warm breeze from the garden into her room. She slipped off her clothes, lay down on the bed, and closed her eyes she was intoxicated by the heat and the strange sense of expectation.

She wished there was some way that she could persuade Peter to let her stay. She couldn't imagine anything she wanted more than to be with him Pulling a sheet up over her shoulders she felt the ache of the bruises on her back – that only served to feed her hunger.

Chapter Ten

As soon as Alex awoke she was aware that someone else was in the cabin. She opened her eyes and was astonished to see Peter gazing down at her. Aware of her nakedness she instinctively tried to cover herself. He smiled.

'How enchanting. I shall miss you very much, Alex.'

She stared up at him. A wave of grief fluttered through her. 'Can't I stay here with you?' she pleaded. 'Please, I'll do anything you want, just let me stay.'

He shook his head. 'No. I'm afraid that's impossible. I have always seen my role as a teacher; a mentor. Here, I want you to wear this for the coming evening.' He handed her a large flat dress box he was carrying.

Alex crept across the bed and undid the ribbon. Inside the box was a long copper coloured dress. She held it up. It looked like something from a medieval painting, with a richly embroidered buttoned yoke and long thin sleeves. The bodice had a low square neckline, below which the body of the dress hung in soft folds. She ran a finger over the silk. It must have cost a fortune, and was very much like a gown she'd painted on one of the figures in the mural. It was a fairytale costume, and certainly unlike anything she had expected.

Peter Tourne nodded towards the box. 'At Simon's party there will be every extreme pleasure you can imagine on offer. His girls and the girls of his guests will be dressed as slaves – in leather, in furs, naked. Only you will be presented as you truly are – a mythical princess amongst slaves. Isn't that what you painted for me in the gallery?'

Alex swallowed hard. 'It's beautiful. Are you leaving me with Mr Bay tonight?'

He shook his head. 'Not tonight – but very soon. Now get ready. Would you like me to send my housekeeper to help you dress?'

She shook her head; she needed to be alone.

Later that evening Peter Tourne's limousine purred along the hilltop roads. Alex stared out into the fading light at the rocky landscape and the sea far below. How easy it was to forget that there was another life outside the villa KaRoche. Sitting beside her in the back seat her current master seemed preoccupied. Before they'd left he'd snapped a fine chain leash onto her collar; a sharp reminder, even a mythical princess could be tamed by the right man.

Alex couldn't take her eyes off the scenery. Olive groves and tiny white houses clung to the steep hillsides. Here and there groups of men meandered along the roads on the way to their local taverna. All these things had eluded Alex until now; she hadn't stepped outside the walls of the villa KaRoche since her arrival. It seemed impossible that life continued normally outside her prison.

Down and down the car went, swinging left and right along the steep roads, until finally below them Alex could see a string of bright silvery lights twinkling through the encroaching darkness. She knew without being told that this was their destination: Simon Bay's luxury seaside villa.

'Ah, at last, Peter. I thought perhaps you'd changed your mind about coming tonight,' Simon Bay welcomed his friend as they made their way up onto the enormous terrace that skirted the villa. Between the palms and neatly clipped hedges music was carried towards them on a soft breeze that blew up from the gently rolling sea.

Alex glanced around. She had never seen such a beautiful house or such a breathtaking setting.

'I should have known you'd arrive fashionably late, even when pleasure is available in abundance. I see you've brought your little protégé. Good, several of my regular customers are here this evening. Come in, come in, everyone else is here already.'

As Simon Bay guided them towards the main party Alex's attention was drawn to the other guests nearby. On the terrace an Arab Prince in long flowing robes sat on a chaise longue. A double ended chain rested in his long fluid fingers, securing two blonde girls at his feet. They were naked except for tiny loin cloths. Behind them, Starn Fettico stood with his two new Asian girls – they too were naked. By the double doors into the main villa a plump well-heeled woman in a sparkling evening dress was being served by a subservient teenage boy clad only in sandals and a mask. As the boy moved Alex could see that his foreskin had been pierced, and a single diamond drop hung from the sensitive skin; it matched those hanging from the woman's ears.

Simon Bay led them through the doors, chattering to Tourne the whole time. Alex was stunned by the number of people in the main reception room there seemed to be a mass of bodies. Some were dressed in opulent splendour, while their slaves were dressed in every erotic and exciting variation of clothing the imagination could create; some in leather, some in harness, some naked except for a bauble or chain. Most of the slaves were masked; rendered anonymous so that only their bodies and their obedience remained on show.

Simon Bay directed his friend towards a small group of people standing by the stairs. Alex found it difficult to concentrate on what was being said as the group exchanged the social pleasantries. The room around them was full of guests and slaves of every hue, shape and nationality. She had no idea that Peter's game had so many players.

A discreet tug on the leash from him brought her attention back to the small group who surrounded them.

The Arab she'd seen earlier on the terrace had joined this inner circle. His two girls crouched at his feet.

'And so this is your latest find, Peter?' purred a statuesque blonde holding a champagne cocktail in one elegant hand and a cigarette with a vivid smudge of bright red lipstick on the filter in the other. Her accent betrayed a soft, cultured American burr. Her clothing, a sleek black evening dress, discreetly whispered wealth. 'We've been hearing *so* much about her.' She pouted her red lips suggestively towards Alex.

Tourne nodded. 'That's right, Monique. She's an artist.'

The woman laughed and proudly swelled her generous bosom towards the beautiful topic of conversation. 'An artist is of no use to me whatsoever, my dear. And why is she dressed like that? What is it you're hiding?' 'I'm hiding nothing I can assure you. It's just that I'm growing a little tired of naked flesh.' Tourne replied as he sipped at the drink Simon Bay had given him.

Monique dismissed this comment with a derisory wave of the hand that sent silvery cigarette smoke curling up towards the high ceiling, and then she nodded towards Alex. 'May I?' The request was directed towards Tourne.

He nodded politely. 'Of course, be my guest.'

The woman gave her drink and the cigarette to a nearby waiter, and casually unbuttoned the bodice of Alex's dress. She slipped a hand inside in a manner that told Alex she was a woman who was used to getting exactly what she wanted. Alex felt her colour rise. The woman squeezed her breasts as though they were ripe fruit. A long fingernail traced the rings that pierced her nipples and the little chain that linked them.

'Very nice,' she breathed and ran her tongue over her full lips. '*Very* nice.' She glanced back at Tourne. 'Not growing tired of marking your conquests then?'

He shrugged. 'Just a trade mark, my dear.'

Alexs' humiliation and colour intensified as the woman

rolled her nipples speculatively between her fingertips. In seconds they hardened into tight peaks. In spite of the shame Alex felt a lovely ripple of desire that unnerved her.

The American woman continued. 'She's quite lovely, and very responsive, but really far too fragile for my tastes. I like them coarser. Bigger tits, bigger bones. Something with a bit more meat on it. It's a pity, I'm in the market for another girl. This one might break if you played too rough.' Her last comment brought a flurry of polite laughter from the other guests.

As her hands dropped away Alex felt exposed and vulnerable. The open bodice of her dress framed her breasts, her tight pink nipples, and the little rings and chain that glittered as she trembled under the group's undisguised examination. Monique waved a hand towards her. Alex knew what the American wanted, and slowly began to inch her skirt up over her legs. Her hands shook as the silky material brushed her thighs, exposing the naked contours of her sex.

The Arab lifted an eyebrow thoughtfully, and then indicated that he wanted her to lift the dress even higher. Alex silently did as she was told.

The Arab nodded his appreciation. 'Very good. She is almost boyish. I have a cousin, Ahmed, who might like her.' He smiled evilly and ran a hand over her creamy flank. 'Soft skin too. Ahmed has a liking for boys. Perhaps I might put a bid in for her – I could buy her as a present for him.'

Alex shuddered, her strongest urge was to turn and run. As the thought passed through her mind she felt the leash tighten and glanced at Peter. His expression revealed nothing.

The prince turned one of the heavy rings on his long fingers. 'I presume we may sample the goods before we make a serious offer?'

Simon Bay nodded. 'Of course, my dear Mustafa. I

may not have trained her myself, but our normal house rules apply. Would you like me to have one of the servants take her to your room now?'

Monique stepped forward holding a fresh champagne cocktail and cigarette. 'Whoa, hang on just one minute! If anyone should be trying her out it should be me! I was here first, remember? I really can't believe you men sometimes!' She looked at Tourne. 'I didn't say I wasn't interested, Peter, just that she wasn't to my usual taste.' She smiled as though contemplating disgustingly naughty thoughts, and her eyes returned to Alex's exposed body. 'Mind you, they do say a change is as good as a rest... now don't they?' She pouted sexily and ran a cool hand down Alex's flat stomach to the soft folds of her quim. Alex shivered.

The brash American grinned. 'Sensitive... I like that.' Her fingers slid provocatively into the crevice between Alex's outer lips. Her fingertip brushed the long ridge of Alex's clitoris, and before she could stop herself, Alex let out a soft moan. The American smiled knowingly, and then pressed her finger deeper still.

Alex hadn't realised she was so wet. Her body offered no resistance as Monique explored her. After a few moments the woman, obviously satisfied, withdrew her finger and rubbed it speculatively against her thumb. 'Tight and wet. What more could a woman ask?' She nodded toward the Arab. 'Why don't you feel for yourself, Mustafa? Tight, hot, and wet. Seems a real shame to waste a body like that on a man who prefers boys.'

The Arab smiled slyly and slid his hands between Alex's legs. She closed her eyes against the humiliation. Mustafa smelt of lemons and something spicy that lingered on her senses. Whereas the American's touch had been deft and businesslike, the Arab's slow and callous inspection made Alex's flesh crawl.

His fingers were like claws, and the rings he wore bit

into her tender flesh as he pressed and prodded. As he breached her sex a single finger strayed further back, stroking the dark puckering of her anus. Alex stiffened – it seemed that Mustafa's brother wasn't the only one interested in the delights a boy could offer. He moved closer, sniffing at her neck and hair.

When he finally stepped away Alex struggled to suppress a shudder of contempt.

Mustafa nodded to Monique. 'You are right. She smells good, almost wholesome. I have a suggestion. What if you try her out tonight, and I have her tomorrow?' He glanced at Simon Bay for confirmation. 'It won't be a problem will it, Simon?'

Alex stared at Peter, waiting for him to protest, but knowing he wouldn't; it seemed he'd handed the responsibility for her further education over to Simon Bay. She didn't like Simon Bay.

'No Mustafa. No problem at all.'

The enormity of Alex's predicament suddenly hit her. More than ever before she realised just how powerless she was to prevent these people from doing anything they wanted with her. Things started happening around her and she was unable to do or say anything.

Monique glanced over her shoulder and beckoned to someone Alex couldn't see. A few seconds later a broad woman pressed between the guests. Alex stared at the new arrival in horror; this was quite obviously the kind of woman Monique preferred. Her slave was no more than five feet tall and almost as wide. Her voluptuous curves were tightly encased in a finely tooled leather basque that squeezed her heavy breasts forward. Her body was contorted into a stunningly exaggerated hourglass. On either side of her cavernous cleavage a small white scar marred the creamy rise of her ample flesh. As Alex looked at the marks she realised with a chilling certainty that the little scars, each about an inch across and in the shape of

159

a rose, where in fact burn marks the woman had been branded by her mistress!

Monique smiled warmly at her slave. 'Gerta, I would like you to take...' she paused and looked at Tourne. 'What's the girl's name?'

'Alex,' he replied. 'Alexander Sanderson.'

Monique nodded and then held out her hand. Without a word he dropped Alex's leash into Monique's palm.

'Take her to my room, Gerta, and get her ready. I'll be up to try her out after we've eaten.' She spoke without taking her lustful gaze from the promising morsel who would be her entertainment for the evening, and passed the leash on to Gerta.

Alex gasped as the plump woman tugged sharply at the strap. She prayed that Peter would grab the leash from Gerta and take her away from Simon Bay and his corrupt hedonistic guests. She looked beseechingly at him, but as she followed Gerta across the crowded room he turned away and took another glass from the tray the waiter offered him.

Peter Tourne dabbed the napkin to his lips and picked up the wine glass at his fingertips.

Sitting opposite him, Starn Fettico grinned. 'A superb meal.'

He nodded.

'You're very quiet tonight,' Starn whispered. 'Simon tells me your latest little kitten has created quite a stir. If Monique and Mustafa are interested you're sure to get a damned good price for her. Not bad, bearing in mind she turned up out of the blue. I wish I had your luck.' He paused, looked at his friend for a second or two, and then snorted. 'Oh come on, Peter, that isn't why you're so damned quiet, it is? For God's sake man, you told me yourself the world is full of women – all ready to serve us.'

Tourne nodded. Starn was right – but even so he'd thought about nothing but Alex since Monique's intimidating slave had led her away. He'd insisted that Alex be returned to him before he left for the villa KaRoche. Mustafa had complained – after all, wasn't Alex supposed to be his for the next day? Reluctantly Tourne had agreed to Simon's arrangement, and then confirmed that he would have Alex delivered to Mustafa first thing in the morning.

He glanced around the room. Monique was lighting a cigarette from the candelabra in the centre of the table. In her everyday life she was an executive in a top New York merchant bank. In her secret life she had a stable of handmaidens – mostly women like Gerta. Tourne acknowledged the nod she gave him.

He'd always thought her choice of plain and homely bed partners reflected her insecurities about her handsome rather than traditionally beautiful face. Whatever her motives, she certainly had the money and influence to indulge her tastes. He'd also met Sven, the Swedish harem master who travelled with her. Ostensibly he was her personal trainer, while the posse of young women masquerading as her PA, her secretary, her housekeeper – each had a fictional role to play in the life she led outside in the real world.

He wondered fleetingly what Alex's role might be in the household if Monique followed through on her promise and bought his protégé – but as he watched her, logic told him that the only reason Monique had insisted on sampling Alex's charms was to assert herself – to prove once again that she was more than equal to any of the men present.

Across the table the rich American woman aped a yawn. 'I'm sure you gentlemen will excuse me,' she said with a sly wink. 'I've had a very busy day. Jet lag, you know how it is.' She fooled no one, least of all Tourne. Monique was eager to get her hands on the exquisite English girl upstairs. Around the table the diners shuffled to their feet, their innate good manners acknowledging Monique's abrupt departure.

Simon Bay smiled and lifted his glass towards Tourne. 'Here's to pleasure,' he said, his eyes firmly fixed on his guest. 'Perhaps you gentleman would care to join me in the drawing room?' he addressed the whole table. 'I believe Tony has organised a little display for our amusement.'

There was a murmur of approval as all eyes turned towards Tony, another of Simon Bay's party guests.

As Peter Tourne got to his feet Mustafa pushed his way through the crowd. When he reached his side he caught hold of his arm and whispered furtively: 'I have no wish to see any more trained apes perform. Simon tells me he has given Monique the Chinese suite.'

Tourne stared at him uncomprehendingly. 'I'm sorry?'

'The rooms overlooking the sea,' the Arab continued whilst trying to contain his obvious enthusiasm. 'Surely you must know about them... the mirrored rooms?' He grinned, and Tourne instantly understood. Several of the suites in Simon Bay's villa were fitted with large mirrored walls. Those in the know were aware that the mirrors concealed secret rooms where the events played out could be observed by a select band of his inner circle.

Tourne discreetly followed the Arab across the room. He wasn't surprised to see that Simon, having waved his guests into the drawing room, was making his way towards them. In one hand he was clutching a bottle of Krug, and in the other three glasses.

He smiled and shrugged philosophically. 'Is there anyone who hasn't already seen Tony's show? They won't notice we're gone.'

Tourne glanced back over his shoulder, hoping that Starn Fettico hadn't seen them leave the main group.

'This way,' said Simon, waving the bottle towards his left. 'Outside, down the steps, through the garden. Just follow the path, but quietly my friends, we have no great desire to give the game away, have we?'

Alex was growing increasingly uneasy. Since her arrival in Monique's room she'd been stripped naked by Gerta, with the help of an intimidating Swede called Sven, and now she hung, powerless, bound to a frame in the centre of the room while her plump little captor oiled her body with some kind of perfumed unguent.

Peter Tourne's indifference had knocked the fight out of her – though she knew she wouldn't be able to overcome Gerta and Sven anyway.

When the doors to the suite opened she struggled to turn to see who had arrived. The collar around her throat made any movement virtually impossible, but from the corner of her eye she saw Monique reflected in one of the huge mirrors that lined the room. Her suspicions were confirmed by the sound of the American's distinctive purr.

'Bring me a scotch, Gerta. Christ, my feet are killing me.'

Alex wondered if the American would give herself a few seconds respite before she turned her attentions to her – she was wrong. The American stroked her back.

'It seems that someone has already taught her about the whip.'

Alex winced as the woman pressed her fingers against one of the weals that marked her spine. A hand circled her torso and cupped a breast, fingers teasing at her nipples.

'I'm not certain about the rings,' Monique continued. 'I much prefer branding – so much more permanent.'

Gerta mumbled her agreement and Alex shuddered as Monique's hands snaked lower to stroke her sex. 'Though here, when the mount is shaved, it is quite effective. Perhaps it's an option I might consider.'

Alex wondered how long this cool and analytical assessment of her body would continue – perhaps the

American's only reason for bringing her here was to ensure Mustafa didn't touch her first.

'How did she behave when you stripped her?'

'She did as she was told,' Sven grunted from somewhere close by.

Monique stepped round in front of her. Alex looked away, intimidated by the merciless look in the other woman's eyes. Monique pensively swirled the ice around in her glass, and then suddenly reached forward, grabbed hold of Alex's hair, and jerked her head up. Fiercely she pressed her lips to Alex's, forcing her mouth open to accept her tongue. As she did, Alex felt something brush her nipples, sending a chill right through her – it was the cruel ice cubes. She stiffened, trying to resist the woman's searching lips.

'Kiss me you little bitch,' hissed the American.

Alex, fighting her revulsion, struggled to respond. The scotch splashed over her breasts, while Monique's hands, still cupping the ice cubes, roamed wherever they pleased. Alex shuddered again in horror as she felt the ice traverse the lips of her sex, and then gasped as Monique slipped the cube inside her. The first was followed by another – and then another. They were so cold they seemed to burn; a hideous combination of ice and fire that made her feel dizzy. Monique's lips and mouth were wet and tasted of wine and acrid cigarette smoke. Instinctively Alex tried to turn away from her, but Monique pulled her closer. Alex squealed as the tormenting fingers returned to her nipples, twisting and pinching at their delicate peaks.

'Please,' Alex whispered in desperation. 'Please...'

Monique stepped away and looked contemptuously at the poor girl. Alex could see the dark outline of the woman's nipples pressing through her expensive evening gown and trembled – Monique was clearly very excited. Deep inside Alex felt the ice beginning to melt, trickling out like chilly fingers over her thighs as the scotch dripped from her belly.

'I think our little friend here needs to be taught that I always get what I want, and I don't expect to have to fight for it. Bring me my toy box, Sven.'

Behind the huge mirror that overlooked Monique's suite, Peter Tourne, Simon Bay and Mustafa were already enjoying the events being played out before them. Tourne was monitoring and savouring Alex's shocked expression as Monique approached her carrying a small ornately cut box, from which she produced two evil looking nipple clamps. Designed like crocodile clips, they were encrusted with precious stones. Alex gasped in horror as Monique lifted then up for her to see, and then groaned as the first one bit home.

The second made her squirm in agony, her fingers clenching and unclenching in anguish. Monique looked triumphant.

'Oh, that's *much* better,' she purred and ran her tongue over Alex's flat tummy.

Tourne felt a warm excitement in his groin as he imagined the delicate cocktail of sweat and scotch.

Gerta circled the English girl slowly, and then tied a blindfold tightly around her head. Once satisfied with her handiwork she handed her mistress an old fashioned teacher's cane. It seemed Alex was to be taught a cruel lesson.

Monique grinned maliciously as the girl struggled in vain against her restraints. She bent the cane into a semi circle before releasing it with a malevolent hiss. Alex whimpered. The American teased the tip along the crack of the girl's sex. As the cane slid over her skin she stopped struggling and began to tremble.

Monique licked her lips hungrily as she circled the girl, letting the tip of the cane trail over her sweating body. Finally she stood behind Alex, flexed the cane once more, and then let go with a stroke of the most astonishing venom. The whole of Alex's body convulsed in the restraints. Even behind the glass the men could hear Alex howl as the pain ripped through her.

'Tourne's playthings are always so soft,' Monique sneered and beckoned Sven to her. The tall blonde slave undid his mistress's evening dress and guided it down over her shoulders. Beneath it she was wearing a leather basque that matched that worn by Gerta. In those few seconds while Monique was undressing, Alex began to sob, struggling frantically to get free of her bonds. Monique smiled without humour and drew the cane back again. Already there was a vivid crimson weal on Alex's slim buttocks.

The second stroke was, if anything, more vicious than the first, and caught Alex on the base of her spine. She sobbed miserably, mouth gaping and gasping for breath. Tourne noticed the trickle of liquid running down between her thighs. Alex slumped forward, gasping as Monique lay on the third and fourth blows. The cry of agony seemed to catch in the girl's pulsating throat.

The cruel American again drew back the cane and brought it down with another terrifying crack. Alex could only whimper now, and Tourne sensed the subtle change in his pupil as she gave herself up to the pain, allowing its dark enchantment to drive away her fear. He wondered if Monique had noticed the change – but knew from her stance and the expression on her face that she had. The girl seemed to almost offer herself up for the next blow, writhing provocatively in the frame. The next blow made her gasp but her hips thrust back, revealing the plump contours of her quim.

Monique smirked. 'Perhaps she isn't so soft after all.' Another blow. Alex moaned and stretched. Monique hastily threw the cane to the floor. 'Cut her down.'

Behind the glass Peter Tourne smiled; Monique was

good.

Gerta looked at her mistress for some kind of explanation as to why the punishment should stop, but was waved away.

'Take off her blindfold, too. I want to see her adorable face.'

Alex stumbled from the frame and was steadied by the powerful arms of Sven. She was still trembling, her eyes glazed, but she turned instinctively towards the sound of Monique's drawl.

'Come here, my little one,' the American woman purred, standing with her legs apart, hands on hips. Alex dropped to her knees and crawled to the woman's feet. Without a word she nuzzled at the proffered and naked sex, her tongue begging entry.

Monique grinned. 'Oh, you *are* good,' she whispered thickly. '*Very* good. No wonder Tourne is so proud of you.' She opened her legs a fraction more to allow the girl greater freedom.

Understanding precisely the requirements of his mistress, Sven handed Monique a huge black dildo. She looked at it with longing while the beautifully inexperienced face continued to work between her legs, and then slipped it into the kneeling girl's hands. Without any instruction Alex lapped at it, her tongue lubricating its thick rubber shaft, and then slowly she pushed it into the mistress's open quim, smoothing its path deep inside with her tongue.

In the hidden room Tourne could feel the growing excitement of his two companions.

'Oh yes!' Mustafa hissed between gritted teeth whilst leaning forward to get as good a view as he could. 'Your young lady is quite, quite superb. Whatever Monique offers you, my friend, I'll double it.'

Tourne smiled. He could sense Alex was almost sharing her mistress's pleasure – it seemed to flow through the two women, rolling back and forth like a tide.

Alex pressed the dildo home, her tongue lapping urgently at Monique's pleasure bud. Her whole body was alive with sensuality as she set a compelling rhythm with the huge phallus. Above her, Monique locked her fingers in Alex's silky hair, ground her hips down onto the thick stem, and then threw back her head, drinking in the attentions of her new and willing slave.

As the first waves of the American's orgasm rolled through her, Simon Bay grunted his approval. 'Are you sure you won't let the girl stay here tonight? I'd most certainly like to slip into that wet little quim of hers myself. Seems such a waste to leave it all to that bull dyke.'

Tourne shook his head. 'Not tonight,' he murmured, his eyes still fixed on the continuing activities inside the room. Still trembling with after shocks of pleasure Monique knelt on the floor beside Alex. Without a word passing between them, Alex gently withdrew the dildo from Monique's body, and impulsively licked the juices which coated it. Monique's whole demeanour had softened significantly, and she looked into Alex's eyes with apparently genuine affection. She gently took Alex's hands, guided the dildo away from her lips, and with no resistance she eased it down and into her grateful sex.

The English girl gasped as the impassive column impaled her, and then lifted her hips to welcome the dark intruder.

Peter Tourne turned away – his job was done. His own intense excitement now needed release. The hard arc of his cock strained angrily inside his expensively tailored trousers. Later, on the way home, he would take his pleasure with Alex. It might be his last chance before he had to hand her over to her new master.

Chapter Eleven

In the early hours of the following morning, in the intimate darkness of the limousine, Peter Tourne ran a warm hand over Alex's smooth thigh. She flinched, but didn't resist.

'Lift up your dress,' he said. 'Let me see where Monique marked you.'

She turned to look at him. 'You should know where Monique marked me,' she said softly, 'you watched her doing it, didn't you?'

He nodded.

'I knew you did. I could sense you there.' As she spoke she slid the dress up to her waist and turned so that he could see her back and legs. Her delicate creamy flesh was covered with livid weals and bruises. Between her legs – even in the gloom, he could see the marks on her thighs where Monique had bitten and pinched her skin as she drove the dildo home. He bent forward and tenderly pressed a kiss to each purple spot. Alex shivered as his tongue traced the perimeter of her injuries.

'Open your legs wider,' he said softly. 'Let me kiss you.'

This was a reward for them both. He gave her tenderness and pleasure where before there had been pain. His tongue caressed and flicked around her clitoris. Alex moaned and sank into the soft leather seat. She allowed his attentions and the quiet movement of the car to relax her. She lifted herself to him, thighs opening, giving everything she was to him. He didn't have to demand her obedience; it was his already.

She moaned deliciously, writhing under him, opening herself wider and wider for his intimate caresses. He could sense that in her heightened state her pleasure was so close to the surface that it wouldn't take a great deal to unleash a maelstrom of delight. Gently he turned her over so that she was crouched on all fours, her knees pressed into the thick carpet, and her face and elbows sank into the seat.

She looked exquisite; ready for him, legs apart, her sex framed by the rich curves of her sore buttocks.

'Hold yourself open for me,' he whispered as he undid his trousers. She did as she was told, and more as her fingers sought out his raging shaft. Eagerly she pulled him closer, her fingers parting the lips of her quim in readiness for his entry. He took her from behind, letting her guide his throbbing cock into the depths of her weary but excited body. She bucked as he slipped home, pressing her buttocks into his groin and then whining like a puppy as he slipped a hand down and began to toy with her engorged pleasure bud. His other hand sought her nipples. They were as hard as cherry pips brushing against his fingers. Alex began to climax almost before he started to touch her.

Her sex closed around him tightly like a closed fist, milking him dry with every stunning contraction. Mutual waves of pleasure roared through them, echoed and intensified by each wild excited thrust – on and on and on until Tourne thought he could happily die inside her. It seemed an eternity before they were still.

As Alex turned over and tidied her dress she caught sight of Mario watching her in the rear-view mirror. She had little doubt that he'd enjoyed her exhibition with his master. Seeing his glittering eyes was an unpleasant reminder that she was still beholden to him. She wondered fleetingly what dark favour Mario might demand as payment for his silence about her phone call to Laurence.

Staring out into the dark balmy night she wondered

whether Laurence had taken her plea for help seriously – surely it wouldn't take him long to arrange a flight to Greece? Where was her rescuer? She tried to block out the events that had taken place at Simon Bay's villa, but it was impossible; there wasn't one part of her body that didn't bear reminders of her time spent with Monique. Her nipples throbbed, the tender folds between her legs felt raw and swollen – and yet, out beyond the humiliation and the pain was a sense of elation and pleasure that drowned almost every other emotion. Peter Tourne's tender caresses had brought the pleasure to the surface. She swallowed hard, confused again by the fact that her rational mind rejected the ecstasy her body demanded. Her rational mind was the part of her that demanded rescue. She slipped down in the seat, trying to avoid Mario's penetrating eyes.

They travelled the rest of the journey back to the villa in silence. Peter pulled her close. She rested her head in his lap, relishing the sensation of closeness. By the time the car drew to a halt Alex was almost asleep. She yawned stretched and uncurled, easing the cramp from her back and shoulders then followed her master inside. As they entered the main hallway Peter turned and said:

'For the remainder of the night you will stay in the guest cabin. I'll have the housekeeper wake you up early. Mustafa has asked that you be delivered first thing tomorrow morning.'

Alex stared at him aghast. 'But... but what about finishing the mural?' was all she could think to say. Every time she felt she was making headway with Peter Tourne he knocked her back by reconstructing the wall between them.

He shrugged. 'It's almost complete, isn't it?'

Alex nodded. 'Yes,' she said sadly. 'Almost... but—'

He turned and began to climb the stairs. 'In that case I'll ask Mustafa to return you as soon as he's finished with you, so you may finish it. Simon's auction is to be held next week, so I want it finished by then…' his voice faded.

Alex nodded sadly. She already knew that Simon Bay wanted her to go to his villa as soon as possible. 'Another day should be enough.'

Peter Tourne didn't reply. With a great sense of loss Alex opened the French windows that overlooked the garden. Someone had lit the lamp in the guest cabin. It glowed at the window like a beacon in the velvety darkness. She hesitated for a few seconds on the steps of the villa, drinking in the perfumed night air, and feeling tears prickling up behind her eyes. It would soon all be over. She rubbed her eyes. Peter had already made up his mind; it didn't matter what she did to try and persuade him otherwise, he intended that she should leave KaRoche.

As she picked her way carefully along the pathway towards the cabin a slight rustling close by caught her attention. Before she could determine what the sound was a hand clamped firmly over her mouth.

She knew at once and with little surprise who her assailant was – Mario, come to collect his debt! One arm locked firmly around her waist, pinning her hands. Alex knew it was pointless to fight or resist. He pushed her down into one of the flowerbeds, turned her over roughly, and knelt heavily across her heaving breasts. He quickly undid his flies and leant closer. His erection was ivory white in the darkness, a fearful scimitar that he pressed to her face. She tried to turn away as he brushed the swollen helmet against her cheek, although she knew it was pointless trying to resist.

'Suck me, English girl,' he sneered as he trailed the moist tip over her closed lips. 'You leave here soon, and I not tell Mr Tourne about your phone call. You owe me.' He grinned and shuffled closer. 'We not got much time. No time to sleep. The boy wants you before you go. I say he could.'

He smelt of raw male musk, his whole body sweating and ripe. Alex felt numb – yet strangely excited – as he guided his throbbing flesh into her stretched mouth. Closing her mind to the discomfort and the taste and smell of his body, she began to work on him. From the undergrowth she heard the houseboy's heavy breathing; it seemed they both intended to make her pay for Mario's silence.

A few hours later Alex rolled off the bed in the cabin. The copper coloured evening dress was stained with earth and splashes of semen. Mario and his accomplice had taken their payment in full. She pulled it off unsteadily and made her way to the bathroom. Looking at her reflection in the steam kissed mirror she wondered how on earth she'd allowed herself to sink so low. The morning sunlight caught the links of the chain that linked her nipples. Either side of the rings were two tiny bruises like fingerprints; the reminder of the nipple clips that Monique had applied to her. As Alex turned slowly she could see the purple stripes that curled across her narrow shoulders. Her whole body was a map of the journey taken through the realms of pleasure and pain. She stepped into the shower and let the refreshing water course over her. It warmed her skin and muscles, soothed away the aches and pains, and massaged her bruises as attentively as any lover could. She closed her eyes and turned her face up into the torrent. The sound stilled her mind and the drumming heat soothed her body – the perfect combination.

When she went back into the sitting room, wrapped in a fluffy white robe, she was surprised to see that in her absence someone had delivered a breakfast tray. Alex had hoped that Peter would invite her to eat with him. She had barely a chance to pour the coffee before the housekeeper appeared in the doorway.

'Mr Tourne say the car be ready for you in half hour.'

Alex nodded, but the old woman didn't move. 'Was there something else?' she asked.

The old woman stepped into the cabin, glancing nervously over her shoulder. 'He ring again for you.'

Alex stared at her. 'I'm sorry?'

The old woman held a bony finger to her lips. 'That man, the one you tell me ring. He ring here last night when Mr Tourne out, and then he ring later when Mr Tourne in.'

Alex stiffened. 'Laurence? He rang here?'

The woman nodded. 'I answer phone. He talk long time with Mr Tourne.'

Alex's stomach knotted. She wondered what Peter had told her agent. What excuse had he spun for her absence? She only hoped that Laurence would still arrive in time to save her – perhaps he'd phoned to confirm his arrival.

'Do you know where he was ringing from?'

The housekeeper shrugged.

Alex pressed on. 'Did you hear what they said?'

This time the old woman shook her head emphatically. 'No,' she said angrily. 'I not listen.'

Alex realised that by asking she was implying that the woman spied on her employer. 'I'm sorry, I didn't mean,' she said quickly, but the old woman fixed her with a cold stare.

'I not listen,' she repeated. 'But I think your man, he is in Greece – the line sound very bad. The local exchange is very old.'

Alex nodded. 'Thank you,' she said softly. She hoped the old woman was right.

She finished breakfast and reluctantly got herself ready for her trip to Mustafa's villa. As she dressed her mind wandered again and again to Laurence Russell. He was hardly a friend, but even so he had to help her. She visualised his face and smiled; she knew his interest in her was not purely business. She'd clearly seen that in his eyes the last time they'd spoken in his office. She picked up her jacket and bag – she only hoped his arrival would be soon. Once the mural was complete there was no telling how long Peter would let her stay at the villa KaRoche – but she knew it wouldn't be for very long.

The car journey back across the island seemed to take hardly any time. Alex peered out of the tinted windows of the limousine, looking again at the sights she had seen on the previous evening. In daylight the island was even more beautiful than she had supposed. It struck her that under different circumstances she could have relished her stay on D'arnos.

As the car headed out along the coast road the beaches below looked magical; each rocky inlet giving way to another with spectacular views out over the rich blue ocean. Mario, divided from the seating compartment by a glass panel, seemed distant and cool. They passed what looked like Simon Bay's villa, curled like a sleek white sphinx at the mouth of a rocky cove. Turning back inland they followed the line of the sea until, amongst a grey green rise of olive trees, Alex saw what looked remarkably like the minaret of a mosque.

She stared in awe as they approached and more and more of the palatial buildings were revealed. Set high on the hillside Mustafa had built or bought what looked remarkably like a Moor palace.

Mario guided the car between a stand of trees towards ornate wrought iron gates. Alex felt her stomach tighten. Until now she had been enjoying the scenery, but as the gates swung smoothly open she realised with a start that she was seconds away from meeting a man who could be her new master – or worse still – was trying her out to see if she might suit his cousin. Alex swallowed hard, grateful that the trees along the steep driveway cast a shadow inside the car, hiding her expression of trepidation. She was being delivered like a parcel – on a sale or return basis. Alex struggled to control the growing sense of panic. She remembered the feeling of unease she'd felt the previous evening when Mustafa had run his hands over her body, and she remembered the strange smell of his cologne. She wished she could go back to Peter Tourne.

She trembled; panic mingling with expectation. It was as though there was another part of her – a dark twin soul – who, far from being afraid, was relishing the moment.

Ahead, in a semicircle of sunlight, Alex could see two dark-skinned men, dressed in long flowing white robes. As the men turned to watched the car approaching Alex saw they were carrying guns, and tucked in their cummerbunds were curved ceremonial swords. They had to be Mustafa's private bodyguards.

The car slowed and stopped in front of imposing double doors.

Mario turned to her. 'I will see you tonight,' he said malevolently as he slid out to open the door for her.

Alex ignored him, her attention was firmly fixed on the entrance to Mustafa's luxurious home. Across the sweeping driveway the doors opened, and in the shadows Alex could see a tall woman, dressed in traditional Muslim robes. Jet black, the robes covered her from the top of her head and down to where they brushed the tiled floor. Only the way the figure moved revealed the fact that she was female.

Alex took a deep breath; this was the moment of truth. In the doorway the woman beckoned to her. Alex climbed nervously from the car, and without looking back she hurried inside.

The smell struck her as soon as she stepped from the sunlight; the perfume of citrus fruits and rich oil. Her hostess – if that was what the woman was – had turned and was already gliding away from her through the opulent hall. Alex followed.

The cool interior of the huge building was quite astonishing. It was decorated in a subtle mixture of traditional Arabic and European styles. When they were beyond earshot of the guards the woman caught Alex's arm and said, in a low and melodic voice, 'I will take you to the harem, to prepare you for my master.'

Alex nodded. She could just see flashing blue green eyes through the black lace eye mask. Silently Alex followed her deeper into the building through a warren of passages. Finally they stood in front of a pair of heavily carved doors; smaller versions of those at the entrance to the house. The woman touched them with a slim pale hand, and at once they folded back on silent hinges to reveal a huge marble lined room. Alex gasped – it was like looking into an ornate bird cage.

On couches around a central fountain girls of every colour and caste relaxed in luxurious splendour. Every one of them was dressed in the traditional costumes of the harem. Every one of them was swathed in jewel bright colours with gems to match. Some were playing cards, others reading, some small groups were talking. Mustafa's harem must have had at least twenty-five exquisite girls in it – and they all turned as one to look at the latest arrival.

'Would you like some tea?' asked the mysterious woman in the black robe.

Somewhat bemused, Alex nodded as a statuesque negress came over to introduce herself.

'Hiya,' she said cheerfully, extending a hand. 'I'm Antia.' Alex was surprised to hear the tall coloured woman had an American accent. She thought for a second of Monique.

'A redhead,' the coloured girl continued whilst eyeing her up and down appreciatively. 'You're not Irish by any chance, are you?'

Alex shook her head. Antia grinned. 'Shame, we think Mustafa is secretly trying to recreate the United Nations. You'd better come with me and have your tea later. I'm supposed to be getting you ready.'

Alex hadn't expected such a warm welcome, and was pleasantly surprised by the confidence and kindness the woman showed her. She began to relax – just a little. As if sensing her confusion Antia took her hand.

'Come on, I'm not going to bite you. We're all sister's here. There's really no need to be so nervous.'

'But… but aren't you all Mustafa's slaves?'

Antia smiled. 'Yeah, and it'll be easier on you if you don't forget that. But we're all here because we want to be with him.' She paused. 'We know what he can offer us, and we all enjoy it.' She lifted her hands to encompass the splendid room. 'It's wonderful the things modern slavery can provide,' she added with a grin. 'Now, come on, I've got to get you ready.'

She indicated another carved door set into one wall. Alex followed her. Beyond the door was another large and splendid room; finished in marble it was much like the previous one. In the centre was a huge sunken bath, and beside it a massage couch and table. It reminded Alex of pictures she'd seen of ancient Roman baths.

Antia nodded to her. 'Take off all of your clothes so we can get started.'

As Alex began to unbutton her summer blouse she glanced up and froze. Set high up in the wall was a balcony. Mustafa was sitting there watching, his face expressionless. He'd come to witness his beautiful sample being made ready. Reddening, Alex slipped off her blouse and skirt. She was naked underneath.

Antia looked at her marked body and winced. 'Wow, who did that to you?' she asked. Alex looked away shamefully, and Antia said: 'Never mind, you don't have to tell me. It's just that it's been a long time since I've

178

seen anyone cut up like that. Mustafa only marks us if we misbehave, and so everyone learns very quickly not to.' She scooped up Alex's clothes and dropped them into a laundry hamper. 'I'm going to wash you down first. Get into the bath.'

Without questioning the woman's instruction, Alex did as she was told, aware as she stepped into the bubbling water that Mustafa's eyes were on her. She couldn't help but admire the graceful negress as she slipped off her harem pants and thin top. Her body was the colour of dark coffee and intimidatingly yet beautifully muscled. Her sex was also shaved, and in one of her outer lips three silver studs sparkled. Seeing Alex's eyes resting on her shaved pubis Antia grinned and stroked them fondly.

'Three sons,' she said in a proud voice.

Alex stared in astonishment. 'You have children?'

Antia nodded. 'That's right. Three sons and a daughter. Mustafa likes his women to breed. He's particularly proud of the boys. He sends them home to be raised as little princes. The more sons you bear him the higher you rise in the pecking order.' She stroked her tight flat belly. It seemed impossible to Alex that she had any children at all.

Slipping effortlessly into the scented water, the coloured woman soaped her hands and began to wash Alex's body. Her touch was both deeply soothing and strangely erotic. Alex's feelings of anticipation were heightened by Mustafa's presence, seated above them bearing silent witness. Alex moaned softly as the coloured girl cupped her breasts, easing away the tension and bruises with her skilful touch. When her long fingers worked lower, down over her belly, Alex felt a tremor of pleasure that shook her to the core. The woman really knew how to excite – was this part of Mustafa's plans for her preparation, or was Antia making the most of the situation? She heard Antia moan softly as a finger found its way into her tight quim. She knew she was already wet, and opened her

179

legs a fraction so that Antia could stroke her with a cupped hand.

Antia's caresses were stunning in their intensity; if this as the treatment she could expect in Mustafa's harem perhaps it wouldn't be so terrible if he did bid for her – this was sheer heaven. Just as the first acute spirals of delight began to form in her belly, Antia's clever hands disappeared. Alex opened her eyes dreamily.

Antia smiled. 'Sorry babe, but we've got to get on – after all, the master's waiting.'

Alex glanced up towards the balcony. Mustafa was staring down into the bathroom, eyes glittering darkly. Alex struggled to suppress a shudder – her previous sense of calm rapidly dissipating. Antia helped her out of the soothing water and up onto the couch. She arranged her so that she was facing the balcony. Totally exposed as she was, Alex wondered what might follow. To her surprise Antia continued the massage, using the same oil that suffused the house with its pungent odour.

This time the coloured girl's touch was deft and professional rather than erotic. Alex winced as she eased her knuckles deep down into her tender flesh. It was deeply satisfying, in an odd way, to be handled with such skill. Glancing up she saw Mustafa had moved closer to the rail to get a better look at the body he would soon be exploring. His expression was intense.

'Now,' purred Antia. 'A little garnish.'

Alex stiffened. 'What do you mean?' she asked softly.

Antia smiled down at her. 'Relax, it won't hurt.' From the table by the couch she took a large bowl containing a brush. 'This is a special stain, it was used by ancient courtesan's at the palace of some king or other to heighten their allure. Mustafa likes us all to use it.' As she spoke she began to outline Alex's nipples. Where the oily paste touched her skin it darkened to a rich crimson. The contrast to her milky white skin was vivid.

'Oh yes, that look's good. You're going to make our master very happy. Now, open your legs.'

Alex glanced up at her hesitantly.

Antia smiled. 'I promise, it won't sting. I just don't want to spill any – it stains whatever it touches.'

Alex did as she asked, closing her eyes tight as the brush worked its way across the most secret recesses of her body. She flinched as Antia opened her legs a little wider, trailing the soft brush back so that it circled her anus. She could imagine the view that Mustafa was enjoying.

Thinking her preparations were over Alex relaxed a little and opened her eyes, just in time to see Antia cracking open a long necked plastic vial.

'Please, what's that?' she queried anxiously.

Antia's eyes sparkled eagerly. 'Lubricant. Breathe deeply, and try to relax – this won't take more than a few seconds. It won't hurt if you don't fight it – I promise. I just want to make sure you're ready for our master.' She paused and eyed Alex, recognising the slight confusion on the English girl's face. 'This'll help to smooth the way.'

Alex blushed deeply as the coloured girl's skilful fingers splayed the tight corona of muscles around her bottom and slid the neck of the vial home. She breathed deeply as advised and waited, and then an oily warmth permeated through her most secret place. She gasped as Antia withdrew the slender container and began to stroke her tightly puckered entrance, working the ointment in deep. After washing her hands in a basin she cracked a second vial and urged it deep inside Alex's sex. The ointment also filled her there to the brim.

Alex lay for a few seconds watching the coloured girl tidying away the remains of her work. Antia smiled down at her.

'Do exactly as he tells you, and don't – whatever you do – fight him. It won't be long now.' From somewhere beneath the couch she produced a pair of ornate wrist bands which were linked by a silver chain. Alex stiffened anxiously as Antia gently but firmly took hold of her wrists and snapped the cuffs into position.

Antia's expression was gentle and comforting. 'Remember,' she whispered, 'just do everything he says – everything. He'll only hurt you if you give him cause to; if you try to resist him.'

Alex stared up into her dark feline eyes; all her fears suddenly returning. Antia helped her to sit up, added ankle chains which matched the wrist chains, and then wrapped a wisp of sheer blue silk around Alex's throat. She folded a matching sliver of silk between her legs, tying it on each hip. Standing back she glanced up towards the balcony and her master. Mustafa nodded.

Antia took a cloak of blue silk and wrapped it around Alex's shoulders. Finally, she produced a matching scarf and used it to blindfold her trembling charge. She took the opportunity of closeness to whisper furtive words of encouragement; she understood the turmoil of emotions the English girl was experiencing.

Alex felt Antia's strong hand close around her elbow.

'He's waiting.'

Alex nodded, her throat suddenly too dry to speak. She allowed Antia to guide her through the cool building, the soft padding of their bare feet on the cold marble the only sound to accompany them.

Peter Tourne hadn't intended to accept Mustafa's invitation to watch his protégé's initiation into the harem – but the temptation had ultimately proved too strong to resist. He'd followed the limousine driven by Mario, to Mustafa's villa, in his Porsche. He'd watched Alex's preparation on close circuit TV, and now sat on one of the plush couches in Mustafa's private first floor suite, sipping strong sweet coffee, and awaiting his host's arrival. Mustafa grinned as he threw open the doors to the room.

'A few minutes more, my friend. I'm very pleased with the way she behaves. You've taught her well, Peter, but then again, I should expect nothing less from you. Would you care to stay here and participate? Or perhaps you would prefer to watch from the privacy of one of the guest suites? There are camera's set up and ready to capture the moment.' The Arab paused. 'I could send one of my girls in to keep you company?'

Tourne hesitated, and then nodded. He knew very well the direction his host's tastes were likely to take, and wasn't sure he wanted to be in the same room when Alex was exposed to them.

'That would be perfect,' he said as evenly as he could. Mustafa clapped his hands. From nowhere a houseboy appeared, dressed in flowing robes that mimicked those of his master.

'Take Mr Tourne to the Peacock Room, and see to it that he has everything he requires.'

Tourne followed the boy from the room. Looking down into the hall below he saw the blindfolded Alex being led by the black masseuse to join Mustafa. She was completely oblivious to his being there.

Alex strained to work out where she was being taken. She could feel a little of the warm oil Antia had applied smearing between her thighs. Her companion was silent now, guiding her only with the lightest of touches on her elbow. They climbed a flight of stairs, and then she heard a knock. Doors opened in front of them. She guessed from the rich smell of oils in the air that she was finally in the presence of Mustafa. Something brushed the chain that linked her wrists – and then she was jerked forward. It took a second or two for her to realise that a leash had been snapped midway along the chain. The thin robe she was wearing was peeled away with a grunt of satisfaction.

As the seconds passed, Alex shifted nervously from foot to foot, aware that unseen eyes were savouring the details of her nakedness. She tried to imagine what Mustafa could see – and what he was thinking. Firm hands turned her around. Fingers brushed intimately between her thighs, and she wondered what on earth would come next... The dark side of her mind had already guessed.

Peter Tourne, ignoring the girl crouched at his feet, watched on the TV screen as one of Mustafa's servants pulled the leash down between Alex's legs; connected to her wrist chain it had the effect of bending her double like a hairpin. It was designed to snap onto the chain that linked her ankles.

He knew that the Arab wasn't interested in the girl's breasts, her face, her talents, or her company; his only real pleasure was in the tight dark closure that nestled between the cheeks of her darling bottom.

The servant untied the loincloth from around Alex's narrow hips and pulled it away. Across the room Mustafa stood unmoving, while the black girl who had prepared Alex ceremonially parted his robes with the air of a squire preparing her brave knight for battle. The Arab was hugely endowed. The coloured girl knelt before him and respectfully cupped his shaft in her fingertips, pressing a kiss to its head before beginning to oil it. Across the room another servant – a handsome boy – was standing in front of Alex, supporting her shoulders.

Mustafa pushed his attendant away and took up his position behind the bending Alex. The coloured girl crawled after him, and without any further preliminaries she guided his cock straight into Alex's sex. Tourne could see Alex flinch as the huge bulk of the Arab breached her. After a stroke or two he saw her stiffen as she felt the Arab withdraw. He saw her hold her breath as Mustafa's cock brushed her tensed buttocks. Tourne willed her to relax – to submit, to give herself over to the insatiable Arab. He watched her mouth open, and then heard her gasping shriek as the coloured girl fed Mustafa into her lubricated anus.

Tourne knew that Mustafa was a far bigger man than his own driver Mario, and he could see Alex's body instinctively trying to repel his advances. He watched Mustafa lock his fingers in her hair and jerk her head back.

'Come along, little English flower,' he heard the Arab hiss. 'This is not what I expect. Let me in or I'll have one of my servants flay the skin off your back. Ahhh, that's *much* better – pant, relax, and let me take you.'

Alex shrieked again as every muscle in her body complained at the cruel contortion. The Arab slid a little deeper into her, making full use of the lubricant Antia had meticulously applied. She understood that compliance would ease the path, but found it hard to overcome her initial revulsion. As the Arab began to move deeper still she thought she would tear. Aside from the throbbing pain in her backside, her whole body complained at the way she was bound. The chain that linked her ankles and wrists was so short that every thrust threatened to rip her arms from their sockets.

Alex struggled for every breath. As she gasped for air she suddenly felt sick, overcome by the pungent odour of the body oil Mustafa was wearing. She felt a delicate touch between her thighs and realised someone else was trying to ease her discomfort. She guessed it was probably Antia. A fingertip brushed her clitoris, and despite the demanding column of flesh in her bottom, she shuddered with a pleasure that could not be denied.

As Mustafa finally reached his goal and his hairy belly came to rest against the up-curve of Alex's perspiring buttocks, she felt dizzy with a mixture of humiliation, suffering, and undiluted rapture.

Chapter Twelve

It was barely lunchtime when Antia took Alex to Peter Tourne's waiting limousine. Used and discarded, Alex felt filthy. Her body was so sore that she could hardly sit down on the plush leather seats. She flushed with shame at the memory of how her body had responded so positively to the strange demands and desires of Mustafa. Once he'd had his fill of her he'd simply walked away, leaving her to be freed by unseen hands. The blindfold had been removed, and she'd been taken back to the bathroom to collect her clothes.

Alex stared unseeing at the countryside as Mario drove her back to the villa. She wondered if Mustafa would now bid for her at Simon Bay's sale; the idea of which horrified her. Worse still, there would be others there, unknown men and women who might demand even more from her. She shivered and wrapped her arms across her chest – she couldn't let Simon Bay sell her, there had to be a way to escape from these people. Where on earth was Laurence? And how could she possibly explain to him what had happened to her since her arrival on the island?

Alex was so deep in thought that it only seemed a few minutes before the car drew up in front of the portico to the villa KaRoche. She barely looked at Mario. Not waiting for him to open the car door for her she slipped across the seats and hurried inside the villa. The housekeeper was dusting in the hallway, and looked up at the sound of Alex entering.

'Is Mr Tourne in?' she asked, some of her old confidence returning.

The old woman shook her head. 'No. He go out after you leave. I not expect him back until after lunch.'

Alex nodded, her mind formulating a plan. 'I'm going to shower and then work on the mural this afternoon,' she said in a firm voice that brooked no contradiction.

To her surprise the old woman was almost deferential. 'Of course. Would you like me bring some lunch?'

Alex paused; the very thought of food made her feel nauseous, but perhaps it was because she still smelt of the Arab's pungent perfume. After a second or two she nodded – she might feel different after a shower, and besides, if she was planning to escape it would be foolish to leave on an empty stomach.

Once back in the guest cabin she sorted through her luggage and found a pair of faded jeans, a thick black cotton shirt, walking boots and a light jacket. Stuffing her passport, wallet, driver's license and a few other essentials into a canvas holdall, she stowed the things at the back of the wardrobe and went into the bathroom. She didn't look in the mirror, afraid of what she might see. After a long shower she ate lunch, then picked up her art box and went downstairs to the gallery. It was cool and silent by the pool. She opened the box and began to work.

Outside, in the heat of the day, Peter Tourne arrived home from his luncheon with Mustafa. He was as preoccupied and distant as his slave girl.

Part of him regretted accepting the Arab's invitation; Mustafa had used Alex like a mindless vessel, as unfeeling and dispassionate as anything he'd ever seen. For Peter Tourne this was not how the game should be played.

He climbed the stone steps to his bedroom, wondering how his protégé was feeling. At the door he hesitated and considered what he might do if he found her waiting for him.

His room was empty the windows open a little to catch the breeze from the sea. Picking up the phone he tapped in a number – he had to ensure that Mustafa didn't get the chance to buy the English girl. His first call was short.

'What do you want me to do with her?'

The reply was a barking laugh. *'You're not getting sentimental are you, Peter? I thought we'd already agreed that I should buy her once she was trained.'*

He felt a sense of relief. 'At the auction? Will you go to the auction? Simon Bay's very keen to take delivery as soon as possible. What worries me is that there's at least one other purchaser who's very keen to get their hands on her. The bidding will go through the roof.'

There was a thoughtful pause at the end of the line. *'Perhaps we can come to a private arrangement then? I'd like to see her on the block, but if you're prepared to deal now…'*

Tourne nodded. 'Yes – yes I am,' he said quickly. 'I'll ring Simon and let him know there's been a change of plan.'

'Good, if we can come to an arrangement over the price I can pick her up tomorrow, if you like.'

He relaxed a little. 'That would be perfect. What'll you offer me for Alex… ?'

When the deal was concluded he dialled Simon Bay's number. After that brief call was finished he pulled off his soft leather shoes and threw himself back onto the large bed.

It was early evening when he went in search of Alex. To his surprise she was sitting downstairs at the poolside staring at her completed creation on the wall. She was so deep in thought that she didn't hear his approach, and for a few seconds he had the chance to watch her unobserved. Alex Sanderson was exquisite – as tiny and delicate as a perfect English flower.

The last of the evening sunlight blazed in her auburn hair, whipping the tumble of curls into a flaming halo. For an instant his eyes moved to the mural she'd created – it was exactly the fantasy woodland peopled by strange mythical animals that he'd envisaged. Erotic images suffused the greenery. It was a masterpiece. Tourne realised that somewhere during Alex's education and initiation he'd lost sight of the work she'd created. It was almost as if he were seeing it – and her – for the first time ever.

Finally sensing his presence she turned, her face tilted towards him, eyes alight and bright with tears.

'It's finished,' she said in a voice cracking with emotion. In her hand she had a small brush, and as he watched she leant forward and signed her name with a flourish. He stepped up behind her and stroked her hair. She let out a long thin sob and turned to embrace his waist, pressing her face into his body. He could feel the tears, hot and angry, soaking into his shirt.

'Please Peter,' she whispered, 'don't make me leave here. Don't send me away with those other people. I don't like them.'

'Let's go and have dinner,' he said quietly. He was afraid if he embraced her or answered her plea he would lose his sense of resolve.

Alex rubbed away the tears with the back of her hand, sniffed miserably, and then nodded.

They ate in virtual silence. Strangely, as they went out onto the terrace for coffee, Alex felt completely at peace for the first time in days. The mural was finished – her work was done and now she would find a way to go home. She had to; if Peter wouldn't protect her, then she had to. She glanced across at him.

'I'm leaving tomorrow,' she said softly.

Tourne nodded.

It was an ambiguous thing to say. She knew he intended to deliver her to Simon Bay's villa – but she had other plans. If he let her spend the night in the guest cabin it would be a simple matter of waiting until the household was asleep and then creeping away into the darkness. Instead of being driven the following morning across the island by Mario, to the fate that awaited her, she would catch the first ferry back to the mainland. Almost exactly as the thought formed in her mind Tourne turned to her.

'You will spend tonight in the cell.'

Alex stiffened. Was it possible he could read her mind? She stared at him, considering her reply, afraid that if she protested too much he might guess her plan. After a few seconds she said softly. 'Why can't I sleep in the guest house?'

'You really are quite astonishing,' Tourne snapped. 'How dare you question my decision? Surely by now, Alex, you've realised that it's extremely unwise to do so? I am the master here – I set the rules. I'm certain your new master will correct your disrespectful failings as a matter of priority.'

Alex felt a flutter of anxiety.

Tourne continued. 'Mario will take care of you tonight, and then I'll have my housekeeper bathe and shave you in preparation for your delivery tomorrow.' He beckoned her closer. She obeyed without another word. 'And don't *ever* question me or any other master or mistress again. Do you understand?' As Alex was about to reply he caught hold of her hair, his face contorted angrily. 'Even now you try to play this game by your own rules. Will you never learn?' He pushed her away roughly. 'Take off your dress.'

Alex lowered her eyes and began to unbutton the bodice. In arriving back from Mustafa's in such a defiant mood, she had accidentally stepped too far back into her old recusant frame of mind. She fumbled nervously with the tiny pearl fastenings. She could sense his growing displeasure, and was relieved when the buttons gave way and she could slide the light cotton dress down over her body. She was afraid to look up at him, and simply stood in the pool of fabric, naked except for her sandals and the rings that he'd inserted.

'Turn around.'

She did so, moving slowly, careful not to let her body posture suggest defiance or flirtatiousness. Even now she was his slave and relished the sensation of his eyes moving over her nakedness. If only there was a way she could stay at KaRoche with him. The thought glowed in her mind like a flare. There was nothing she would not do for him or give him; he owned her in every sense of the word, and she couldn't imagine ever feeling the same way about any other man.

Her train of thought was broken by the arrival of the houseboy carrying a mobile phone. Tourne took it from him, and as he began to speak Alex realised with a jolt that the caller was Mustafa.

'Actually, she's with me now,' Tourne said, once the niceties had been exchanged. There was a pause and he laughed without humour. 'No, my mind is already made up, though I'm not saying your offer isn't a good one. On the contrary – it's highly flattering.'

Alex felt a cold chill of fear trickle down her spine – it seemed that Mustafa was pleased with her, and wanted her for his own. She prayed for Peter's resolve to hold, and that he wouldn't be swayed by the obviously tempting offers coming from the insatiable Arab.

Tourne was still speaking. 'My dear friend, you know I would never set out to offend you, but the decision has already been made.'

Alex's mind was racing. She assumed Mustafa was attempting to put in a bid before the auction to secure her services. She shivered. Only moments before she had brooded for the umpteenth time whether escaping was what she really wanted, and that what she longed for deep down was to stay with Peter Tourne, but she now realised that was impossible. For her own sake she had to finally accept that he had no intention whatsoever of keeping her – and that being the case, she had no choice but to escape from KaRoche.

As he continued to speak he beckoned her closer. She moved to his side, and trembled as he began to stroke her breasts with idle familiarity. Oddly his touch was of great comfort, and she crept even closer to him, relishing the smell and heat of his body as his fingers moved down to the folds of her sex. For a while he toyed with the ring that pierced her, and then casually slipped a finger into her moist quim. It wasn't until he'd finished his conversation and handed the phone back to the waiting houseboy that she remembered they were being observed.

Tourne put a finger under her chin and tipped her face up to his. 'It would appear that you've created a great deal of interest in my friend Mustafa.'

Alex fought to control her anxiety.

He grinned salaciously. 'He just offered me at least twice what I might expect to get for you at auction. Believe me, that is quite a sizeable offer, and tempting to say the least.'

Alex swallowed hard, wondering whether he would be swayed by greed. He pulled her closer, pressing her down onto her knees. 'But I told him your fate has already been decided.'

Alex tried not to show her fear; what did he mean? Had Simon Bay already put in an offer for her. Or perhaps Monique? Or Starn? Or was it someone else who'd been at Simon Bay's party? What was going to become of her?

'Undo my belt,' Tourne said.

With trembling hands and heavy heart she did as he ordered.

'Now, pull it free.' He looked across the terrace to the

still hovering servant as her fingers guided the leather through his trouser loops. 'Come here boy, put the phone down. I have a job for you.' He looked down at Alex. 'Give my young friend here the belt, and then get down on all fours. Perhaps I can teach him a few new tricks.'

Alex tried hard not to meet the houseboy's excited eyes as she handed him the belt. She could see his hands trembling as they closed around the buckle. Crouched at his feet she braced herself for the first kiss of leather. She wondered if his lack of experience would make him timid – it didn't.

His first stroke was a terrifyingly ragged explosion that wrapped tight around her waist, cutting into her delicate flesh like razor wire. She heard Tourne say something in Greek, and closed her eyes and hid her face in the crook of her trembling arm in preparation for the second blow. This time it hit her squarely across the buttocks with a terrifying crack. The blow was so hard that it seemed to ricochet through her skull. Her every sinew tensed in readiness for the next strike. She heard her tormentor take a deep breath, and then she yelped in shock as the belt caught her low, flaring against the soft folds of her pouting sex.

The dark twin inside her mind was beginning to stir. She could feel a web of pleasure weaving itself in her belly as the next stroke, as hot as molten steel, blasted across her buttocks. Then there was another, and another, and another. As the boy laboured on the myriad of sensations he unleashed became a blur. She gave herself up to the pain; a willing supplicant, riding it like surf as it crashed over her. Every thought and every fibre of her was fastened to the belt's kiss. When the boy finally stopped she almost felt as if she'd been robbed of her pleasure. Hands grabbed her hips and she felt the urgent press of a cock seeking entry. She had no idea whether her rider was the houseboy or Peter Tourne – her only desire now was to give herself freely.

As the cock opened her, driving deep into her throbbing quim, she shrieked with pleasure. It felt as if she might drown and pull her unseen lover down into the water with her. The merest brush of the groin against her buttocks was enough to spark the first heady contractions of orgasm. On and on the waves swept, rolling out from the centre of her soul, until finally, exhausted and breathless, she collapsed onto the flagstones of the terrace. She was totally drained – all passion was spent.

When the penis eventually slipped away and she opened her eyes, she was pleased to see she was alone with Peter. It seemed his words to the houseboy had been a dismissal. She curled up against his broad chest, making soft noises of pleasure and affection. He gently disentangled himself from her.

'Don't Alex. Put your dress back on, and I'll send for Mario. You must be ready to leave tomorrow.'

Alex stared at him, the sense of cruel reality returning. Despite everything she was still nothing more than a commodity; he'd done with her and now she was dismissed. She got to her feet, eyes downcast to disguise her pain and sense of loss. With clumsy fingers she pulled on her clothes. Once again the truth hit her that escape was imperative, and before the next sunrise.

Mario silent appeared and snapped the lead onto her collar without being instructed. He then led her away from Peter Tourne and away from the villa. His eyes were alight with lust.

'What did big Arab do to you?' he teased with a wicked leer as they made their way into the shadowy garden. Alex suspected he already knew, and wondered how much of the day he'd spent thinking and lusting about what had happened to her. As he jerked her close she could smell stale wine. She could see he was a little drunk.

'You like it maybe? You know Mario like it.' He stumbled

a little on the steep steps and held out a hand to steady himself. As he did Alex, without thinking twice, seized her chance.

Grabbing hold of the leash with both hands she gave it a hefty tug, completely unbalancing her gaoler. As he staggered towards her she lifted her knee and felt a satisfying crunch as his testicles squashed against it. Speechless, gasping for air, and completely unable to move, Mario let go of the leash and collapsed into the bushes. He curled into a ball and rolled onto his back, his large hands clutched to his groin. Without considering the consequences Alex grabbed a garden hoe that lay carelessly nearby, and brought the handle crashing down onto the slob's head. He slumped instantly, and ceased moving or making any noise.

Turning sharply, Alex sped away, running down through the archway that led to the guest cabin. Without daring to look back she threw open the door and grabbed the holdall she'd hidden in the wardrobe earlier. It may have lost her a few seconds, but it would be far easier to get away dressed in sensible outdoor clothes with money and a passport. She checked quickly and was relieved to find both her money and passport still inside. She tried not to think of Mario and the enormity of what she'd done, lest her frail courage suddenly desert her. Despite her haste she had the presence of mind to grab a couple of succulent oranges from the bowl by the window for sustenance. Then, bag in hand, she hurried back down through the gardens, desperately seeking a way out that didn't involve going back into the villa.

Removing her sandals she ran down flight after flight of stone steps. As the darkness closed around her she thought she heard voices from the terrace. Perhaps Mario had recovered already. Just as she was about to hide in the relative safety of the bushes, she saw a gate set in the perimeter wall, and headed for it. Carefully easing it open, she was delighted to find it led onto a steep coastal track – it was hardly a road. Panting heavily, Alex quietly closed the gate behind her and slipped into the oily shadows.

In the moonlight she could see the track was cut into a deep gorge, its high sides creating dark pockets of inky blackness. She scurried for cover and changed into the clothes she'd brought with her. Rolling the discarded things into a tight bundle she stuffed them deep into a patch of scrub and headed downhill on what, she hoped, would be the pathway leading to the main harbour. She could now distinctly hear voices on the hillside above. She had no head start to speak of – if she wanted to be safe she knew she'd have to find someone to help her, or somewhere to hide.

The track, which skirted the walls of KaRoche, was steep and uneven. Alex was glad she'd had the sense to bring boots. The heavy rubber soles not only gave her good grip but also muted her footsteps. In the darkness she was certain no one could see her from the grounds of the villa, but her heart still beat a calypso rhythm in her chest, and the downy hairs on the back of her neck prickled. Gingerly she clambered up the steep walls of the track, trying to get her bearings.

Far below, away to her right and along the edge of the shoreline, she could make out the lights of the harbour. Above her she heard the sound of a car starting up – either Mario had alerted Peter, or Mario intended to take the car to search for her himself. He would now be in a foul mood – to say the least, and she certainly didn't relish the thought of being caught and subsequently punished by him.

Overhead the moon broke through the clouds, and for a few seconds Alex could see that amongst the rocks and bushes on the seaward side of her was a path that led down towards the rocky shoreline; it looked impassable to anything but foot traffic. She scrambled up between the bushes and began to pick her way down towards the sea. The path was steep and precarious, twisting backwards and forwards between the tumbles of boulders and wind contorted trees.

It seemed to take an eternity to get down to the shoreline. With every step she was afraid she might fall or lose her footing in the darkness. Finally, though, the path flattened out, and Alex was at last aware of the peaceful lapping of the warm Mediterranean. Another few steps and she was finally walking on sand, and a gentle sea breeze played through her hair. Relief popped in her stomach as she spotted a cluster of lights through the silvery darkness. It wasn't the main harbour, but at least here she might get some much needed help.

A hundred or so metres along the beach she realised that what she could see was a low cottage or a boatshed, with a small fishing vessel hauled up onto the shore beside it. A lantern swung and squeaked in the breeze. Figures huddled around the boat, the sound of their voices and an occasional laugh drifting towards her. As she got closer one of the figures looked up; a pale face in the dark night. Before she considered the possible dangers she called out to them.

'P-please…' her timid voice strained nervously. 'Can – can anyone help me?'

A man called back in Greek. Something about his voice startled her. The lantern swung higher and two of the figures headed towards her at a brisk trot. She sensed instantly that she'd come across a clandestine meeting that was supposed to be secret, though she had no idea what it could be. Calling out had been a terrible mistake. Turning frantically she scrambled around in the darkness for the cliff path. Behind her she could hear raised voices getting rapidly closer, and she knew she'd escaped from one nightmare, only to foolishly stumble into another.

As she stumbled around in the stamina sapping sand a

pair of steely hands clamped onto her shoulders. She shrieked in terror. She was utterly unable to resist as her captor flipped her over onto her back. Pinned down in the darkness she struggled and twisted back and forth to try and unseat the shadowy stranger who held her down in the sand. After a few seconds another figure appeared with the lantern, and lifted it up so they could see what it was they'd caught.

Alex, breasts heaving and breath rasping in her lungs, glanced up into the lamp's glare. Four male faces peered down at her. One of them mumbled something in Greek, and a second leaned closer. His rough fingers slipped under the leather collar Peter Tourne had fastened around her throat. The man sitting heavily on Alex said a few words to his colleagues. She didn't need to speak Greek to understand that they knew exactly what the collar meant. The man who'd touched the collar now tugged at the front of her shirt. It was strained tightly across her breasts, and the buttons easily popped open. The delicate silver chain and the rings that pierced her nipples glittered in the lamplight. There was a split second of silence. Alex felt the lust rising in the men as clearly as she could hear the sea rolling in, and had little doubt as to what would follow.

One of the men mumbled Peter Tourne's name, and there was a contemptuous laugh from the man sitting on her as he squeezed and mauled her vulnerable breasts. His breath reeked of cheap wine.

Jerking their prize to her feet, he picked her up as if she weighed no more than a child, and threw her over his shoulder. She gasped and thumped his back with her fists, her feet kicking wildly. Her strong captor merely laughed, slapped her bottom, and tightened his grip on her thighs.

When the party reached the boat the man threw her unceremoniously onto the sand. One of the other's knelt across her and pinned her hands back above her head. She was surprised when another pressed the mouth of a bottle to her lips and grunted something at her. Unable to resist, she took a long drink. Wine poured down her throat, making her gasp for breath. The lamp was put down in the sand and the soft light draped across Alex's bewildered face. Another pair of hands closed around her waist, while someone else pulled and tugged her boots and jeans off.

In the orange arc from the lamp she could see the four men were swarthy local fishermen, on a late night drinking spree. The alcohol had stripped away any vestiges of control. The wine bottle was forced back into her mouth, while she felt a hand pawing at her shaved sex. Eager fingers splayed her open, diving deep into the warm moist confines of her sex. She froze, terrified they might tear the delicate flesh around the ring.

Someone picked up the lantern and held it high, and the man who'd been pinning her down slid off so they could admire their prize. There was an earthy grunt of approval from each of them, and then the one who'd first caught her unbuckled his belt; it seemed he was to be the first to have her; his prize for bringing in such a fine catch. Her legs were forced apart and he straddled her, hauling her back onto his raging cock. Dragging her face closer he pressed a wine-tainted kiss on her lips. His cruel and hungry eyes stared down into hers, savouring her humiliation and distress. He grinned, and stroked her leather collar.

'Slave,' he whispered in heavily accented English.

Alex shivered, and then gasped for breath as he suddenly plunged his cock into her.

The next few hours were a jumbled tapestry of insanely wild sex. The fishermen poured more and more wine down Alex's throat, forcing her to drink, making her head spin and her stomach churn. And they fucked her again, and again, and again. There was not an orifice they did not fill; her mouth, her anus, her quim. If they noticed the weal marks and bruises on her exhausted body it didn't stop them from using her for their seemingly endless round of pleasure.

Alex crouched on all fours in the sand, feeling like a stud bitch as one man slipped his cock into her dripping sex while another lifted her head up and fed himself into her mouth. Every sense was drowned with the sounds, sight, and smell of sex. In her muddled, drink-numbed mind, she begged them to stop, to take her home, to set her free – but her plea's fell on deaf ears.

At long last, as the grey light of a new day began to break, the man who'd initially caught her hoisted her up into his arms and carried her to the hut. It seemed to be the signal for the others to depart.

Alex curled up on his rough bed, assuming that she would be allowed now – finally – to go to sleep. But quickly his hands running between her legs told her otherwise. He rolled her onto her back and began to lap at her sex, awash with the spent semen of his companions. She moaned for him to stop, but he was relentless. He grinned up at her, his lips slick and wet.

'Pleasure. You to give me pleasure, you're slave,' he stumbled with the English. Alex moaned and sobbed as his tongue worked its way over her clitoris. Her exhausted body responded at once. She was so tired, but she adored what this peasant could do to her. She was stunned and ashamed; how could her body find so much pleasure in the aftermath of their squalid orgy? Her tormentor eased his fingers into the warm confines of her sex, stroking her towards the darkest of ecstasies. She writhed miserably, trying to suppress the passion that was growing inexorably in her belly.

'Please don't,' she sobbed as the first white hot shard of orgasm exploded inside her. 'Please let me go. You have to help me, please...' Her whole body convulsed with the wonderful sensations he was inducing, and she knew then that she was beyond help.

Whatever vestige of self-respect she had remaining shattered like glass, and she relinquished every part of herself to the slave mentality that drove her on and on, taking pleasure from her own humiliation and shame. Her captor finally pulled away, still grinning. Almost idly he crawled up alongside her and dragged his cock out of his trousers. He rubbed the rejuvenated shaft across her open lips.

'Pleasure,' he purred again. 'You give me much pleasure, or I beat you too… like Peter Tourne.' As he spoke he ran his fingers through her sweat-soaked hair. She had no choice but to take him into her mouth. As her lips closed around him she could taste her juices mingled with the sweat and semen of his companions. He threw back his head and pulled her up onto him, while her fingers and tongue struggled to give him the pleasure he demanded. He bucked against her face, and she sucked hard as she slowly admitted to herself that she enjoyed the way he used her purely for his own gratification; there was no consideration for her needs, and that realisation re-lit the fire deep in her belly. He quickly groaned and filled her mouth, and Alex swallowed and shuddered pleasurably in unison with the heavy man.

When he was still and breathing evenly she curled up like a child against his hairy belly. He smiled and stroked her tenderly. 'You a good slave,' he murmured and dragged a blanket up over them both. Alex closed her eyes, willing sleep to steal her thoughts away.

Chapter Thirteen

As Alex's eyes fluttered open the morning light filtering through a small window reminded her of the guest cabin, but the reality of her predicament filled her mind an instant later. She blinked and stared around the rough interior of the beachside building. It was little more than a shed and smelled of rotten fish. On the far side of the room, piled on a table, were a heap of fishing nets. The wooden floor was bare and sandy, the walls covered with faded yellowing whitewash. The odd sticks of furniture were sun-bleached and looked like salvage. Alex rubbed her eyes. The makeshift bed smelt of sweat and sex. She shivered. The only crumb of comfort was that she was alone.

Memories of the previous night came flooding back in an intense rush of disjointed images; her escape from Tourne had delivered her straight into the hands of drunken ruffians. Far from making an escape, it appeared she had merely exchanged one horrible prison for another. Her head ached violently from the after effects of the wine they'd forced upon her, and every other part of her body felt tired and tender.

She gingerly tried to slide off the bed. As she rolled over something caught on the tangle of dirty blankets. She stretched across to free herself, and was instantly horrified at what she saw. The fisherman had tied her to the bed with a length of greasy rope. One end was knotted through her collar, and the other was fastened around the metal frame by her head. It certainly wouldn't prevent her from escaping, but the gesture made her cringe. She was tied in the same way a man would tie a stray dog.

Tears trickled down her face. Did the fisherman truly believe she would wait there for him to return? How could she have sunk so low?

Beside the pile of fishing nets her gaoler had left a bucket of water, a tin cup and a half loaf of bread. Alex stared at it and tried to shake off the sense of resignation and despair that threatened to engulf her. Her clothes had to be on the beach – if she found them, got washed and dressed, she could still make her ultimate escape.

It took seconds to free herself from the rope. She hobbled across the rough floor and used the cold water from the bucket to wash away the evidence of the night before as best she could. She was thankful there wasn't a mirror around to bear witness to her degradation. Wrapping herself in one of the blankets she crept cautiously out onto the beach – it was deserted. Under the hull of the boat she found her jeans and boots. She picked them up, trying to ignore the cache of empty wine bottles littered around in a rough circle. It was here the men had held her down, their arena marked by discarded rubbish.

Across the sand in the shadow of the rocks she found her shirt, jacket and bag. Even though her clothes were stained and torn she pulled them on. Dropping the blanket to the sand she dressed where she stood in the cool rising sun, the fresh sea air helping to revive her – just a little. She checked her meagre possessions, and was relieved to find the men had not taken her money or passport. She then started to explore, trying to get some idea of where she was in relation to the harbour.

The cove she was in appeared to be completely encircled by rocks, but as she had come down a steep path from the villa, she reasoned that there had to be another way out which led in the direction of the village – after all, the boat was still on the beach, so her captors hadn't left by sea, and she doubted they'd climbed up to Peter Tourne's villa, because it was situated so far away from the village.

Alex circled the warming beach. Her senses concentrated on any unexpected sounds in the distance; the last thing she wanted was for the fishermen to reappear and find her still there.

After nearly half an hour she came across a well worn trail that seemed to lead up into the hillside but ran in the general direction of where she guessed the harbour to be. There were probably other paths, but she was desperate to get away from the beach and its vivid memories, and the possibility of recapture. Shouldering her holdall, she set off determinedly without looking back; she wanted to put the events in the cove, and at KaRoche, well and truly behind her.

After the first hundred yards or so the path veered steeply up into the hills. What had appeared to be an easy escape route quickly turned into a tortuous climb. The path that had seemed so well trodden close to the cove twisted back and forth between rocks and boulders, at some points fading away totally. The loose stones made it difficult for her to get any decent footing, and the muscles in her thighs and calves soon ached and burned. She considered whether to climb down and try to find another way out, but was afraid she might come across the fishermen again. She was rapidly losing her bearings – which way was the harbour now?

Eventually, after a tortuous climb that tested Alex's resolve to the limit, she clambered up between a rise of steep rocks and found herself in a deserted olive grove. She paused a moment to gain her breath, and then followed the meandering path until she was beyond the trees, where she found a narrow track which she presumed to be the one she'd crossed the previous night. To her right it climbed back up into the hillside towards the villa, and to the left it ran down in the direction of the sea, which glistened far below.

Alex stopped for a quick rest. She quelled her nagging

hunger by devouring the two juicy oranges, and despite her desperate predicament, was unable to resist the spectacular views her elevated position afforded her. She shaded her eyes from the sun and watched the tiny dots offshore that were the local fishing boats. Some were stationary, and accompanied by a mass of white flecks which circled and swooped to feed on any discarded scraps, but others were moving slowly in a line, and Alex knew then that they were coming out from the harbour, and in which direction she needed to be walking. Surely she couldn't now be more than half an hour from the village and the harbour?

Slinging the holdall over her back she set off with a new feeling of optimism. Sadly that optimism was punctured fatally as she rounded a large boulder a little way down the track. Below her, parked in the curve of the bend, was Peter Tourne's distinctive Mercedes. She stopped abruptly, almost losing her footing, and inadvertently sent a number of large stones clattering noisily down towards the car. Spinning round to flee back the way she'd come, she came face to face with Peter Tourne and Starn Fettico.

'No!' she screamed in horror and frustration. 'No! Where did you...? How did you... ?'

She quickly turned again trying desperately to locate an escape route, and saw Mario was now leaning cockily against the car. They had cut her off. She stared at Mario, then at the track, then back to Mario, wondering if she dare try to run past him. Even from a distance she could see he had a sore looking lump across the side of his head, and she knew that if he caught her he would be eager to repay her for the blows she'd struck the night before. He grinned malevolently as their eyes met. She sensed he would be only too pleased for her to try and make a break for it. She knew she was lost. Her shoulders sagged in defeat, and she turned and looked up at Peter

Tourne.

'How… how did you find me so easily?' she asked quietly.

He smiled with his usual, infuriating confidence. 'Your little friends were eager to let me know they'd found one of my girls. I hope you enjoyed their company. We'd already guessed where you were; there are only three paths up from the cove, and someone would've let me know if you appeared down in the harbour.' He paused, his eyes resting on her ruined clothes. 'You wouldn't have got very far on the island anyway – my marks are well known all over.'

Alex's wrists were suddenly seized and twisted painfully up behind her back. She shrieked with agony and arched onto tiptoes in an attempt to decrease the discomfort of Mario's rough and unnecessary treatment. Both Tourne and Starn enjoyed the way her shirt stretched tightly over her vulnerable breasts, her nipples clearly visible, and then the former waved Mario away.

'Let her go, that won't be necessary. Will it, Alex?'

She shook her head miserably as she rubbed her freed wrists.

Starn grunted and mopped his brow with a handkerchief. 'You're too damned soft, Peter. I'd flay the skin off the little bitch if she was mine.'

Tourne smiled. 'Then I'm sure she'll be relieved to know that you haven't bought her, Starn. But as it is, her punishment is no longer my concern.'

Alex stared at him. 'What do you mean?' she whispered.

Tourne reached forward and gently brushed the hair back off her forehead. As he did he snapped the lead onto her collar. 'You are no longer my property, Alex. At lunchtime today I hand you over to your new owner. I think under the circumstances it would be better if we went back to the villa and prepared you for their arrival.'

Alex stood rooted to the spot. Mustafa's face formed in

206

her mind, followed rapidly by Monique's. 'Who is it?'

Tourne smiled and then tugged at her leash. 'You never learn, do you? Let's just say he's an old friend of mine. I'm certain you'll make him very happy.'

Alex's thoughts raced. Was it Simon Bay? Was he to be her new owner? She silently fell into step between Peter Tourne and Starn Fettico, and contemplated the fate that awaited her back at KaRoche as they led her to the waiting car.

When they reached the villa Tourne turned to her. 'I'm going to chain you in the gallery room. My housekeeper will come and get you ready for your presentation to your new owner.' He stared intently into her eyes. 'Don't ever lose sight of the game, Alex. I told you before that I make the rules, and despite how it may seem to you at this moment, I promise I will do all I can to ensure you are well treated when you leave here.'

Alex barely heard his words of scant comfort. She was looking up the garden steps at Mario, who was already standing beneath the shady archway that led into the gallery. He was obviously waiting for her. She wondered with a shudder what revenge he might exact upon her for having the audacity to escape.

Peter Tourne tugged at the lead. 'Come on, we don't have much time.'

The gallery was cool and dark after the glare of the bright morning sun. Alex would have been grateful to have shed her filthy clothes if it hadn't been for Mario watching her undress with his lust filled eyes. He hadn't spoken since his boss had handed him Alex's leash. To ensure she made no further escape attempts the collar was now connected to an overhead chain, like the one in the cells.

The room had already been prepared for her return – she wondered how it was that Tourne had been so confident he would find her so quickly. Once she was undressed the housekeeper re-shaved her sex with deftly confident fingers. Alex could hardly believe she now found such intimacy acceptable. Her sex and nipples still bore the crimson stain that Antia had applied to them. Climbing into the steaming bath Alex tried hard to concentrate her mind. If she thought for more than an instant about who her new owner might be she could feel a sense of panic growing low in her belly. Mario remained unmoving against the wall – his expression was dark, thunderous.

As the housekeeper helped Alex from the bath and wrapped her in a fluffy towel, Mario mumbled threateningly: 'You soon get what it is coming to you, English girl.'

Alex flinched. The housekeeper glared at him, but he continued unperturbed. 'I am everywhere. Every house has a Mario.'

Alex felt an icy chill run down her spine. He was right – every master would have a friend or a servant, who would demand or steal her favours. She straightened her back and squared her shoulders, and challenged him with a confidence she didn't feel. 'I'll be ready for him next time, you've taught me a great deal.'

Mario's eyes flashed furiously and he lunged towards her. It must have hurt his pride to let a girl like Alex escape his clutches. Alex leapt back in alarm as he raised his fist. The little housekeeper intervened.

'No!' she snapped at the corpulent driver. 'I get her ready now! You don't mark her face, you fool!'

Mario spat in disgust. 'Bitch!' he growled. He was genuinely very angry.

Alex prayed that whoever had bought her intended to take her away from KaRoche straight away – if she was left alone with Mario she dreaded to think what might happen. The housekeeper waved her towards the leather surgical couch. Glad to break eye contact with the driver, Alex climbed onto the padded top and stared at the ceiling.

The old woman secured her wrists to the framework. It wasn't until she was totally immobilised that Alex wondered why she had been secured.

Mario's distinctive features came into her field her vision. He was grinning like an imbecile.

'He going to brand you now. Your new boss want you marked so everyone know you belong to him,' the housekeeper said as if she could read her mind. Alex gasped and began to struggle frantically, rolling sideways off the couch. With her wrists secured any real chance of escape was impossible. Mario grabbed her and dragged a heavy leather strap around her waist.

'Please! Please don't do this!' Alex pleaded as he turned his attentions to her ankles. 'Let me go! I'll do whatever you want... please Mario!'

The sweating driver merely laughed. She should have known that there was no point in appealing to him; he would be only too pleased to see her hurt and humiliated, as he had been. Despite her frantic despair Alex heard a door open, and then saw Peter Tourne approaching her.

'We've come a very long way, you and I,' he said with a casualness that belied the insanity of her situation. She stared at him, longing for him to untie her. At his shoulder Mario reached across her and took a cloth bag from the housekeeper. Before Alex could really focus on what he was doing, he lifted her head and pulled the bag down over her face, plunging her into stuffy darkness. She heard the door to the gallery open again and strained to pick up any sounds that might give a clue as to who was with Tourne.

'It's good to see you again,' she heard his muffled voice greet the unseen guest. As you can see, we have her ready for you. What do you think?'

The reply was too indistinct to catch. Alex closed her eyes and struggled to concentrate on the voice of the new arrival. It had to be the man Peter had sold her to;

her new owner. A cool hand stroked her thighs and then lifted to outline her breasts. A fingertip lingered on the rings that pierced her nipples.

'Ummm,' murmured her unseen examiner. It was impossibly frustrating, not to mention alarming. The hand returned to her thighs, easing them wider and then stroking her exposed sex. Alex instinctively strained her hips against the leather strap that held her waist to the couch, and a low chuckle told her that her rude movement had been noted. A thought formed in Alex's mind, but quickly fluttered away as a probing finger slipped inside her.

'Very nice… very tight. You've done a good job,' said a man. 'I'd like my mark in the usual place.' The finger slid from her and was gone.

Unseen hands loosened the strap at her waist and rolled her over. They pinned her firmly to the couch. Something pliable but hard was pressed between her lips. She bit down hard and held her breath. An instant later a searing lightening strike exploded on her buttock. The pain roared through her body. The scream caught in her lungs. She bucked and twisted against the excruciating heat of the branding iron. Sobbing incoherently, she clenched her fists, refusing to be overtaken by the shadowy waves of unconsciousness that beckoned. Despite her determination the darkness draped over her. The voices around her fragmented and broke into abstract sounds, floating on a swirling wind, and she slipped effortlessly into oblivion.

When Alex recovered she was laying on her side on the uncomfortable mattress in the cell. Surely she couldn't have been unconscious for more than a second or two? She stared around, struggling to get her bearings. The cell door was slightly ajar. As she watched it opened and a figure appeared from the shadows.

Alex stiffened – it was impossible. A name formed in her mind and then on her parched lips.

'Laurence?' she whispered in total astonishment. Her agent, her would-be rescuer, the man who'd sent her to the villa in the first place, stepped into the tiny room. She struggled to lift her head, and repeated his name. 'Laurence? Oh my, it is you.' A great wave of relief swept over her. 'I'm so glad you're here.' Her eyes filled with tears. 'Why did you take so long – ?'

Laurence smiled gently. 'Hello Alex. I've come to take you home. That's what you rang me for, wasn't it? You wanted me to rescue you from Peter Tourne's clutches?'

She began to nod, but something in his tone and expression made her stop. Why was it he showed no surprise or shock at finding her bound and naked in a tiny cell? And why didn't he seem concerned for his own safety?

'Why didn't you come straight away, when I first rang you?'

He smiled again. 'What, and spoil Peter's fun? I don't think so Alex. I came here today because he told me you're ready – and I can see that you are.'

He stared down at her, relishing the details of her body. Alex shivered, realisation trickling down her spine like icy water. Looking up into his eyes she knew exactly why he'd come to KaRoche.

'Was this your idea all along, Laurence?'

'I'm afraid so,' he grinned and shrugged as though he'd merely been uncovered as the perpetrator of a harmless prank. 'Peter Tourne and I have been friends for years. When I took the commission for the mural I didn't tell him you were a beautiful woman, but I knew he wouldn't be able to resist breaking you in once he saw you.' He moved closer, as though about to tell her a secret. 'And that's precisely why I sent you here in the first place. I wanted to possess you from the first moment you came into my office for an interview. You look quite lovely, Alex. But then again, I always knew you would.' He ran his fingers lightly over her forehead. 'Peter gave you a light sedative to help with the pain, are you feeling okay?'

Alex nodded weakly. 'And so you're my new master?'

'That's right, my dear. We couldn't have Mustafa taking you off to God knows where, now could we? The man's an animal, let's face it, Monique is not much better. Such a waste to let either of them have you. I'd planned to bid for you at Simon Bay's auction – it seemed like a suitably melodramatic conclusion to your training – but as you generated so much interest amongst his associates, Peter and I came to a private arrangement; we couldn't risk losing you. I must say, he seems commendably interested in your future welfare. He knows you'll be well looked after in my stable; my companions are part of a very exclusive coterie. You've been marked with my initials, as are all the girl's I own. You can meet the rest of them when we get back to London.'

He gently unfastened the leash from her collar. She made no attempt to escape – what was the point?

Lawrence nodded towards the cell door. 'When we're done here I'd like you to collect your things together so that we can catch the evening ferry. I'd like to get back to London as soon as possible.' He paused and smiled with genuine warmth. 'You'll like the rest of my clique, I'm quite certain. The girls are all like you; artists, sculptors – a very select band of England's most talented young stars…' he gently touched the dressing which soothed the smarting area of the branding. 'It'll look quite exquisite once it's healed, believe me. Oh, I ought to tell you that I've already arranged for all of your things to be delivered to my house. I expect my slave to be on hand for my every whim.' He patted his thigh. 'Now, come here, Alex. Show me that you understand totally what I expect from you.'

Alex swallowed hard, almost unable to believe what she was hearing. Hadn't she always suspected that Laurence

Russell's interest in her was more than just professional? Wasn't his carefully hidden desire what she'd hoped would spur him on to come to D'arnos to rescue her?

She slowly slipped from the mattress and crept towards the man who'd delivered her into the hands of Peter Tourne. He was her rescuer turned master. She didn't need to ask what he wanted from her. His penis was jutting forward like a rapier against the soft fabric of his trousers. Catching hold of her collar he pulled her up onto her knees and bent from the waist to kiss her passionately.

'Oh Alex,' he murmured. 'You have no idea how much I've dreamt about this moment.'

Without a word she undid his belt and, kneeling at his feet, ran her tongue along his exposed shaft in an ancient act of worship.

Even as she tasted his first salty offering she could feel the excitement stirring deep inside her own body. Her sex moistened, her nipples hardened, and the dark half of her mind had finally won the battle.

More exciting titles available from Chimera

***

The full range of our wonderfully erotic titles are now available as downloadable e-books at our great new website:

www.chimerabooks.co.uk

You've enjoyed *Captivation*, so you'll love these great titles from *Sarah Fisher* too!

Dr Casswell's Student

When Sarah Morgan is invited to help her employer, Doctor Casswell, translate an antique journal at his isolated country mansion, she finds herself drawn into the dark and sensual world of medieval slave girl, Beatrice de Fleur.

As past and present meet, Sarah is caught in an intense web of passion and pain. Stripped and bound for Casswell's pleasure, Sarah soon discovers what it is like to be a student of desire...

1-901388-21-2 ● £5.99

Dr Casswell's Plaything

On the trail of medieval slave girl, Beatrice de Fleur, Sarah Morgan and her enigmatic master, Dr Casswell, find themselves caught up in the exotic surroundings of a Turkish port.

And when their hosts trade Sarah's body as payment for access to Beatrice's diaries, past and present mingle once again as they uncover more of the slave's sensual secrets. Naked, bound, and at the mercy of an unscrupulous museum curator, Sarah understands only too well how Casswell's passion and pain collide.

1-903931-08-8 ● £5.99

And we're releasing *Sarah's* latest steamy novel of domination and submission in September 2003...

Maggie and the Master

When Maggie Howard takes in a new lodger she gets a glimpse of a dark, sensual, forbidden world that has always fascinated and intrigued her.

With the lodger's input she meets Max Jordan, a notorious Slave Master whose speciality is training wilful, spirited young women to be auctioned off to the highest bidder.

Naked and tormented, eyes bright with conflicting tears of trepidation and longing, Maggie finds herself at the mercy of the Master, and begins to learn the true meaning of submission.

1-903931-52-5 ● £6.99

Visit our all new website to order online from our full range of over **one hundred** titles, download them as e-books, enjoy discounts and special offers, enter competitions with great prizes, make contact and chat to others who enjoy **Chimera's** quality erotica... **plus**, keep an eye out for our forthcoming audio books, films, and a whole lot more...

www.chimerabooks.co.uk

And **New** from **Chimera!**

Brighten up your desk with a quality mousemat featuring a stunning **Chimera** image. Enhance your computer time at work or at home with one or both of these beautiful girls for only £4.99* + p&p each (£8.99* + p&p if you fancy treating yourself to both). Or how about treating a friend or partner?

And we'll be adding to the tasteful-but-saucy range of **Chimera** merchandise, so keep visiting our great new website and enjoying our extensive list of erotic books for news and updates!

*Price may be subject to change in the future

Chimera Publishing Ltd

22b Picton House
Hussar Court
Waterlooville
Hants
PO7 7SQ

www.chimerabooks.co.uk
chimera@chimerabooks.co.uk

***

Sales and Distribution in the USA and Canada

Client Distribution Services, Inc
193 Edwards Drive
Jackson
TN 38301
USA

***

Sales and Distribution in Australia

Dennis Jones & Associates Pty Ltd
19a Michellan Ct
Bayswater
Victoria
Australia 3153